VIRTUALLY HARMLESS

VIRTUALLY HARMLESS

HIGH-TECH CRIME SOLVERS #3

P.D. WORKMAN

ISBN: 9781989415504 (IS Hardcover)

ISBN: 9781989415498 (IS Paperback)

ISBN: 9781989415467 (KDP Paperback)

ISBN: 9781989415474 (Kindle)

ISBN: 9781989415481 (ePub)

ISBN: 9781989415924 (Retail audiobook)

ISBN: 9781989415931 (Library audiobook)

pdworkman

ALSO BY P.D. WORKMAN

MYSTERY/SUSPENSE:

Zachary Goldman Mysteries

She Wore Mourning

His Hands Were Quiet

She Was Dying Anyway

He Was Walking Alone

They Thought He was Safe

He Was Not There

Her Work Was Everything

She Told a Lie (Coming soon)

He Never Forgot (Coming soon)

She Was At Risk (Coming soon)

Kenzie Kirsch Medical Thrillers

Unlawful Harvest

Auntie Clem's Bakery

Gluten-Free Murder

Dairy-Free Death

Allergen-Free Assignation

Witch-Free Halloween (Halloween Short)

Dog-Free Dinner (Christmas Short)

Stirring Up Murder

Brewing Death

Coup de Glace

Sour Cherry Turnover

Apple-achian Treasure

Vegan Baked Alaska

Muffins Masks Murder

Tai Chi and Chai Tea

Santa Shortbread

Reg Rawlins, Psychic Detective

What the Cat Knew

A Psychic with Catitude

A Catastrophic Theft

Night of Nine Tails

Telepathy of Gardens

Delusions of the Past

Fairy Blade Unmade

Web of Nightmares

A Whisker's Breadth (Coming soon)

High-Tech Crime Solvers Series

Virtually Harmless

Stand Alone Suspense Novels

Looking Over Your Shoulder

Lion Within

Pursued by the Past

In the Tick of Time

Loose the Dogs

AND MORE AT PDWORKMAN.COM

From USA Today Bestselling Author, P.D. Workman, comes a gripping techno-thriller, part of a multi-author series tied together by an interlocking cast of characters, all centered around the fantastic new promise of high technology and the endless possibilities for crime that technology offers, in a world where getting away with murder can be not only plausible, but easy… if you just know how.

ACKNOWLEDGMENTS

My sincerest thanks to my readers and fans for their support and encouragement. To my coauthors in the series and especially Uvi Poznansky for spearheading it and keeping us all on track. Thanks to Jim Grusendorf for editing faithfully month after month. And thank you to my family and friends for supporting my writing career and recommending my books to others.

To all of those striving to put a face on crime.
Thank you for your heroism every day.

He thought that he was safe. It was the perfect crime. No witnesses left alive, no one to point the finger at him.

He'd shown her who was boss. She thought she could go behind his back? Cheat on him? Every day acting like she was the perfect little girlfriend, so naive and innocent and happy to please him, and all along, she'd been sneaking around behind his back. Well, he'd shown her.

And there was nothing to lead the cops back to him. Neither of them had shared the details of their relationship with anyone. She'd been even more concerned about her family and friends finding out than he'd been. He'd warned her about how she would be treated if people knew about them. So he was sure she hadn't talked, and now it was too late.

They'd always met away from their homes or usual haunts, the danger of being found out adding an extra layer of excitement to the illicit relationship.

And surveillance cameras. He'd even thought of that, casing their meeting place and the streets around it for surveillance cameras and nosy neighbors. Wearing an oversized hoodie, ball cap, and glasses as he arrived and left afterward to hide his identity in case he did get caught on camera.

It had been a thrill, satisfying a lust in him even deeper than their secret rendezvous. He was high and satisfied and exultant all at the same time.

He'd gotten away with it.

The perfect crime.

Only he hadn't known about Micah Miller.

<hr>

"They got him," Aaron Kwong told the team, a smile spreading across his usually impassive face.

Micah was momentarily distracted by the itch to sketch Kwong's face. In a population that was ninety percent white, her artist's eye was immediately drawn to those who stood out. The Asian cast of his features, skin smooth even at the end of the day when he was tired and other men would have been showing a five o'clock shadow. Neat, close-cropped hair. And the glasses. She thought that the narrow, rectangular frames were new. A little bit different from the last time she had seen him.

He wore a white lab coat to match the dress of most of his team, buttoned up with a light blue shirt and perfectly-knotted silk tie underneath. But he was rarely in the lab. Like Micah, most of his work took place in front of a computer, not a test tube.

"David Beggs was just arrested by the Toole County Sheriff's Department for the murder of fifteen-year-old Jessica Johnson."

A smattering of applause went up from the assembled team. Micah joined the lab techs a few seconds later, clapping quietly. It wouldn't bring Jessica Johnson back, but it was one less predator on the street. One less violent pedophile. Who knew how many children they had saved from a similar fate.

"Most of you were involved in getting the Sheriff's Department the evidence they needed to collar David Beggs," Kwong went on, "but I wanted to mention Micah particularly. Without your work, Micah, we wouldn't have had a face to put to the killer. That was the one key piece of evidence that helped the cops identify the killer. Because of you, Jessica's family can at least be assured that their daughter's killer is behind bars."

All faces turned toward Micah, renewing the quiet applause for a few seconds. Micah shifted her feet and looked away, slightly uncomfortable with their attention. She smiled and nodded, waiting for Kwong to go on and take the spotlight off of her.

There was more work to be done. She wanted to be back at her desk, working on the next case.

2

Micah sketched as she waited for the Snohomish Police Department Duty Officer to figure out who to put her through to. Drawing was something that kept her fingers occupied for hours every day. She wasn't the kind of person who could just sit and be still. Whenever she wasn't doing something that occupied her brain, she had to be doing something with her hands. And ever since she was a child, that had been drawing.

She ran through several different faces, cases that she had been working on lately, trying them out with different hairstyles, facial hair, accessories, or expressions. Sometimes, something just clicked, and she would create a new composite with those details to add to the file. She couldn't count the number of times when sketching while bored had led to the creation of the composite picture that would crack a case.

But none of them was prompting any special thrill today. Micah switched tactics and drew her own face, just like she would one of the composites, naked of anything but the essential shape and features to start with. She didn't hold any illusions that she was a beauty. She was a plain Jane. Nothing particularly striking about her. She'd analyzed her face piece by piece many times. Her face was mostly well-proportioned—nose just a little too prominent, jawline just a little too square.

You could be pretty if you put some effort into it.

How she had come to hate that comment. It had been made by both men and women who disdained the fact that she rarely wore any makeup or did anything with her dark hair but brush it out and put it in an elastic to keep it out of her face. People didn't seem to understand that she didn't care about being pretty. She had good hygiene; she didn't wear the same set of clothes every day—though she did have a sort of a work 'uniform' that made it easy to get ready for the day each morning—she didn't smell bad or have mussed-up hair. She just couldn't be bothered to go to all that trouble for no good reason.

For what? So she could attract a mate? She enjoyed her friendships with men, had an easy camaraderie with most of the men that she worked with, both cop types and geeks. But she far preferred a meeting of the minds to the possibility of a romantic relationship. She had guy friends, not boyfriends. And she didn't often hit it off with women. Too many of them were distracted by girly things. Fashion, shopping, chasing men, talking endlessly about their children or pets. It was hard to have a good intellectual discussion with someone whose brain was busy with so many other things.

Micah filled in some new details on the sketch of her face. She gave herself bobbed hair that curled around her face, softening the lines. Earrings. No glasses. All different from her real-life look. She picked up some colored pencils and added skin tones that were a little warmer than her natural complexion, dusky red lips, roses in the cheeks. Sure, she could be pretty, or at least prettier, if she cared to change those things. But the face that looked back at her was fake. A mask to be put on every day instead of being able to be her own true self. Start down that road, and who knew how many concessions she would make to societal expectations? As a combination of geek, artist, and forensic detective, people allowed her latitude, shrugging off her eccentricities, and that was the way she liked it.

"Is this Micah Miller?" a gravelly man's voice spoke in her ear.

Micah was startled, but managed not to drop the phone and quickly recovered.

"This is Micah," she said briskly.

"This is Detective Rasmussen. Not sure why you didn't call me directly, honey. I left you all of my details."

"As I told your duty officer, the voicemail you left me was garbled. I don't know whether there was a problem with your phone service or mine, but I could barely figure out your police department name after listening to it half a dozen times."

"Oh. Well, no harm done, I guess. You're the one who had to wait around while my DO tied himself in knots."

"What can I do for you?" Micah asked, getting straight to the point.

"I'm told that you are the go-to man—er, woman—for those whatchamacallits, virtual mugshots for perps you don't have photos of."

"Composite pictures."

"Composite, yes," Rasmussen agreed.

"Do you have an eyewitness?"

"If I did, there are folks around here who can do sketches or use the computer programs that make them. My problem is that I don't. One of the techies here said that you could make pictures from DNA samples. I told him there's no freaking way, if you'll pardon my French. But he says you can do it, and some of these virtual pictures you've done have been so on-point that they've been able to identify the perp and get an arrest."

"Yes, I can do Forensic DNA phenotyping," Micah told him. She knew that he wouldn't know what the phrase meant, but if she dumbed it down for him, he'd never learn and would keep calling them virtual mugshots. "These are graphic representations of what your suspect may look like according to his or her DNA. You will also get a listing of observable characteristics that will help you to eliminate suspects. For example, I may be able to tell you that the suspect's eyes could range from green to brown, but they are absolutely not blue. Or I may be able to tell you that your suspect's skin and hair are fair, which will allow you to eliminate those with darker complexions."

"And these pictures can be used to identify the perp."

"The picture gives you an idea of what he or she looks like. I'll produce a series of photos with different hairstyle or facial hair, accessories, age range, weight range, and so on, in the hopes that one of them will be close. But that will not be sufficient evidence to charge him or her. You will need to gather other evidence, try to get a direct DNA match, and so on. The court will still expect you to have done your homework."

Micah spoke slowly and precisely to give him a chance to soak it all in. She'd given the explanation many times and, although she felt it was perfectly clear, LEOs—law enforcement officers—still seemed to think that the pictures she produced would magically provide the identity of the subject and they would have enough to make an arrest without all of the difficult in-between work.

"Can you give me some examples of what we would get?" Rasmussen's tone was petulant. "We can't afford to be shelling out money to private contractors without being sure that we're going to get something out of it."

"Can you use an internet browser, Detective?"

"Can I use a—?" Rasmussen sputtered. "Of course I can use an internet browser! I may not have grown up with the technology like some of the young folks coming up now, but I've learned how to use it!"

"Great. That will save us some time. Are you at a computer right now?"

"Yes."

"Excellent. Fire up your browser and type in this URL." Micah waited for Rasmussen's verbal confirmation that he was ready.

"Up in the top bar?" Rasmussen asked, a little sheepish, since he had just told her he knew what he was doing.

"Yes. Are you ready? Here it is." She spoke and then spelled out the URL for him character by character. His typing was slow and uneven. Hunt and peck.

She waited for him to load the page and look it over.

"Are these all yours?" Rasmussen's voice held new respect, almost reverence. Micah clicked her home button and loaded the page on her own display. Up came the images of FDP composites that had been released to the public, some of which were paired with photos of the suspects who had been convicted of the crime. She never tired of looking at the page.

"Yes, anything from the past three years is mine," she informed him. "They are in reverse date order, so that's the top five rows."

She could hear him breathing as he looked through them. "Good grief. I owe Darius a beer. These are incredible."

"As you can see, some of them are better likenesses than others, and we have put the best match at the top of each picture stack. If you click on a stack of composites, they will fan out so you can see the various hairstyles, ages, and weights that I produced for that file."

She could hear his clicks through the phone as he tried a couple.

"I've seen what sketch artists and computer programs produced from witness testimony in the past," Rasmussen said. "They always look flat, and darned if I can see the likeness to a suspect. But yours look like… well, like he was sitting across the table from you."

"Thank you," Micah acknowledged. "I take the information the DNA provides to come up with a computer composite, and then I finish the details by hand, like a portrait artist. I use the genetic and epigenetic clues and any crime-scene evidence available to piece together things like age, height, likely body build, and facial hair and hairstyles that are typical to that generation and region. And as you can see, sometimes I couldn't have gotten much closer if he or she *had* been sitting across the table from me."

3

Micah got back to her house late. It was dark, the nip of autumn in the air. Her eyes caught a movement in the dark, and she froze, every sense straining, trying to identify if she were in danger. There was another movement in the shadows, but it was down low, in the bushes, below knee level. Micah approached slowly, prepared for an exploring skunk or raccoon. It wouldn't be the first time. Living on the edge of town as she did, she often ended up with critters in her yard.

There was a movement and, looking down into the reflective eyes, she saw a small, skinny kitten.

"Where did you come from?" Micah murmured.

It clearly wasn't someone's pet, too young to be let out on its own. A feral cat or the kitten of one of the barn cats on a nearby farm. It wouldn't stand much chance out there on its own, with coyotes and other predators venturing close to the houses, habituated to humans.

"Hopefully, your mommy is close by to take you home."

Micah unlocked her door, gathered the flyers and mail from her mailbox. Mostly flyers. Like everyone else in the modern world, she preferred to have her bills delivered to her virtual inbox rather than physical copies through the mail. A lot of the new communities were using centralized neighborhood boxes rather than delivering directly to homes.

She pushed the door open, put everything down on the side table inside the door, and swiveled to shut and lock the door behind her. A dirty gray form zipped by her.

"Hey!"

Micah stood there for a moment, not sure what to do. Yelling and chasing the kitten wasn't likely to be very productive. If she just left the door open a few inches, chances were it would leave on its own. As long as she didn't feed it or make it comfortable, it would wander back out again. She didn't have a litter box or any cat food.

She removed her shoes and coat and put them away. She took the mail and flyers to her desk and sorted them into her in-tray or recycling bin. That done, it was time to get herself something to eat.

Whenever she saw the kitten poke its head out, she did her best to shoo it toward the open door. But it seemed determined to stay, and she didn't like the idea of leaving the door open for so long.

It had been a long day, so she wasn't in the mood for anything that required much effort. She drained a can of white beans, added some herbs from her windowsill garden and marinara sauce and warmed it up while she made a quick salad. The cat hadn't appeared again, so she sat down at her table to eat. If she ignored it, it would give up on getting anything from her and leave again. Hopefully, before the house got too cold. The temperature was going to drop below freezing, judging by the biting wind that was getting gradually more brisk.

She browsed through her social networks as she ate, even though she knew that the experts said one should not do anything else while eating, just focusing on the food. Her restless brain and body would never allow that.

Despite the amount of time and energy Micah put into her work, she was very active in a number of social forums. She found it a satisfying way to engage with other people and share interests on her own schedule and at her own pace. The internet made it easier to compose her thoughts in a detailed post that others would appreciate, a significant advantage over water cooler or cocktail party chit-chat.

There was a post by Michael Morse in one of the social forums on computer-generated imaging systems, and Micah stopped and read through it. Michael was a brilliant computer coder EvPro had engaged from time to time to track down some bugs and improve the quality of the composites the computer generated from DNA analysis. As Micah was the person at EvPro who lived in the nexus of the scientific data and produced the faces of victims and suspects and took them to the next level, she had worked closely with him on several occasions. She had come to admire the unique way he visualized computer code and was able to use it to generate faces, places, and everything needed to create his own virtual reality worlds. He worked remotely from the lab in his garage, the whole blue-painted interior acting as a virtual screen for his computer-generated images.

While much of what he posted was too technical for her to comprehend fully, she always read his posts, and was fascinated with his ideas and how he was able to transform data points into his own version of reality. She was fully engrossed in Michael's latest post when there was a crash from the kitchen. Micah shot out of her seat.

She knew before she got there what had happened.

The kitten was nowhere in sight. The crash had probably scared the crap out of it. The bean can was on the floor, evidence that the cat had been licking up the remains of the juice. The cat had also made significant inroads in the beans in marinara sauce that Micah had left on the counter. Micah had mistakenly assumed that the kitten wouldn't be interested in anything but cat food or meat or fish. But if the poor thing was starving, it would probably eat whatever it could drag out of the trash.

"Kitty, kitty?" she called softly. "Where did you go?"

Her house was sparsely decorated, even spartan. That was the way she liked it. Clean lines, little to distract her attention. So it didn't take long to find the kitten in the gap between the fridge and the counter. It peered up at her with big, frightened eyes.

"I can see I'm not going to be able to get rid of you tonight!"

Micah left the kitten in its hiding place and went back out to the front room to shut the door. She had goosebumps from the chilly air that had blown in. She grabbed a hoodie from the front closet and pulled it on over her head. She warmed her hands in the kangaroo pouch and went back to the kitchen to deal with her unwanted visitor.

***

For a long time, they just watched each other. Micah sat down on the floor with her legs crossed and watched the kitten. The kitten stared back out at her.

A few times, it mewed silently at her, mouth opening wide and nothing coming out. Maybe its voice was too high, out of the range of human hearing. Micah put some of the beans in a little aluminum pie plate and set it on the floor. She sat and waited some more.

Eventually, the cat's hungry tummy drew it back out of the hiding place, and it quickly licked up the bean mixture, purring a tiny rumbling purr. When it was done, the kitten sat back to wash, looking at Micah most of the time, wondering who or what she was and what she was going to do. Micah spoke a few words, trying to reassure it and get it used to her voice.

When the kitten was finished its bath, it crept toward her, tail held up high and eyes wide and curious. Micah held out her hand and allowed the cat to sniff her thoroughly. When she petted its head, it jumped back at first, but as she continued to pat it or rub its ears and chin, it calmed.

The next thing Micah knew, it was sleeping curled up in the big pocket of her hoodie, and she was wondering what she was going to do with a kitten.

4

Micah scrolled through the items in her email inbox, scanning the subject lines for any new cases or updates on old ones. Too much spam and corporate junk. It was unbelievable how much people chattered back and forth over nothing.

Her phone rang. Micah looked down at the screen. Wes Watley. Ex-FBI and Army CID, Wes was now a private security consultant that she'd had the opportunity to do some work for once or twice. Micah tapped the phone to answer the call.

"Wes."

"Micah, how are things going in your part of the country?"

"Getting cold. What can I do for you?"

Like her, Wes was not one for chit-chat and didn't see the need to continue with the small talk.

"Heard about a lost baby that must not be too far from you. Wondered what you had heard."

"A lost baby?" Micah repeated. She clicked her daily news email and skimmed it for details. "Missing person? Kidnapping?"

"Well, I suppose I should say a found baby. Abandoned. They don't know who the parents are or why the baby was left there."

Micah's body shuddered with a chill. She looked around for her sweater and pulled it on, but the shakiness did not pass.

"Where was she found?" she asked Wes.

"In the Sweetgrass Hills. That's the mountain range close to you, isn't it? Part of the Rockies?"

"It's near here. But it's an island range," Micah repeated. "Not part of the Rockies. Out in the prairie on its own."

"Huh. Never knew that."

"No reason you would, unless you went to school here. So is she okay? The baby?"

"Cold and hungry, but the hospital said she would make a full recovery."

"Is this related to one of your files?" Micah couldn't imagine how an abandoned baby would be within his purview. That was strictly a police matter.

"I had a client inquire about it, ask me if I could get any intel."

"Why?"

In her mind's eye, she could see Wes's shrug. "I guess he was curious. It could be part of a pattern. I knew it was out there near you and wondered if you'd heard any water cooler gossip."

"You know me. I'm not the type to hang around the water cooler. And I haven't finished checking my email this morning, hadn't even seen the news about her being found."

Wes grunted. "Okay. I wouldn't mind hearing about it if you happen to come across something."

"I'm not likely to hear anything that isn't in the news. They won't likely need my services."

"I don't suppose they would need yours specifically, but the police could ask EvPro to do lab work on trace evidence."

"What did they find?" Micah closed her eyes and envisioned the scene. A tiny baby. Diaper, onesie undershirt, sleeper. If the person who had abandoned her wanted her to survive, then probably a warm hat and blanket or sleep sack. Maybe a pacifier or bottle. How old was she? Where exactly had she been left? Micah was picturing a newborn lying in a little hollow of leaves, but that might be far from what had happened. More than likely, she had been left in a store or a car—one of those little gas station convenience stores that serviced the Sweetgrass area.

"Not much to go on. The baby herself—a girl, by the way, not sure how you knew that—some soiled clothes, a diaper bag."

"They'll be wanting to process the trace," Micah agreed. "But I don't know if they'll involve us. If it looks like it's just a routine case, they'll send it to the city lab and let it wait in line. If there's a reason to rush it, they might give us a call."

"I suspect there will be a lot of public engagement. Leaving a baby exposed like that, someone so helpless and harmless, just walking away and abandoning her… it tugs at people's heartstrings. They'll be making signs and sending letters. Or tweets, or whatever."

"I'll give Kwong a heads-up. Make sure that our decks are clear if it gets shipped here."

"Alright. Let me know if you hear anything that's not in the papers. Or if you have any theories."

"Theories?" Micah repeated. "Somebody decided she was inconvenient." Just saying it felt like a punch in the gut. "There's not much to theorize about."

Wes chuckled. "It's the truth," he agreed. "It's an emotional case, but probably not a complicated one."

5

Sunday was dinner with her parents. Micah didn't go every Sunday, but she couldn't stay away too long and let them feel neglected. They had raised her, after all, and she owed them that. No matter what any of her other feelings were about them.

As someone who was fascinated with faces, Micah loved the character in her mother's face. Despite over-tweezed penciled eyebrows and thin, lipsticked mouth, Marianna Miller's face was the face of an angel. That was how she had thought of her mother when she was a little girl. As the angel who had been sent to earth to watch over Micah. Maybe Micah had misunderstood something that some Sunday School teacher had told her. Or perhaps she had heard something on TV that planted the idea. Whatever it was, she had not believed, in those early years, that her mother could do any wrong.

Marianna had not aged well. Micah couldn't remember her ever being young, but she had seen pictures. Her mother had been pretty when she was a girl. But the wrinkles and bags and sags that she had acquired as she got older gave her a permanently worried look, which pretty much matched her emotional state. She was always concerned about something. Fearful of an uncertain future. Sure that they had not done something they should have, or had done something they should not have. What had been lively brown curls when she was young now looked flat and tattered. A wide part to one side showed how thin it was getting.

Her father had become more distinguished with age. His hair had silvered but not receded. He wore the lines on his face like a suit, or like a uniform. She'd seen pictures of her father in his police uniform. She couldn't remember ever seeing him in it as she was growing up. Probably he only wore it for funerals or meetings with visiting dignitaries by then. His wrinkles looked like they had been drawn on for maximum effect. A cop's cop. A man who had done his duty, served his town, and eventually retired with honor. If Cole Miller had ever made a mistake, he hadn't confessed it. He stood by every decision he had ever made, giving a logical reason for each one.

"How was your week, Micah?" Marianna inquired. "I haven't heard from you all week. Are you feeling alright?"

"Yes, I'm fine. No complaints. It was just a busy week. I'm sorry. I should have at least dropped you an email."

"Well, I know how busy and all-consuming law enforcement can be. Forty years a police widow. It was quite a shock to our relationship when Cole finally retired."

Things had definitely been rocky. Micah had, luckily, been out of the house at that point, so she hadn't had to deal with the constant tension and arguments, but some of it had still boiled over into conversations she had with each of them and into visits home, which she still tended to avoid. Things had eventually settled into a rhythm as her parents each learned to give the other the space they needed, but Micah still found the new dynamic uncomfortable. It was strange to have her father at home every time she went by, and the stories that he told were all the same stories as she had heard before instead of new cases.

"I heard about the arrest of that pervert, David Beggs," Cole commented, his voice louder than necessary. "That was one of your cases, wasn't it? It was your pictures that helped to identify him?"

Micah nodded. She poked at the oversalted macaroni casserole on her plate, wondering how much of it she would have to eat to be polite. She didn't want her mother to think that she was sick or that she didn't like Marianna's cooking. Even though she never had.

"The picture helped to narrow the suspect pool and bore a strong resemblance to David Beggs," she agreed. "But it was good old-fashioned police work that brought him in. The police working his case did a good job."

Cole beamed, the wrinkles in his face turning upward, as pleased as if he'd still been on the police force and instrumental in making the arrest himself. Blue pride.

"They showed your pictures of him beside his mugshot on the TV," Marianna contributed. "It always amazes me how you can predict how these criminals will look. It's a special gift."

Micah shrugged. She took a couple of bites of the casserole and washed it down with milk. Nonfat milk now, one of her mother's efforts to keep herself and Cole from putting on more weight than they already had. It had been a constant battle since menopause, she had confided in Micah. Her body had never been the same after the change. And Cole, well, he had put on a few pounds in his years as a detective, not as active as he had been as a street cop, but still with a penchant for Boston Creams. He claimed that he could still wear the uniform that he had worn as a rookie policeman, but Micah suspected that was either an exaggeration, or that what he meant was that he could pull it on, even if he couldn't button it up.

"You're always so modest about your talent," Marianna persisted. "I knew that you had a gift for drawing right from the time you were tiny. The other children your age were drawing stick figures with no noses, and you…" Marianna shook her head, eyes smiling. "You were drawing portraits. Nothing like what you can do now, of course, but faces with depth. And hair. And noses."

Micah laughed. Drawing had always been a passion of hers. She had never imagined it would lead her where it had. She had wanted to be a cop like her father. Even though she was nothing like him. They had nothing in common.

"Working on anything else interesting right now?" Cole asked, pouring himself a second glass of wine, pretending not to see the disapproving gaze his wife leveled at him.

"Well… mostly routine cases right now. I keep busy with it, but I don't always know the outcomes. Whether they catch the perp or whether it goes cold. Not all of them are as newsworthy as David Beggs." She sipped her milk. Marianna's eyes were on Micah's plate, and she knew she was going to have to make an effort to get more of her dinner down. She sighed and stirred it around with her fork. "Have you heard anything about Baby Doe? The baby abandoned in the hills?"

Cole and Marianna exchanged glances. How many secrets did they still keep? And why did they still feel the need to protect her? She was a grown woman, independent. Old enough to have a few children of her own, if she had felt the desire to get married and produce offspring. Micah laid down her fork, resentment starting to bubble up.

"It was in the news," she pointed out. "You heard about the baby, right? You couldn't have *not* heard." She'd been reading everything she could on the case. The police had circulated one picture of the baby, and Micah couldn't get it out of her mind.

"I saw it on the TV," Marianna admitted. She gave a little shrug, as if it had been nothing more than the latest sports scores. "It's very sad. You have to wonder what her parents were thinking, to leave a baby all on her own like that."

"Outside in the cold," Micah pointed out. "You don't just leave a baby under a bush and walk away. Somebody would have to be really disturbed to do something like that."

Marianna's eyes drifted away. "Yes," she murmured. "I don't know what goes through people's minds."

"Do they have any leads on who her parents are?" Cole demanded, pretending that he didn't feel any of the tension or awkwardness.

"I don't have anything to do with the case," Micah said. "I only know what I've seen in the news myself. No undisclosed details."

"The police have a lot more tools at their disposal now than they did thirty or forty years ago. Back then, we had the phone and shoe leather. Asking people questions. Asking if they know of anyone who had a baby but didn't anymore. Even the baby's race was only a guess. What you could see with your own eyes. Now, there are so many more inquiry channels— internet social media and bulletin boards and news stations. DNA analysis. Surveillance cameras everywhere, watching all the time. It's getting harder and harder for criminals to go undetected."

Micah thought about surveillance cameras. Maybe that was why the baby had been abandoned in such a secluded area. Not so she wouldn't be found until it was too late, but so there were no cameras to get Baby Doe's mother—or kidnapper—on film.

"It was such an isolated area," she said. "No cameras out there."

"Are you sure of that? You know, there could be hikers or bikers with helmet-mounted cameras. Automatic wildlife cameras on game trails. And they would have had to park somewhere. You can't just walk into the mountains carrying a baby. They have to have parked somewhere close, within a mile or two, and the parking lot could have surveillance."

"Yes, probably." Micah forced a couple more bites of casserole down. "I wouldn't know. It's not my case."

After supper, the conversation moved to happier topics, with Micah telling her parents about the stray kitten, showing a delighted Marianna pictures and video clips of the furry baby sleeping and playing.

"Oh, she's just darling! Why didn't you tell me? I would have gone over to see her. I can't believe that you finally got a cat. You were one of the few children who never asked for a pet of any kind."

"That's not true," Micah objected immediately. "I asked for a Venus flytrap."

"That's a plant, not a pet."

"It moves, it eats, it grows."

"A plant can't be a pet. A pet is an animal. Like a cat."

"Just higher up the food chain."

"You've always had such strange ideas." Marianna shook her head, bemused. "You were always surprising me."

Micah supposed that not all six-year-old girls had an interest in law enforcement or science. She'd always been happier playing cops and robbers with the boys—she was always one of the cops—than she had been in playing whatever it was the girls played.

And when she was older, she'd been fascinated with the dissection labs in Biology, feeling absolutely no need to pretend that it made her sick or faint. It was like the best field trip ever, that journey of discovery into what made creatures tick. Being able to see and touch and hold the life-giving organs in her hand, rather than just to look at them in a book. The various parts that were so neatly labeled in the textbook were not always so easily recognizable or perfectly-shaped in real life. Or rather, in death.

"I'm sorry I was never one of those girly girls," she told Marianna. "You probably would have liked it better if I was interested in clothes and boys and having a pet cat."

"No," Marianna put her hand on Micah's arm and spoke to her intensely. "No, I would not have preferred to have raised anyone else, or for you to have been any different than what you were. You're unique and you're special. You don't have to be anyone else."

"I don't imagine all of the parenting books were much help."

"Well, to be honest, you never needed that much parenting!" Marianna stared off into space. Cole was sitting in front of the TV, watching reruns of Hunter and McCall from an internet subscription package. "You were always very mature and always tried to do things the right way. I hardly ever had to tell you anything more than once. You wanted to know what the rules were and you wanted to follow them."

Micah wondered why she didn't still feel the same way. As she got older, she found herself bristling at society's expectations and the rules at work or in other places. When she was young, she had needed the guidelines. It had been a relief to know what was expected of her and to be given specific instructions as to what she should or shouldn't do. But now that she was older, an independent adult living her own life, she had less and less patience for being told what to do. Instead, she wanted to do things her own way. Delayed adolescence? Midlife crisis? Early change of life?

"So I was an easy child?"

"Oh… I don't know if I'd put it that way." Her mother laughed. "Easy is not a word I would have picked to describe you. You didn't need much parenting… but you had a mind of your own. And such a voracious learner. You were so full of questions about everything, never satisfied with the answers I gave you."

That did sound like Micah. Anything that tweaked her interest could lead to a full-blown research project and an avalanche of information to be absorbed.

She loved it.

She could never get enough answers.

6

Micah was normally a good sleeper. She kept a strict bedtime and rising schedule and was usually asleep within minutes of her head hitting the pillow. But after getting back from her parents' house, her brain was whirling with questions, concerns, and anxieties, and she couldn't sweep them aside to go to sleep.

Her mind kept going back to Baby Doe. That lonely little baby, being taken away from everything she knew and abandoned there, in the dark and cold. It was inhuman. Who would do something like that to a baby? Harm something so harmless? And if it was a kidnapper, then why hadn't he just killed her? If he didn't intend to return her to her family, why didn't he smother her and bury her in a shallow grave somewhere in the mountains? Why leave her alive and chance someone finding her? Maybe he had been interrupted. Maybe that had been part of the plan, but he hadn't been able to follow through.

Or if it was Doe's mother, her biological parent, then why hadn't she abandoned the baby somewhere she would be sure to be found? A church or fire station or some other sanctuary. Like most other places in the USA, Montana had a safe haven law. A newborn could be handed over to any emergency services personnel with no recourse being taken against the parent. She wouldn't have to give her name or any other identifying information if she didn't want to. She could safely abandon the baby if she didn't feel she could take care of her.

Was the biological mother mentally ill, then? Maybe she didn't know what she was doing or didn't have the mental capacity to understand how to take care of an infant. Maybe she came from a culture where child abandonment, especially of a baby girl, was more acceptable. Maybe she had postpartum syndrome so severe that she couldn't function, even to call in an anonymous tip to tell the police or first responders where to find the baby.

Micah tossed and turned. Every time she moved around, the kitten started crying, snuggling against her and kneading Micah's stomach or whatever body part was closest to her, clearly still missing her mommy cat. What had happened to the kitten's mother? Had she been caught by a fox or coyote or another predator? Hit by a car? Taken in by some kind soul who had no way of knowing that she had a helpless kitten out there somewhere that still needed her?

Micah made soothing sounds and stroked the kitten, trying to settle it back to sleep again. But then after another twenty minutes of trying to quiet her busy brain, she would have to move again, disturbing the kitten once more. She was going to be exhausted by the time morning rolled around. She would call in sick, but was staying up all night worrying about an abandoned baby and trying to soothe a motherless kitten a good excuse for skipping a day of work?

She didn't skip work, but she wasn't feeling like herself. She piddled around with a few composites, losing herself in the work, but all the time she was trying to envision the faces behind the DNA sequences, she was thinking of Baby Doe and how she had come to be abandoned in the Sweetgrass Hills that day. Was it a kidnapping? Abandonment? A ritual of some sort? Did the person who had left her there think there was something wrong with her? Did he or she want Baby Doe to die or to survive?

Kwong knocked quietly on Micah's door, trying to get her attention without startling her from her focused state. Micah finished a couple more lines, then sighed and put her pencil down. She saw it was Kwong and nodded.

"What can I help you with?"

"I just wanted to know how you were coming along with the Bertie Wilson case."

Micah turned around the composite she had been working on. Kwong studied the man's face thoughtfully.

"This really is amazing technology. And the life that you bring into a picture makes all the difference in the world. The difference between a flat computer graphic and something that you have worked up can mean the difference between solving a case and not solving it."

"Thank you, sir," Micah acknowledged. Kwong was not one who was usually effusive in his praise, and she didn't know whether to take his words as evidence that she really was doing something remarkable or whether he was buttering her up before asking for something.

"Are you okay?" He studied her, frowning slightly.

"Just tired. I haven't been sleeping very well." She decided that telling him that she was being kept awake by a stray kitten would not do her any good. "To be honest… I've been thinking a lot about the Baby Doe case. I know it isn't one of ours, but I want to do something to help."

He pursed his lips. "I've been watching the case. So far, they haven't indicated that they have anything for us. I don't think there's anything requiring your particular skills. Maybe they'll have some trace that they need to be processed quickly, but that won't be anything for you."

Micah could process trace. She had the training for it. But he was right, it wasn't her area of expertise and she couldn't contribute anything more to it than the others in the lab.

"We need to identify her parents," Micah said slowly.

"Yes. Clearly. And the police are publishing her picture, asking for anyone who has knowledge of who she might be to come forward. Asking for the mother to come forward with the promise that she won't be charged." His mouth twisted. "They're only concerned about her well-being."

Micah rolled her eyes. She suspected, as Kwong did, that the line was nonsense. They said they were concerned about the mother's health and safety, but they wouldn't hesitate to charge her with abandonment or neglect once she came forward.

"The baby is a genetic amalgam of both of her parents. We can test her

DNA to find out specific things about her heritage. Traits that she got from either parent."

"But most of those traits, you can't sort between the mother's DNA and the father's. And even if you could, you are only going to get a half-set of DNA for each of them. That won't give you enough for an accurate composite, even with your skills."

Micah thought about it, sitting back in her chair, tilting the seat back until it creaked in protest. Kwong grimaced at the sound.

"Sorry. But what about trace on the baby or her clothing? Has it been properly processed? What about mother's skin cells, hair, blood, tears? The Calgary police released a composite of the mother of an abandoned baby based on trace at the scene. Or if Baby Doe was kidnapped, what about the kidnapper's DNA? I could do a composite on whoever has left trace evidence on her. And if one of them is the parent, then I can use that profile to sort the baby's genetic traits and build a partial profile of the other parent."

"We haven't been given the evidence to process, so I can't tell you whether there are any biological samples on the clothing. If it wasn't handled properly from the time she was found… there could be all kinds of contamination from the hikers who found her, the first responders, CFS, doctors and nurses at the hospital, her foster parents… There could be a dozen different donors."

Micah closed her eyes, focusing. "I'll think about it. Do some research into whether there is any way for us to separate the mother's DNA and the father's…"

"I think you're reaching. We'd have mitochondrial DNA, but we both know that except in a few very specific circumstances, it is impossible to tell what DNA came from which parent. Especially in a baby girl. With a boy, at least we'd have a Y chromosome from the father."

Micah ground her teeth. "There are XY females. Has anyone tested the baby's DNA to see?"

Kwong rubbed his forehead between his eyebrows, which Micah recognized as a gesture of frustration, a warning that she was taxing his patience. "AIS is pretty rare. I don't think we can expect a break like that."

Micah rolled her eyes. "No way to know if no one tests Baby Doe's DNA."

"No," Kwong agreed. "And we don't even have a contract. I'll reach out to the PD, but no guarantees. They aren't going to throw money our way just because you're feeling bad about the baby. There has to be a compelling case."

7

It was a few days before Micah heard anything else from Kwong on the Baby Doe case. She had to focus her attention on the other routine cases coming through the office. Though, of course, none of them were routine to the victims or their families. Micah didn't lose sight of the fact that each file represented a tragedy that someone had to deal with personally.

While she was working on those other files, she continued to research the possibility that she could do something constructive on the Baby Doe case. She loaded scientific papers that might be helpful onto her phone and had a TTS app read them to her as she studied the computer predictions and composites, DNA and methylation results, and other clues provided by the scene or trace evidence collection, working on her own drawings and variations to develop a variety of lifelike composites for each file.

She set up a newsfeed alert to notify her of any breaking stories on the Baby "Sweetgrass" Doe case, but each story was just a rehash of what the public already knew and appeals for anyone who had any tips or knowledge of Baby Doe's identity or parentage to come forward. Forty-eight hours came and went without any news, seventy-two hours, and before long it was a week since the discovery of the infant and as far as Micah could tell, there was a complete lack of any evidence of the baby's identity or an explanation as to why she had been left there.

Micah walked through the lab, glancing around to take the temperature of the room. Veronica Clang, the blond, middle-aged lab tech and Mr. Hawkins, a senior who, despite his age, was very into computer technologies and had boundless energy for scientific research, both looked up from their work.

"What's up?" Veronica asked, leaning back in her chair and rolling stiff shoulders.

"Wanted to talk to Aaron," Micah said, nodding toward Kwong's office. "How is he?"

She found it difficult to read Kwong's face and body language, but the lab assistants were close enough to his office to overhear any phone conversations, especially if Kwong raised his voice.

Veronica shrugged. "Seems to be having a pretty good day. I haven't noticed any issues." She looked at Mr. Hawkins, who nodded his agreement.

"All quiet on this front."

"Good." Micah raised her brows. "Hopefully, that won't change."

Veronica laughed. "Good luck."

Micah continued on her way to Kwong's office and knocked on the open door. Kwong, facing away from the door looking at his computer, swiveled to greet her.

"Ah, Micah. What can I do for you?"

"I had some thoughts on the Baby Doe case. If you have a few minutes…?"

He looked back at his computer, considering, then nodded toward the guest chair on Micah's side of his desk. Micah entered the room and sat down. The chair was uncomfortable. Deliberately so, she assumed, to discourage people from landing there and overstaying their welcome. Kwong folded his hands on his desk.

"How have you been doing?"

"Oh, I'm okay."

"You haven't been worrying too much over this case, I hope."

"No." Micah hesitated, considering how much to say about it. "It does bother me. I want to help out. But it hasn't been affecting my performance."

"Right. Good. I think we're all feeling a little bit helpless about it. Baby shows up, abandoned, and no one knows where she came from or what happened to her parents. Why was she left there? Who could just abandon an infant in a wilderness area like that?"

"And was she supposed to be found dead or alive?" Micah contributed.

Kwong nodded slowly, chewing on his lip. "So, I understand your desire to help. I'm just not sure we have anything to offer the police."

"I might," Micah said cautiously.

"What are you thinking?"

"Do you know anything about microchimerism?"

"Microchimerism. Not really. I'm aware of chimeras in general, of course—a person carrying multiple sets of DNA. Possibly due to a twin being absorbed in the womb or anomalies in fertilization or cell division. Or from organ or bone marrow donation."

Micah nodded. She was in her zone now, talking about science and her latest research.

"Microchimerism is something they have just recently begun to research and test for. Researchers found that mothers who had borne sons had some Y-chromosome genetic material in their bodies. Especially in the brain. It would seem that some of the fetal genetic tissue crosses the placental barrier and enters the mother's bloodstream."

"Okay. So if we found the mother, we could test to see if she had any of Baby Doe's genetic material in her blood. But we could already do a maternity test to verify that she is the mother. I don't see how that gets us any farther in this case."

"It turns out that the opposite is also true. Some of the mother's DNA also crosses the placental barrier and is present in the child's blood."

Kwong just looked at her, one eyebrow raised. Micah said nothing, waiting for him to process what she had said. Kwong blinked and straightened up. He leaned toward her.

"Baby Doe could have her mother's full DNA profile in her blood?"

Micah nodded. "Exactly."

"And with her full DNA profile, we could do a composite of the mother."

"Yes."

His eyes moved back and forth as he examined this hypothesis from different angles, identifying potential weak points.

"How hard is it for us to separate the mother's DNA from the child's? Can it even be done? How much blood would we need? This is an infant we are talking about; we can't request more than a couple of vials."

"We can do that. We are already set up to extract multiple DNA profiles from one blood sample much smaller than a vial. If there are multiple contributors, we can extract as many as ten unique profiles."

"But the baby's and the mother's would not be unique. The baby has half of her mother's genetic material. Will the computer be able to differentiate them?"

"I can talk to Michael Morse and get help tweaking the programming. He knows the system. Chastity can help with the deep knowledge."

"Has this been done before?"

"Well... not that I've been able to identify. But from all of the journals that I've read, it is theoretically possible. We're not sure that DNA is exchanged between the mother and fetus in every pregnancy. Most of the studies that have been done so far have focused on mothers of sons, because the Y chromosome is simple to flag, and those tests did not find a Y chromosome in the mother's blood in every case. They haven't had the ability like we do to break full profiles out of a single blood sample. That's proprietary technology."

"So we could test Sweetgrass Doe and not find any of her mother's DNA."

"It's possible. But taking a little blood is not a risky procedure. If we don't find what we're looking for, no harm done. We're no farther ahead, but we haven't destroyed any evidence or harmed the donor."

"Just expended our time and resources."

"Right. I think it's worth a shot. Think of how much it would advance this case."

"The PD isn't going to want to pay for something with the risk of no results. In a case of homicide, they are more likely to risk it, but something like this, where it is just child abandonment? It's an emotional topic, but it's not worth pouring money into."

Micah rubbed her thumb along the arm of the chair, thinking about his arguments. "Can we offer it on contingency? We'll run the blood sample. If there's no maternal DNA, they don't have to pay anything. If there is, they foot the bill."

Kwong scratched the back of his neck. "How likely are we to find maternal DNA?"

"In the brain studies, sixty-three percent," Micah told him reluctantly. "But that's brains, not blood, and decades after the pregnancy. In this case, we're talking about a DNA exchange that occurred within the past month.

Even when you get a blood transfusion, the donor's DNA profile can stay in your system for fourteen days or more. I would put the chances much higher than sixty-three percent, with the DNA exchange occurring so recently."

"Quantifiable?"

Micah hesitated. "I'm not aware of any studies that could provide those statistics. There's no precedent, but if we mathematically 'split the difference' between the decades-old maternal brains and the possibility that microchimerism occurring in one hundred percent of cases, then we would be left with somewhere around eighty percent."

Kwong considered that. He jotted some notes on the scratch pad in front of him. "Let's just say greater than sixty-three percent," he decided.

Micah sighed in relief, glad not to be held to her speculation. "Will you approach them, then? Suggest that we give it a try?"

"I'm going to talk it over with Amy Bradshaw first. I know it's just one case, so our losses would not be great, and we are pioneering new ground here."

Amy Bradshaw was the Vice President over their team. With the looks of a porcelain doll in a pinstripe charcoal suit tailored to her figure, Amy was everything Micah didn't want to be. The perfect makeup and feathery, shoulder-length hair that must take an hour to achieve with a blow-dryer, uncomfortable clothing patterned after a man's, a corporate-level job that required her to supervise people and work long hours, to kowtow to the CEO, the board, and the clients. It all sounded like a nightmare to Micah. No amount of money could compensate for having to live that kind of life.

"Do you think she'll approve it?"

Kwong tapped the end of his pen on his pad of paper, considering. "I'm not making any promises. But EvPro prides itself with being on the cutting edge of forensic technology. Being on the cutting edge necessitates risk-taking. If we can make use of this technology in a way that has never been done before, and the only thing we are risking is a few hours of your and Chastity's time, it seems like a reasonable trade-off to me. But I'm not the one in a position to make that choice."

"And maybe some consultant fees from Michael to tweak the multiple profile algorithm," Micah reminded him. "And computer processing time."

He nodded and added these items to his notes. He looked up at her. "I'll let you know. It may take a little finessing."

"Don't let it go for too long. We don't know how long maternal DNA stays in the offspring's blood, and we don't want the case to get too cold while we're waiting."

"We're used to coming into cases late, after the police have exhausted all other avenues. The DNA isn't going to change. But I understand your point about the unknown timeline on the maternal DNA. We don't know if it stays for days or decades."

Micah nodded. "My guess would be that it stays, just like fetal DNA in the mother's brain, but that's only a guess. It could be gone in a few weeks, like a blood donor's."

"I'll do what I can to convey the urgency. The fact is, there's lots of public attention on this case as well, which makes it attractive for PR reasons, even if the technology fails. At least people would hear our name and know that we tried."

Micah stood up, satisfied that he would do his best to get them the case. Whether Amy Bradshaw would approve approaching the PD to lobby for the file or whether the PD would give it to them were out of her control.

"Thanks for following up on this, Micah," Kwong said with a note of dismissal, and swiveled his chair back toward the computer.

8

After getting home, Micah scanned her newsfeed for any information on progress in the *Sweetgrass Doe* case, but there was nothing new. Even the filler articles with the speculations of the self-proclaimed experts were starting to fade out. Before long, everybody would forget all about the baby girl. The case would go cold.

Sweetgrass Doe was probably already with a foster family. They wouldn't have kept her in the hospital for more than a day or two unless there was something really wrong with her, and the news reports had indicated she was just hungry and cold.

The kitten had been yowling and rubbing up against her, but Micah was focused on her tablet until the kitten grew impatient and tried to climb her leg.

"Ouch!" Micah reached down and detached the kitten from her leg, snagging her slacks. Her leg stung. She was getting quite the collection of pinpricks and scratches on her legs. "No claws! I'm not going to forget to feed you."

The kitten snuggled in her arms, starting to purr. Micah laughed and shook her head, pressing her cheek against the kitten's soft, fluffy fur. "You suck-up. Come on, let's get you something to eat."

There was still dry kibble in the cat's dish, but the second dish Micah used for the moist canned food was empty. She didn't like to put too much food out and have it sitting at room temperature all day, getting dry and icky and multiplying bacteria. Micah got more canned food out of the fridge, the kitten yipping and yowling like she was starving to death. Of course, if she were that hungry, she would have eaten more of the dry kibble, so Micah wasn't fooled, but she laughed at the cat's histrionics.

"Believe me; you could be a lot worse off, kitty."

***

Micah was sitting at her desk working on a sketch when she got a text from Kwong.

Meeting in the lab. We got the contract.

He didn't say which contract, but it had to be the Sweetgrass Doe file. Any other contract, and he would have had to specify which one he was talking about. 'The contract' could only have one meaning.

She grabbed a scratch pad to make notes on and headed into the lab.

The lab techs were talking quietly with each other, looking around, speculating on what was going on. Veronica raised her eyebrows at Micah, a query as to whether she knew what was going on. Micah nodded. She pulled a stool to where the others were sitting, but didn't have time to explain anything to Veronica before Kwong entered.

He didn't sit, but stayed on his feet close to a whiteboard that had been wiped clean.

"I'm sure everyone here is familiar with the Baby Sweetgrass Doe case that has been in the news."

The techs looked at each other and then back at Kwong.

"I wasn't aware that there was any trace evidence in that case," Chastity commented. "Why haven't they followed it up before now? Or is the city lab too backed up and they decided they need to get it processed before the case gets too cold?"

Chastity was their DNA analysis expert, so her time and input would be required on the case. She had a few sharp edges, and Micah sometimes found herself at odds with the woman. Micah wasn't sure whether there was some sort of rivalry between them, if maybe Chastity was threatened by Micah's success as a Forensic DNA Phenotyping artist. Micah wasn't sure, but didn't spend any time worrying about it. If Chastity had any objections to being involved in the file, Kwong could handle her.

Kwong nodded gravely at Chastity's question. "It turns out that they have evidence that they didn't realize they had," he explained. He turned toward the whiteboard and outlined Micah's suggestion that they could get the mother's full DNA profile from the baby's blood and develop a phenotype and composite from there.

"This is untested technology," Chastity pointed out. "No one has tried to do this before."

Kwong turned around, raising an eyebrow questioningly. Chastity looked confused at his reaction and turned toward the other lab techs for their support.

"The concept is sound," Mr. Hawkins said, warming to it. "The fact that no one has ever tried to apply it this way is beside the point. I can do some more research into the studies that have been done up until now, but we're moving into uncharted territory, so I'm not sure how much help it will be to see what's been done before."

"The best way to find out is by trying it," Veronica said. "If we can't get the maternal profile, then we can't. No way to know without putting it to the test."

"If we can, it could break the case," Micah pointed out. "It would be a great addition to your CV."

Looking somewhat disgruntled, Chastity turned back to face Kwong. "We might need to make some changes to the programming," she warned. "We can pull separate profiles from the same blood sample, but the assumption is usually that they are unrelated. I'm not sure what the impact will be of such large SNP's when trying to separate the profiles."

"I've already given Michael Morse a heads-up. He'll be expecting your call. I brought him up to speed on the possible difficulties, and he figured he could handle it."

Chastity's mouth was a thin, straight line. She didn't voice any further objection, but Micah could tell she was thinking it through, looking for holes in the theory.

"Blood samples will be coming over this afternoon. I want to make this a priority. Find out as quickly as we can whether we can isolate the maternal profile. We don't want to look like we're sitting on our hands. The police don't know why this baby was abandoned and what happened to her parents, whether they are suspects or victims. They haven't been able to move the case forward, and this could be the break they need."

Chastity nodded grudgingly. The others seemed more positive about it, but it was Chastity who would be working on the initial steps. If she wasn't committed to giving it her best effort, she could derail the whole thing. Micah looked away. She didn't want some resentment getting in the way of the file. She didn't want it to be a competition between the two of them. Chastity knew enough about what Micah did to recognize her hand behind Kwong's explanation.

Kwong asked for any other comments or questions, cleared up the last few non-issues, and gave a firm nod. "Alright. Those of you who will be involved, please do the best you can to clear the decks of other work so that you can give this priority. We'll leave this whiteboard up and you can make notes as you move forward and either have more progress or roadblocks."

—

Micah knew that they wouldn't have the fully-sequenced DNA that day, even if they did manage to immediately extract the mother's profile, but she was still hyped up and anxious for the results. She paced her office, unable to work on anything else in her inbox.

It had been a while since she had talked to Wes Watley, the investigator who had first called her about the case. She finally had something to tell him, even if she didn't have anything concrete yet. But she would soon. Or might. Hopefully. She found his contact record on her phone and tapped it.

"Wes Watley," he answered briskly.

"It's Micah."

"Oh, Micah. How are you doing?"

"Good. I thought I would let you know about the Sweetgrass Doe case."

"Sweetgrass…? Oh. The abandoned baby. Yes, how is that going? Do you have any news? It's been pretty quiet."

"The police don't seem to have made very much progress. But in a way, that's good, because I've managed to get the file. And maybe…"

"Maybe you can crack it?" he suggested. "You've done it before."

"Well, I'm hopeful."

"There was DNA evidence, then? They didn't release that information to the public."

"That's because they didn't know they had it. And we still don't know, actually, but maybe by tonight, we'll at least have some indication. In a few days... maybe enough data for phenotyping."

"Explain," Wes suggested succinctly.

Micah smiled. As an ex-FBI SAC and Army CID investigator, Wes was not one to waste words. He was a very... *efficient* communicator. She appreciated the quality. She gave him an efficient summary of the possible existence of the mother's DNA in the baby's blood. There was silence on the line as Wes thought this through.

"So you're not talking about the half of the baby's DNA that is inherited from the mother. You're talking about her full DNA actually being in the baby's blood, like a... like a bacteria or something. A foreign body."

"Yes, exactly. Up until now, we didn't have the technology to detect the separate profile reliably. Researchers have been testing and speculating based just on flagging Y chromosomes in the maternal blood. And some companies will test the maternal blood for gender or for fetal defects like Down Syndrome instead of doing amniocentesis. But no one has been doing the reverse, pulling the maternal DNA from the baby's blood. They haven't had reason to. With a case like this, though, it could be the breakthrough. We could be able to identify the mother from the baby's blood."

"Incredible. Well, if anyone can do it, it's EvPro. And Micah Miller."

"I won't be doing the actual separating and sequencing, though I'll stand by with suggestions if they run into any problems. But once they have the mom's DNA sequenced... it's going to be a few days, and I don't know how I'm going to sleep between now and then."

Wes chuckled. "You're like a kid on Christmas Eve, aren't you? This is like your favorite crossword book or something."

"Better than Christmas! I never got anything I wanted for Christmas."

"No? You probably wanted something nerdy, eh?"

Micah closed her eyes, remembering. "I wasn't your typical kid. The things I wanted were out of my parents' price range, and they could never understand why I would want them in the first place. It was like getting socks when you were expecting the latest video game."

"You wanted your own DNA sequencer when you were twelve?"

"Something like that. Instead... I probably got a china doll or something similarly useless. Maybe something other girls my age would have loved, but that I didn't have any use for."

"I know the feeling—I always wanted a detective kit instead of toy trucks. I think my parents really wondered about me." Wes chuckled again. "Poor Micah. Well, now you're a big girl, you can buy the DNA sequencer yourself."

"Yeah." Opening her eyes, Micah paced across the room and back again. "Can you see what a great tool this will be? If this works… there's no telling all of the applications there might be. It's… a game-changer."

"It sounds like it. Well, thank you for the update. Let me know what you find, okay? As soon as you know anything."

"Sure," Micah agreed. She would have to be careful about confidentiality. She wouldn't be giving him any details about the identity of the mother, but that didn't mean she couldn't tell him how they were getting on. "I'll keep in touch."

"Good luck. Blessings on your computers."

"Thanks, Wes."

Micah hung up, grinning to herself.

9

Micah looked at the phone when it buzzed. She wasn't expecting it to be anything important. A green text slid onto the screen.

We got it.

She looked at the sender. Chastity's number. Micah leaped out of her chair and was in the lab in an instant.

"You got it?" she asked Chastity, her heart thumping in excitement. She didn't see anything else in the room, totally focused on the other woman in her blue lab clothes, gloves already removed and tossed in the garbage as she examined a report on the screen of the nearest computer. "You got the maternal DNA?"

"I had my reservations about whether we would be able to get anything, but there it is," Chastity said. Her cheeks were pink with excitement. Her doubts didn't stop her from being pleased with the results.

"Full sequence?" Micah asked, moving in closer for a look at the screen. "No missing information?"

"It's all here." Chastity pointed to the two sides of the split-screen. "Here is Sweetie's raw genome data, and here is Mama's."

Micah skimmed it with interest. The shared sequences were highlighted, showing DNA that had been inherited from her mother. Roughly half of the letters on the screen as Chastity scrolled through it.

"Some nice long shared SNP's," she observed. She would download everything into the company's proprietary software and it would start spitting out observable characteristics and predicting the most likely facial structure for the composite pictures. Micah would be able to see how many of the traits were shared between the baby and her mother. She considered that for a moment, the letters blurring in front of her eyes. She wondered how long maternal DNA remained in the child's blood. Were her own mother's DNA sequences still swimming around in her blood, an artifact to be examined like the traces of a civilization long extinct dug up by an archaeologist? She had never been able to look at Marianna and see features that they shared. But maybe, there in her blood…

"Micah?" Chastity poked her arm. "Everything okay?"

"Yeah, fine. Just thinking. I can't wait to start running this through the imager." She looked at the clock on the wall. "Can we start it going now so that I'll have results in the morning and can start working on some sketches?"

Chastity nodded. "I've already started it loading." She stared at the screen. "What do you think we're going to find?"

Micah shrugged. She'd seen pictures of the baby, so she imagined they would find that the mother was white with brown hair and brown eyes. She could be wrong, but that was her expectation. The baby didn't look biracial, but not all biracial children did, especially as babies. It was hard to tell what the planes of the face would be like when she got older, puffed out as they were with baby fat. There was no one around to say 'she has Uncle Ray's nose' or 'Mama's ears.'

"I don't know yet what she's going to look like," Micah offered. "Your guess is as good as mine."

"Yours is probably better than mine," Chastity confessed, looking at the letters. "But visualization is your job."

"How about epigenetic data?" Micah asked, changing the subject. "Can we still get methylation from the maternal DNA?"

"Yes. I'll run it, see what we can get out of it… but you know that's still experimental."

"It's new," Micah corrected. "That means that people don't trust it yet, but that doesn't make it any less correct than the DNA sequence."

"We know less about how it works and what the different methylation switches mean."

"Yes," Micah admitted, "but we know what we know. Epigenetic switches that point to age, adult height, dietary habits, trauma. There's a host of other switches that we haven't gathered enough information on yet. But what we know, we know."

Chastity nodded. "We'll see what it spits out."

Micah turned to survey the rest of the room. She had blocked everything and everyone else out in her excitement to see the results with her own eyes. Veronica and Mr. Hawkins were watching with interest. Kwong was right beside her, and Micah hadn't even registered his presence.

"What else do we have? Do we have any evidence from the crime scene? Any trace? Other details?"

Kwong knew that she would study all of the other details from the scene in trying to construct an accurate composite. The tiniest things could give her clues as to what the mother might look like.

"There's not much," he said. "We have the baby's clothing to check for any skin cells, fibers, or other trace. The blanket she was swaddled in. The police department picked up any litter close to the scene in case the unsub happened to drop something, but on a quick visual, nothing was fresh, it had all been sitting there for some time."

"Send me pictures of the clothes and blanket. Manufacturer labels too. They might give me some clues as to where the mom shopped and what style of clothes she wore herself. Pictures of the scene?"

"Didn't get any. You think they might have missed something?" Kwong asked skeptically.

"No. Just… her choice of location might tell us something. I know it was the Sweetgrass Hills and 'under a bush,' but I'd like to see the surroundings and positioning… I won't know what it will tell me until I see it."

Kwong nodded. "I'll ask the PD to send us what they have."

Surprisingly, Micah slept soundly that night. If she'd had to predict, she would have expected to lie awake half the night, tossing and turning and thinking about the work she would be doing the next day. The process of studying the computer composites and identifiable characteristics index, developing ideas of how the mother might have done her hair and makeup, clothing and accessories, experimenting with different ages and weights. She was eager to get started the next morning.

But it was the first night's sound sleep since she had first heard about the discovery of Baby Sweetgrass Doe. Maybe it was knowing that she could finally do something to contribute to the investigation. Maybe the kitten slept better and didn't wake her up wanting to play or cuddle. Whatever it was, she slept through the night and woke up feeling refreshed and ready to tackle her project.

She normally went to bed and woke up at the same time every day. Even though she had an alarm set in case of oversleeping, she was usually awake a minute or two before it sounded, immediately swinging her feet over the side of the bed and rising with no thought of snoozing the alarm or lingering in bed just a little longer. This time, she was up an hour before her usual rising time, and by the time her reminder alarm rang, she was showered and dressed, had eaten her breakfast and fed and played with the kitten, and was nearly ready to step out the door.

The kitten followed her around, probably confused about the deviation from her usual schedule, but she was used to Micah's routine and jumped up onto the windowsill as she put her shoes on so that she could watch Micah leave.

"I'll see you after work," Micah told her. "Might be late today, but I'll be home." The cat had enough crunchy kibble that she wouldn't suffer if Micah were away for longer than usual. She might be restless not having someone to play with in all that time, but Micah had accumulated enough cat toys for her to find things to entertain herself if she were bored.

The kitten meowed silently. Micah gave her ears a scratch and petted her for a couple of minutes, listening to the cat's tiny rumbly purr.

"Okay. Sorry for the long day," she apologized in advance and headed out the door.

10

Micah stared at the computer screen. Sweetie's mother was, as Micah had expected, white with brown hair and hazel to brown eyes. Her heritage was mostly European, with a bit of Nordic and Native American. All pretty common for Montana. Those were the basics. The composite program gave a predicted facial structure: Oval, Nordic cheekbones, prominent chin.

She skimmed through some of the suggested hairstyles and makeup, picking out a few that seemed likely and sending them to the printer, but she needed more data to make the face lifelike. What kind of life had the woman led? How old was she? How much fat did she have on her face? What was her predicted height?

Some of that information would be in the epigenetic analysis, so Micah minimized the composite program and opened the epigenetic data for Mama Doe. As Chastity had said, this analysis was not yet widely accepted, but they had run thousands of samples against known subjects to analyze what different epigenetic switches indicated. Science was still discussing the reliability of epigenetic data; EvPro was establishing and refining their database of traits.

Micah was distracted by her inbox notifications and reluctantly clicked on the icon before reviewing Mama Doe's epigenetic traits. A couple of emails from the Toole County Sheriff's Department asking about her

42

progress. One from Kwong with links to the crime scene photos she had requested. Even one from Wes Watley. Everyone was waiting for her composites. But she couldn't let them hurry her. She needed to be thorough in her analysis before releasing any information.

Hoping that personal contact would be a more efficient way to reassure the Sheriff's Department that she would be getting them the information they had paid for as soon as possible, she dialed the number at the bottom of the most recent email.

"Sheriff's," was the curt answer.

"Deputy Bellows, this is Micah Miller."

"Ah, Miss Miller. Thank you for calling me back."

"I wanted to let you know that I am working on Mama Doe's profile right now. I have preliminary phenotyping now, but I have other data to run through and a portfolio of pictures to sketch for you. It is going to take some time."

"Can you send me what you have now? Then we can get a head start on this…"

Micah rolled her eyes. They were already behind where they should be, the case going cold. Waiting for her to give them a good set of composites was worth the wait.

"As much as I would like to hurry the process, that won't be helpful to your case. I can tell you that the mother was white, brown hair, brown eyes. I'm working on filling in some additional details and then I'll get going on some sketches. Is there any other evidence that you are aware of that we have not been provided? Even if it doesn't seem like something we could use for the composite sketch, sometimes the most obscure details can inform the sketches."

"Yes, of course, we gave your company everything we have."

"How about vehicles? Do you have any pictures or videos of the cars parked in the nearest parking lot during the twenty-four hours before Sweetie was found?"

"Well, yes," he admitted. "But I don't see what good those will be to you. We don't have any pictures of the unsub, don't know which car might have been the one transporting the baby."

"But you must be able to narrow it down to a handful that were there during the time she was abandoned. And license plates…"

"They are not going to help you."

"They might. The registered owners of the vehicles must have driver's licenses, and if one of them matches the phenotype…"

"We have approached the owners of those vehicles already, nothing suspicious."

"Are there other license holders at the same address as the registered owner?"

"We have done the footwork, Miss Miller. We haven't just been sitting around here."

"I'd like pictures of the cars that were in the parking lot around the time that she was abandoned. They might inspire something."

She could practically hear him rolling his eyes. "Fine. I'll get you pictures of the cars."

It was odd that following up on the cars in the parking lot hadn't led to anything. How far would someone walk or hike in to abandon a baby? If it had been the mother, she was probably weak and tired. If it were a kidnapper, he wouldn't want to be seen carrying the baby around; he'd want to have it in his possession for as little time as possible.

"Is there anything else I should know about?" Micah asked. "Any physical evidence? Anything suggested by the surroundings? By the time of day or any other circumstances?"

"We believe she was abandoned the evening before she was found. She was probably there all night. I don't know what that tells you."

Probably that she was not supposed to survive. In the evening, and no car nearby, that probably meant that whoever had left her there had thought it out ahead of time and didn't want to be caught.

"Anything else?"

"No, can't think of anything, ma'am. So when do you think you're going to have those pictures?"

"I'll have something to you tonight or early tomorrow."

"Well, I guess that will have to do. I was hoping it would be earlier than that, since the computer work is all done. I thought that was most of the work."

"The picture that the computer produces and the observable characteristics list is just the beginning. I need to play with the data, make some changes to the hair, jewelry, clothing, makeup, age, weight, and anything else that might help you to identify her more easily. There are a lot of variables to be considered. Even after I give you the first set of pictures, I may develop more farther down the line as I think about her circumstances and what her DNA and epigenetic information tells me."

"Alright, then," the deputy sounded slightly mollified. "You get it to me when you can. We need to make some progress on this case, and the mother's picture would be a big step."

"What we've done so far is groundbreaking, Deputy Bellows. It's like landing on the moon. Brand new unexplored territory. Who knows what kind of doors this could open in the future."

He didn't seem to know what to say to that. Not that Micah could blame him. It was almost inconceivable that they'd been able to do what they had done.

"I'll be in touch," she promised, and hung up.

Micah took a look at the pictures in her inbox of Sweetie's clothing, frowning and zooming in on the cloth and the labels. She rubbed her eyes, too dry from staring at the screen. Her energy was dipping and she needed to recaffeinate. Walking through the lab to the kitchenette, she stopped by Hawkins's workstation.

"Mr. Hawkins, I have a little research project for you."

"Sure!" Mr. Hawkins beamed and turned toward her, arching his back and rubbing the lumbar region. He needed a better chair. Or better posture.

"The clothing that Sweetie was wearing. Do you have access to the clothes? Or even just the pictures?"

"The pictures are in the workspace. Do I need physical access?"

"Maybe not." Micah leaned on the corner of his desk. "I was just looking at the pictures, and… the clothes don't look new. They look outdated, and it looks like there is wear in the fabric. Some rubbing and pilling."

"Okay, sure."

"Baby clothes don't wear out very fast. With newborns, they get worn a handful of times, and as long as they are kept clean, they are still good enough to pass on to someone else."

He nodded his agreement. Micah glanced at Mr. Hawkins's desk for any pictures. Did he have children? Grandchildren?

"I'd like you to take a look at the brands and styles. See if you can tell when they were manufactured or if anyone is still selling them. I think they're either hand-me-downs or purchased at a thrift store."

"Sure. I'll take a look. And if they're second-hand, does that tell you anything?"

"It tells me that Mama is probably wearing second-hand clothes too. Something that might be slightly out of style. Nothing fancy, just very basic. The baby's clothes weren't frilly or dressy. And Mama probably doesn't have much by way of jewelry. If she has glasses, they'll be an older style frame."

Hawkins was nodding along rapidly, understanding where she was going with her analysis. The shape of a person's glasses or collars could make a big difference to the look of her face and how people perceived her. To whether they even saw her. "I'll get on it ASAP," he promised.

Micah continued on her way to get a refill on her coffee, and returned to her desk. She closed her door. No distractions. She wasn't going to look at any more emails or answer any phone calls. If people wanted her to get the pictures done, they needed to give her the time and space to do it.

She opened the file detailing the epigenetic features they had been able to catalog and started to work her way down the list, referring back to the observable features that the computer had worked out, and even back to individual genes with EvPro's proprietary genome browser for the finest details.

She fed information back into the composite generator, adjusting age, freckles, earlobes, and the lines and expression on Mama Doe's face.

She was deep into the files when a knock at the door pulled her out of her groove. Micah slapped her hand down on her desk, frustrated.

"Who is it?"

Kwong opened the door and walked in. He looked at the pictures scattered over Micah's desktop and turned them around to look at them, studying the girl's face. Micah intentionally didn't have a guest chair in her office, so he sat on the edge of her desk.

"This is her?" he asked unnecessarily, picking a couple up.

"So far. Still making adjustments."

"You've age-adjusted her to be younger than the default profile."

"Mothers who abandon their newborns are typically quite young, often teenagers who didn't want anyone to know that they were pregnant and weren't prepared to be parents. And her epigenetic data suggests that she was under twenty."

"Telomeres?" Kwong inquired.

Micah shook her head in irritation. As the head of the team, Kwong really should have a better handle on the science behind what they did.

"Telomeres have been used to identify how much someone has aged, but they are not a reliable indicator of someone's actual biological age." Micah squared a few of the pictures on the desk. "Not everyone starts with the same length of telomeres, and you need to know how long they were to start with and how rapidly they are shortening to calculate someone's age. But we can use other methylation data that is far more accurate, making it so that we are able to predict biological age within three years."

"And the range of Mama Doe's is…?"

"Definitely under twenty. Lower range fifteen or sixteen. You probably won't see a lot of full-term pregnancies much younger than that anyway. And the person who abandoned her needed to have access to a car. So, let's say fifteen as the minimum."

"Fifteen to twenty." Kwong gave a low whistle. "I hadn't thought of her being so young." He looked down at the composite pictures once more. "Tell me what else you have adjusted for."

Despite wanting to get the work done so she could get pictures out to Deputy Bellows and anyone else involved in the investigation, Micah enjoyed discussing her work and the unraveling of the DNA puzzle.

"Her epigenome suggests that she is a smoker, so I have deepened the lines of her face more than I normally would for a teenager. I aged a photo of Sweetie, with reference to their unique and shared heritages, and made a few adjustments to Mama's facial structure to match. Other traits included unattached earlobes, no dimples or freckles, probably straight hair." Micah paused, considering the details she had been poring through. "The data suggests some level of malnutrition. So I have gone with a slightly lower than expected height and thinned her face."

"Malnutrition," Kwong repeated. "Really? Was she an immigrant? She's white."

"Even in America, there are still children who don't get enough to eat. Not just immigrants from poorer countries."

Kwong looked like he would argue the point, then shook his head.

"Well, I guess that helps to narrow the pool. Someone who may be living below the poverty line, making use of county services."

"I've been digging down deeper into dietary and environmental factors and their effect on the epigenome. I might get Mr. Hawkins to do a bit more research for me if he's not too busy."

Kwong raised an eyebrow. "Which would tell us what?"

"I may be able to get an idea of what her diet and environment were like. What she was eating, where she was living. Whether she's from this area or somewhere else."

"How accurate would that be? It would narrow it down to what kind of area?"

Micah blew out her breath slowly, considering. She'd gone off down a rabbit trail, chasing what other information they could extract from Mama's epigenome, but how useful would that information be? How would it help them to identify her?

"Hard to say… no one has done it before, as far as I am aware. But it would be good for us to at least start a database, start tracking this internally so that we can make better predictions in the future…"

"What would it tell us?" Kwong persisted. "That she grew up in this county? This area? Montana?"

"Uh… probably not that narrow. Maybe… western states, or Rocky Mountain or prairie states…"

"That doesn't really help us to identify Mama Doe. It's too broad. We already know that she lives in this region, and if she is just a teenager and indigent, chances are she grew up here."

"I suppose," Micah agreed.

"Don't waste any more time on that. Yes, it's something you can suggest to R&D that they work on for the future, to stay ahead of the competition, but don't get bogged down with it now. There isn't enough data to make it worth our while on this file."

"Okay. I'll send them a memo."

He nodded, satisfied, and put down the pictures. He tapped one with the pads of a couple of fingers. "I like these. It's good work. If you can get the first couple to the Sheriff's Department tonight, then you can work on whatever variations you wanted to try over the next couple of days, send them over as you complete them."

Micah looked at the time on her phone and realized that it was time to close up for the day. She stretched her shoulders and back. "I'll touch a couple of these up and send them over," she agreed. She opened her drawer and removed a tray of colored pencils. "Won't take long."

"Great. I'll let them know they're on the way."

Micah sat on the couch, petting the kitten and staring at the dark window, visualizing Mama Doe's face and thinking about everything she had learned and the pictures she had produced over the previous few days. Despite the fact that the streetlights were on, she did not notice the figures moving up the sidewalk and was startled when the doorbell rang, followed by a sharp rap.

The cat immediately sat up, staring at the door in alarm. Micah didn't encourage visitors, so the kitten was unused to anyone else coming to the door, and certainly not to anyone knocking or ringing the doorbell. When Micah rose to go to the door, the kitten streaked away, claws skittering over the slippery wood floor, and hid.

Micah peered out the peephole, but she knew who was at the door without looking. Not many people would come to her house unannounced, and it was too late and too dark out for door-to-door salesmen or missionaries. Besides, she knew that knock. She'd heard it many times before, and it was always exactly the same. She confirmed the identity of the visitors and opened her door.

"Hi, Mom, Dad. I wasn't expecting you."

"No," Marianna agreed, stepping forward to give Micah a brief hug and brush her cheek with a kiss. "You never do ask, do you? I've been telling you that I wanted to come over and see your new little one, but you're always too busy."

Micah made sure that the door was shut before looking around for the kitten. Her parents began to take off their jackets and gloves. Micah called the kitten, checking her usual hiding spots. She had wedged herself between a counter and the fridge and was backed right up against the wall, eyes wide with worry.

"It's okay," Micah soothed. "There's nothing to be scared of. Just some new people to meet. It's okay."

She could hear her parents getting settled in the living room, talking in low voices, commenting on her decorating or the reception they had received or speculating about the kitten.

"Come on out," Micah invited. She shook the kitten's kibble bowl. "Come on. Come here. Nothing is going to hurt you."

It took some minutes of encouraging but, eventually, the kitten crept out, still jumpy and looking around anxiously. Micah fed her a few pieces of food by hand, then picked her up gently. The cat made one protest, then was quiet, and Micah carried her out to the living room.

"Here she is. This is Marianna and Cole, my mom and dad," she told the kitten, getting closer. The kitten's nose moved as she sniffed the air to get the scent of the new arrivals. Micah wondered what she could smell and whether she thought they smelled safe. They would smell different from Micah, not living in the same household and eating the same food. She wouldn't be able to discern the relationship between them.

"Oh, isn't she precious!" Marianna crooned. "Give her here. Let me hold her."

Micah shook her head, sitting down with the kitten. The cat burrowed her head into Micah's elbow, hiding from the intruders. "No, she doesn't know you yet. Give her a chance to get used to you first."

They both looked at Micah, saying nothing at first, waiting awkwardly.

"How has work been?" Cole asked eventually, looking around the living room and finding nothing to comment on.

"Good." Micah stroked the cat, enjoying the feel of her silky soft fur. "We got the file for the Sweetgrass Doe case. I've been working on composites of her mother."

"Her mother? How did you do that?" Marianna asked. "I didn't think there was any blood at the scene. Was there... blood or something else?"

"No. We weren't able to get trace from anything else. Or at least not yet —another department is trying to find anything useful from the clothing. But we analyzed Sweetie's blood." Micah gave a short explanation of the technology.

Neither parent said anything. They looked at each other, communicating without speech. That always weirded Micah out. She couldn't imagine knowing someone so well that she could communicate with them by facial expression and body language alone.

"How long does the mother's DNA stay in the baby's blood?" Cole asked eventually.

"We don't know. The studies that have been done have mostly focused on the fetal DNA in the mother's body. So that they can test for genetic anomalies like Down Syndrome before the baby is born without putting him or her at risk with amniocentesis, identify the baby's gender in the first few weeks, things like that. They have done studies that show that the baby's DNA remains in the mother's body, in places like the brain, for decades after the baby's birth. At this point, we don't know. It hasn't been studied widely enough. Until recently, we didn't have the technology to separate multiple profiles from the same blood sample, especially at such low concentrations."

"The world is changing," Marianna observed, looking frightened. She turned to look at Cole again. He made a calming motion with his hands. Micah knew what they were worried about. But she didn't have an answer for them. She was still trying to figure it all out herself.

"No one would ever have guessed twenty years ago that we would have this kind of technology someday," she said. "And thirty or forty years ago... no one was even talking about DNA."

Marianna shook her head, distressed. "All of the adoptions back then were sealed. They were always supposed to stay sealed and confidential. And now even if the governments don't open the records up, adoptees can still track their biological families down!"

"With technology like this," Cole said, "if children carry their mother's full DNA and mothers carry their children's... then there's no privacy at all. Upload it to one of those genealogy matching sites, and suddenly you know everything there is to know about your family."

"Well, it's not quite that easy. Sometimes the links to other people in the database are quite distant, but you can find some connections to your biological family, even if they're not immediate."

Another department at EvPro would, Micah knew, search for genetic connections to Mama Doe and Sweetie in the genealogical databases. But there were more and more rules about what information law enforcement could access even in public databases. People were still trying to hold on to their ability to keep their genetic information private, but technology was outstripping the laws. Did a murderer or rapist—or someone who had kidnapped or abandoned an infant—deserve to have their identity protected? Did their relatives' privacy rights outweigh the social good of getting a violent offender off the streets?

Micah didn't meet her mother's eyes. She looked down at the kitten. The cat was getting braver, poking her head up and watching the strangers. Curious as a cat. Micah had never known how apt the expression was before.

"What did you name her?" Marianna asked.

Micah squirmed. "Uh… Meow."

Cole laughed loudly, making the kitten burrow her head back down into Micah's arm and side. "*Meow?* You know, they have sites on the internet where you can look up good names for cats."

Micah rolled her eyes. "I know. I looked at some of them. But they're just… too cutesy. I don't want a silly pun on some actor's name, or something based on her color or something ironic like a dog's name. I wanted… something suited to a cat."

"Well, I guess I can't argue with the suitability of a cat being named Meow, but really! It's not very inventive, is it?"

"It's how she communicates. Why wouldn't you… pick a name that your pet can actually say?"

"But if everyone went by that principle, then all cats would be named Meow and all dogs would be named Bark."

"But not everyone does."

"No." Cole chuckled again. "You are… you have always had your own way of thinking about things."

Micah tried to shrug it off. She knew that her brain worked differently from either of theirs. She had always felt like an alien observing another culture. She looked like the people around her, but another kind of brain had been dropped into her human body. Something that was only a near approximation of the rest of the human race.

"He didn't mean that," Marianna said, touching Cole's arm. "Cole, tell her you didn't mean anything negative. You're brilliant, Micah, we've always known that. There's nothing wrong with your brain or the way you think."

"I didn't say there was anything wrong with it," Cole muttered, shaking his head.

"You *laughed* at her. You're making fun of her difference."

"It's okay, Mom. I know he didn't mean it that way."

Even while she was talking to them, trying to smooth things over before it became a real argument, the gears were turning in Micah's head. Adoption. The baby. The mother. The traits she had seen in Mama Doe's epigenome analysis. Malnourished. Early smoker. Early pregnancy. No one calling in to report a mother whose baby had suddenly disappeared.

"Micah? Micah! You see, Cole, it did bother her. Micah, you can call your cat whatever you like. Nobody cares."

The way the kitten had shown up on her doorstep. No mother. No owner. No one missing her. The mother cat had to have been feral, maybe killed by a predator and never returning to the nest where her babies sheltered. Because she didn't have a place in the community, in its social structure.

"No, it's okay, Mom," she told Marianna absently. "I'll be back in a minute; I have to…" She stood up, handed the kitten to Marianna, and hurried to the desk in her home office. She had a whiteboard, various scratch pads, notebooks, and sketch pads, so she always had a place to jot down her thoughts and start mapping her ideas out. She had her computer too, with several outlining or mind-mapping programs on them, but she never achieved the same flow as she did if she drew things out with a pencil or marker. She sat down and started to connect words and ideas, stood up and went to the whiteboard, and sat down again with another notepad to develop her thoughts further. It fit. It made sense, like nothing else in the case had.

She wasn't sure what time it was when Marianna ventured into the doorway of Micah's home office to say goodbye. She carried the kitten, who was blinking sleepily and had probably been asleep in Marianna's lap for however long Micah had been lost in thought in the office.

"We really should be heading home now, and you'll be wanting to get to bed too, I guess. Will you come over Sunday for dinner?"

"I'm not sure." Micah didn't look at her calendar. "I'll have to see."

"Don't let what Dad says get to you. You know he loves you."

"I know," Micah agreed. And she preferred his gruff, blunt manner to Marianna's fussing and political and social correctness, but she would never tell Marianna that. "It's fine. It's forgotten."

And it was; she could barely remember what they had been talking about. She was too wrapped up in her thoughts about the Sweetgrass Doe case.

13

M icah called Deputy Bellows as soon as she got to her desk, hoping that he would be on duty and not have been on night shift.

The phone rang a few times, and she suspected he wasn't going to answer. She swore under her breath, something she almost never did. She waited for his voicemail, preparing to hang up. She didn't want to leave a message. She wanted to talk to him directly. This was a message that required voice-to-voice communication.

"Sheriff's."

"Deputy Bellows?"

"Yeah, who's this?" He apparently looked at his caller ID "Miss Miller. I'm afraid we're not getting very far with your pictures. I'm sure they're fine, but we haven't had any calls. I have men checking wants and warrants and missing persons reports. They've looked at everything in the region and are working their way out. Some possibilities, but nothing that is looking too promising."

"I know where you need to look."

He sputtered. Micah worried she had caught him in the middle of taking a drink of coffee. "Are you okay, Deputy?"

He cleared his throat. "I'm fine. What do you mean, you know where to look?"

"Foster care. You need to get CFS checking their files."

"Foster care." Bellows didn't sound enthused. "If she was a foster kid, there would be a missing report on her. They would already have been looking for her. A teen mom disappears with her baby? Or loses the baby? They would be having kittens."

"Not if she had already aged out. If she was eighteen…"

He considered that. "She wouldn't be in a foster family anymore, unless they decided to foot the bills themselves, and most parents can't afford to do that. She might still have a social worker."

"Maybe. But not for sure. And if she lost touch, they wouldn't be that worried about it. Once she's an adult and on her own, she can decide for herself not to have contact."

She could hear him turning pages. "I still think there would be a report if a new mom went missing, or if her baby disappeared."

"There are lots of ways around that. Some women hide their pregnancies. Or she could tell anyone who knew that she'd given the baby up for adoption. Or that it was stillborn. As long as she doesn't say anything to make them suspicious…"

"I'll look into it. What made you think of it?"

Micah thought back to the previous evening. "Just a discussion I had with someone… I got to thinking about the epigenome. Malnourished at some point, she could have been a neglected child. Mother a junkie, or on the streets, or just didn't want to have to take care of a child. So CFS apprehends her. Puts her into foster care. Tries to get the parent back on track or maybe Mom is in jail. The child takes up smoking early in life, barely a teen or maybe even younger. Gets pregnant. All very common for a displaced or neglected child. Probably drinks, too. And then the lack of social connections. No family to report her or the baby missing. No one who suspects that anything was wrong. She's invisible."

"It fits," Bellows admitted. "There are other possibilities, but when you hear hoofbeats…"

"Think horses, not zebras," Micah finished, impressed that he knew the expression. She supposed that, like with medical research, police too had to focus on the obvious answers and not get sidetracked with 'what if's' and chase down rabbit trails.

"I'll put in some calls to CFS and see if anyone can identify her from the description and the pictures. If we can at least identify Mama, we'll have much better chances at finding her and getting her story."

Micah let out her breath, happy that he had agreed to follow her lead. "Thank you."

"No, thank you. It's a good suggestion. Fits together nicely. I just hope it's not another dead end."

***

Micah had other things to do. There were plenty of new files for her to play with. And plenty of old ones that the police hadn't been able to make arrests on yet where they would be happy to have another picture or two with other possible variations. But she wanted to stay focused on the Sweetgrass Doe case, to move it forward even further, if she could.

She wandered out to the lab and stood near Chastity's bench, waiting for her to finish preparing a sample for analysis. Chastity looked up, brows drawn together, when she was done.

"Micah."

"I wondered if you could do a Lazarus for me."

Chastity dutifully labeled and logged the sample and put it on the shelf with samples to be processed.

"For who?"

"For Sweetgrass Doe's father."

Chastity considered, lips pursed. "Start with Sweetie's profile, remove Mama's contribution, and we get Daddy."

Micah nodded.

"Well, half of Daddy," Chastity pointed out. "It's not going to give us a very good phenotype. We can pin down the dominant traits. Go with the most common pairs for the rest. It's a lot of guesswork, and it's not going to be accurate. Not without a sample from him or other offspring."

"I know. I just want… to have something. It's going to be pretty broad, I know. I'd just like to have something in my back pocket. A place to start."

Chastity shrugged. "Yeah, I can run it through the system. If trace recovers anything from the clothing that matches, maybe we'll be able to build a better profile."

"Yeah, good idea. I haven't heard anything, though I don't think they've been able to find anything usable."

"That's the way some of them go. We haven't been able to get very far with this file."

Micah didn't tell her about her idea that Mama might have been a foster child. If it didn't pan out, there would be no need to explain what had happened. If it did, then the Sheriff's Department would make the fact known. They would probably give Micah the credit for the idea, but if they didn't, it didn't matter. She was more concerned about solving the case than she was with getting credit. EvPro already knew how good she was and what she could do with a computer and some colored pencils.

Micah was getting ready to go home at the end of the day when her email notification flashed. She looked at it, hesitating between ignoring it and leaving the email until the next day, and taking a quick peek to make sure it wasn't urgent. If she left without looking at it, she could honestly say that she hadn't known there was anything urgent waiting for her when she left at the end of the day.

Curiosity killed the cat. Maybe some of the kitten's curiosity was rubbing off on Micah. She tapped the mouse and opened the email window.

Deputy Bellows.

The unread email was bolded. The subject line read *Mama Doe.*

Micah sat back down. She double-clicked the email to read it. The first thing she saw was a photograph. A teenager. Brown hair and eyes. Narrow face. A tentative, uncertain smile. Eyes somewhere beyond the photographer.

It was a very close match to Micah's picture of Mama Doe.

She read the information below the picture.

Trisha Madro. Seventeen. She had disappeared from her group home a year earlier. She was a chronic runaway, so CFS hadn't put all of their resources into tracking her down yet again. She knew how to get help if she needed it. She'd been in the system for long enough to know how it worked.

"They never filed a missing person report?" Micah asked aloud.

There was no one there to respond to her.

Maybe they had, and maybe they hadn't, but the police would not have been inclined to put a lot of effort into it either. She was a voluntary. People walked away from their lives sometimes; that wasn't a crime. Mama Doe was couch surfing at a friend's. Or had run off with a boy. Or preferred sleeping rough to having to answer to group home supervisors.

Considering the outcome—Sweetgrass Doe—Micah guessed that she had run off with a boy. Maybe they had thought that they were old enough to manage on their own. But things hadn't turned out to be as easy as she had thought.

No contact in the past year, Bellows had noted.

That seemed like a red flag to Micah. Yes, kids ran off sometimes, preferred partying to having to answer to someone in authority, but they usually surfaced again. Picked up for drugs or shoplifting, borrowing a car without permission. Returning to a previous family or showing up at a homeless shelter, looking for a place to sleep. Maybe involved with a gang. A social worker couldn't do anything about it, couldn't force a girl back into foster care or a group home situation when she refused. Sometimes she could be incarcerated on a minor charge or evaluated for mental health concerns but, before long, she would be back on the street looking for the next high.

But disappearing completely?

Obviously, Mama Doe—Trisha Madro—had not been killed. She had survived without institutionalized care for another year, long enough to get pregnant and deliver a healthy baby girl.

She picked up the phone and called Bellows. There was too much for her to put into an email response. She wanted to hear the inflections in his voice.

"Hello, Miss Miller."

"Can you call me Micah, Deputy Bellows?"

"If you'll call me Frank."

Micah smiled, feeling like things were moving forward. They had a professional relationship now. Bellows was willing to give her information and to accept her ideas. If the two of them put their heads together, maybe they could figure it all out.

"Okay, Frank. So tell me everything you know about Trisha Madro."

"I summarized it in the email."

"I know, but… did anyone look for her? Run into her at any shelters or youth outreach events? Did they have sightings? Have an idea where she had gone?"

"I'm going to meet with her social worker tomorrow. Do you want to come with me?"

"Could I?" Micah was surprised.

"I wouldn't ask you and then tell you no. It's not exactly regular, but you've been instrumental in getting us this far. You have some insight into her lifestyle and experience. I don't know how much we'll get from the social worker, or if it will intersect with any of this… genetic stuff… but it's easier than trying to relay everything to you after the fact, and then finding out that there was a question I should have asked."

"That would be great. I'd love to be involved. You're sure it's okay? I'm not law enforcement."

"I'm aware of that. And I wouldn't take a private citizen just anywhere. But I don't think we're walking into a dangerous situation. I'm not expecting the social worker to come after me with a blade."

Micah laughed. "No, I guess not."

"I'll give you a call tomorrow once I've had a chance to organize my day. It will probably be early afternoon but, as a cop, my schedule is subject to change."

"Okay. I'm pretty flexible. Early afternoon is fine. Just let me know."

14

It was a chilly day, the air crisp and the sky blue and smooth as glass. Micah checked the forecast before dressing and tried to pretend that it was just a routine day, like any other. If Bellows ended up having to follow up on breaking cases, their interview might not even happen for another day or two. It wasn't written in stone.

But she didn't believe it. It was the first major break in the case. If the social worker had any idea where Trish was or what kind of life she was leading, it could be the interview that led them to her door. They might get all of their answers about why Sweetie had been abandoned in the Sweetgrass Hills.

The kitten meowed and purred around her feet, and Micah had to take care not to step on her while she was walking around the house, getting her breakfast ready and trying to put her thoughts in order.

In a few hours, she could know the story behind what had happened to Sweetie.

"Social Worker is Ardith Pitz," Bellows advised as he drove. He looked much like Micah had pictured him, hearing his voice over the phone. A large man, stomach a little too big for his duty belt, his hair in a buzz cut receding around the temples. He had a grim, stern sort of face, but Micah judged that was mostly genes and lifestyle, not a sour temperament. He seemed pleasant enough as he greeted her and filled her in on the details he knew. "I've dealt with her a time or two in the past. She'll be cooperative, but that won't necessarily help. She has her ethics to think about, which include not sharing private information about her children. In addition to that, social workers learn pretty quickly that there is only so much they can do." He turned a corner smoothly. "They can't afford to get emotionally wrapped up in every child. They know they can't 'save' them all, especially teens. So I don't know how much she's had to do with Trish Madro."

"Right. The social worker might know a lot about her, or practically nothing."

Bellows nodded his agreement. "We have to be ready for either scenario."

"I'm trying not to expect too much from her."

"Good plan. And before we talk to her... I don't know what your thoughts are on Trish Madro. We don't know what kind of kid she was. We don't know if she is a victim or a criminal. Right now, she's a person of interest."

"Which means suspect."

He glanced at her. "It means person of interest. But yeah, we don't know yet what her involvement in the abandonment was. So keep an open mind. Maybe something happened to her, and maybe she's just a cold-hearted..." he cleared his throat and didn't voice his chosen noun.

Micah stared out the window as they approached the CFS office. She had never understood child abandonment. How could anyone neglect her own flesh and blood or leave her alone, with no one to care for her? She couldn't fathom it. She couldn't help feeling judgmental whenever she heard of or read an article about a child being abandoned. How could anyone be so cold-hearted?

"We're here," Bellows advised quietly. Micah wondered whether he had noticed her distraction. Whether he had any idea what it meant.

"Sorry. I was just thinking."

"You ready?"

Micah unlatched her seatbelt and opened her door, letting her actions be her answer. Bellows preceded her, but stopped at the door to the social services building and motioned her to enter, though he didn't actually open the door and hold it for her.

He followed her into the reception area and spoke to the woman at the desk.

"Bellows. Here to see Ardith."

"Yes, she'll just be a moment, Deputy."

Neither of them sat down. They moved around the reception room restlessly, looking at the paintings and pictures on the walls, the certificates and awards, ignoring the worn state of the carpet, the chipped paint, and the dreary little toys in the toy box awaiting children who might go there for evaluation or supervised meetings with parents.

Eventually, a woman came out to meet them. She was a heavy woman in slacks and a print blouse. No skirt suit or plaid. She did have a lanyard around her neck with her identification badge on display—an older woman, probably around Marianna's age. Her red-brown hair was undoubtedly dyed.

"Deputy Bellows, come in. And you are…" Ardith Pitz looked at Micah, frowning.

"I'm Micah Miller." Micah stretched out her hand to shake. Ardith Pitz took it in a smooth, cool grasp, looking into her eyes for a moment.

"Miller…" she repeated thoughtfully.

Miller wasn't an uncommon name. No reason she would have known who Micah was. Maybe she had dealt with Cole Miller on a case sometime in the past. But Micah didn't bring him up.

"Well, let's get started, then," Mrs. Pitz turned and led them down the hall to a meeting room. A room that looked more like the room a board would meet in than a place for families to meet. Micah chose a chair and sat down, trying to look comfortable. Which she was not.

"Trish Madro," Mrs. Pitz said, before she was even seated. There was a thick file open on the table. "I'm not sure I have anything useful to tell you. As I indicated on the phone, she left her last group home a year ago. She hasn't been under the care of CFS again since then."

"That's not quite the same as never having heard of her again," Micah said.

Mrs. Pitz cocked her head, looking at Micah. "No," she admitted. "That's not what I said."

"So you have seen her since then. Or know something about where she could be."

"I wouldn't go that far," Mrs. Pitz countered.

"Maybe you could be more clear," Bellows suggested. "This meeting will be a lot more successful if we all just lay our cards on the table. What do you know about what happened to Trisha after she left her last group home?"

Mrs. Pitz smoothed the papers in the file before her. She picked up a water bottle, opened it, and had a small sip. "I have not seen Trish since she left. I have not talked to her."

"But you've heard something," Micah said. "Maybe a rumor."

"She was a difficult child. She came into the system when she was… oh, nine or ten."

"She'd been neglected. Malnourished."

Mrs. Pitz nodded her agreement. She glanced over at Bellows, waiting for one of them to explain why Micah was there and what her role was supposed to be. Neither of them did.

"She was very quiet. Timid. I hoped that by placing her in a home with a nurturing mother, she would open up. Blossom. Sometimes, all you need to do is give these kids an environment they can grow in, and the changes are remarkable. You wouldn't even guess that there was anything out of place. Unfortunately… that's not the way things turned out with Trish."

"She doesn't have a juvenile record," Bellows said. "I checked."

"No. She didn't get into trouble with the law. From the beginning, she had problems with school. I don't know how much she had attended before she was apprehended. Things didn't work out. Whether it was because she hadn't gone to school in those early years, or because the neglect and abuse had caused brain damage, or maybe she was just born with a learning disability. We tried several programs that we hoped would help her, but nothing seemed to click."

With such a small population, maybe the county hadn't had the money to run the kind of programs Trish had needed. Or maybe it didn't matter; her brain was just programmed the way it was. The same way Micah's wiring was different, making her feel like she was operating on a different plane from others.

"So with the problems she was having at school, she fell in with the wrong crowd," Bellows suggested.

"She grew angry and resentful. Even though many people were trying to help her—parents, social workers, psychologists, tutors, teachers—she acted like no one cared. She didn't bond with her family. She had… an attitude."

Micah thought of the photograph Deputy Bellows had sent to her. Trish hadn't looked sullen and angry, but she certainly hadn't looked comfortable or happy. An outsider. Someone who wouldn't let others in.

"We tried some other families. Therapeutic programs. Group homes. She broke the rules. She failed at school, wouldn't complete her work even in special education. She didn't make friends."

Micah could see where it was going. Trish moved on to smoking and drinking, maybe partying with drugs. She became more promiscuous, not observing boundaries.

"We did our best to meet her needs," Mrs. Pitz said regretfully. "But she was… damaged."

"So you're not surprised that she would abandon her child," Bellows suggested, jumping ahead.

"I doubt if she was qualified to care for an infant. I don't know if she could bond with a child or comprehend its needs. If she had still been in care when she delivered, we would have done some very intensive training with her. Or if she wasn't willing to do that, we would have seized the baby at the first opportunity."

Micah's chest hurt. She felt like there was a fist-sized hole in it. What a tragedy. Trish's own neglect had set her up for failure as a mother.

"What did you hear about her during the past year?"

"People had seen her. It's not the big city. You really can't go anywhere and be sure you won't run into previous acquaintances."

"Do you know who her boyfriend was?" Micah asked

Mrs. Pitz shook her head.

"How was she living? Was she on the street? Rooming with someone? In a shelter?"

"Living with someone, I suppose. I don't know details. She wasn't accessing any public welfare services. We didn't have any direct contact."

"She wasn't ever reported missing?"

"She wasn't missing. She was a runaway. She had taken off many times before, for days or weeks at a time. We did our best to keep her safe, but she didn't want that. She didn't want people looking after her or supervising her."

"Do you know where she is now?" Bellows asked.

Mrs. Pitz looked away. "I knew you were going to ask that. I've made inquiries. But no one has seen her recently. Wherever she has been living, she's been keeping her head down. Not telling people what she's doing. No one who has been aware of her said anything about her being pregnant. I don't think I would have believed it, if I hadn't seen that picture."

Micah felt unaccountably guilty. By making the composites, she had brought attention to Trish. And now Trish, failed by society and the system, would face the justice system for failing at something no one thought her capable of.

"A composite isn't definitive," she reminded Bellows. "It's just the starting point. You still need evidence that Trish was pregnant and chose to abandon her baby. You need to get a maternity test done to prove that she is Sweetie's mother. You need to show that she understood what she was doing."

"That's why we're here." Bellows looked at Mrs. Pitz. "We're going to need the names of people who have seen her, so we can start looking for her."

When they left the building, Micah took in deep lungfuls of crisp, clean air, trying to focus on the feeling of being free again, escaping the oppressive feelings of the CFS offices.

"Are you okay?" Bellows asked. "Do you want me to take you back to your office?"

"Aren't you going to follow up on these people today?" Micah asked, surprised.

"Yes. But you didn't seem very comfortable with what went on in there. I thought maybe you lost your taste for the investigation."

"I still want to do it. It's just... sad."

"You knew going into it that kids in foster care have a tough time. It is sad. Tragic. But I need to determine exactly what happened and how responsible Trisha is for what happened. You have to be a little hard-hearted about something like this. I think you're too invested emotionally."

"I... it's not that."

"You're feeling bad because of what she went through. Before that, you were only thinking about Sweetie. How someone could do that to a baby. How bad you felt for her. You wanted to catch the culprit."

"I still want to find Trisha."

"To put her behind bars?"

"I don't know. That isn't my job."

"What is it, then? You didn't seem like you were willing to pursue this. If you want to go back to your office, that's fine. Like you said, you're not law enforcement. You were just tagging along to help with any questions. There's no reason you have to take it any further."

Micah leaned against the car, looking over the roof at Bellows. "You can't understand, because you don't know."

15

He looked back at her steadily. "Understand what?"

"*I* was abandoned as a baby."

Bellows's mouth dropped open. He stared at her. "You were abandoned."

Micah nodded. "They never found my biological mother. My mom and dad adopted me. They raised me as their own. But we are not genetically related."

"Wow. So seeing the kind of life that Trisha had growing up, that's pretty intense. It makes you wonder what kind of mother you had. What happened in her life that made her abandon you."

Micah nodded and got into the car. She sighed. "I've dealt with all of the emotions. Abandonment, anger, guilt, grieving, fantasizing... believe me; there are a lot of different ways it can hit you. Every time I feel like I've finished dealing with it, something else comes along."

"What are you feeling right now?"

Micah was startled. Surprised that he didn't ask her about the circumstances of her own abandonment, but what she was feeling at that moment.

"I'm not sure I even know. Confusion. Anger and pain. Regret." She shook her head. "Just... I feel like there's a hole in my heart."

"For your mother?"

"Maybe… because of what she took from me. I wish I could answer that, but I can't. It just hurts."

He started the engine. For a few minutes, they both sat there, breathing clouds of warm air into the cold car, waiting for it to warm enough that they wouldn't fog up the windows.

"Where am I going?" Bellows asked. "Do you want to go back to your office? Or home?"

"No. I can deal with it. Let's go on, see if we can find out where she went."

Unfortunately, one of the people who had seen Trish since she had run away the last time was Carolyn Dublin, one of her foster mothers from the early years. It was unfortunate because the conversation clearly brought Mrs. Dublin pain, regret over the fact that they had never been able to reach Trish, that they'd let her go, hoping that another family would be able to do more for her.

"You know your kids when you see them again," Mrs. Dublin said, dabbing at her eyes with the cuff of her green pullover. "Even though it's been years and they've grown up, you love them, and the years don't erase that relationship."

"How did she look?" Micah asked.

"Not good." Mrs. Dublin shook her head. "She was thin, she was smoking, and her face looked very… she had on makeup that was very… grown-up. Dramatic. Like a little girl pretending to be a woman."

"Jewelry?" Micah suggested. "What did her clothes look like? Did you think she was living on the street?"

"No. I just thought… I don't know… that she looked too grown up. I guess she's seventeen now, so she's almost an adult, but I wanted so much for her just to be a little girl again, to try one more time."

"Was she with anyone?" Bellows asked.

"Yes. Some other girls around her age. Standing around, smoking and talking to each other. Like kids do. I thought… skipping school… ducking classes."

"Do you remember what day this was? What month, even?"

"I don't know. May, June. Something like that."

"You couldn't tell that she was pregnant?"

"No." Mrs. Dublin scowled and shook her head harder. "I didn't notice any baby bump. She was thin. Her face especially. No one would have thought she was pregnant."

Bellows nodded. Micah had seen so many similar stories play out in the media that she had to believe what Mrs. Dublin said. Some people, teenage girls especially, just never showed. They gained only a few pounds and managed to hide any bulge or symptoms.

Mrs. Dublin described the area that Trish had been in, and Micah closed her eyes and pictured it. Lots of traffic, both foot traffic and cars. Nowhere near the Sweetgrass Hills. What had Trish been up to? Was she just hanging out with friends? Part of the invisible homeless, never counted, couch-surfing or finding other ways to survive? Or had she found a job and rented a little apartment, with one or two of those girl friends? There were ways for a young woman her age to make money, both legitimate and not.

"Did she see you?" Micah asked.

"I'm pretty sure she did. She was looking my way, and she went quiet, stopped talking to the other girls. They kind of closed around her, blocked her from my sight. I don't know. I couldn't just stand there, watching. So I went on."

Micah nodded. She wasn't a foster mother, so she couldn't be sure what she would have done. Mrs. Dublin no longer had anything to do with Trisha's life. She couldn't walk up and demand to know what she was doing, or tell her to get in the car because they were going home. If she hadn't had anything to do with Trish recently, she wouldn't know Trish was a runaway. Even if she did, it had never been reported as such, and there was no reason to call the police.

"I called the caseworker who had been working with us when Trish was with us. That's when I found out that she had run away. I wished I had done something… but I don't know what else I could have done. She seemed okay." Mrs. Dublin shrugged. "I drove by there a couple more times in the weeks after that, but I didn't see her again. I guess she just happened to be there once, shopping with her friends. I kept my eyes open, but I never saw her again."

Bellows made a couple of notations in his notebook. Micah wondered what he'd found to be of interest.

"Did anything else stand out to you?" he asked. "She was smoking.

Did you suspect alcohol or drug use? You thought she was skipping school, so you didn't have the impression that she was homeless or out on her own."

Mrs. Dublin hesitated, her eyes distant, replaying the memory. "I remember being disappointed that she was smoking, but not surprised. I figured she was probably abusing other substances as well. Smoking is a gateway."

"And school?" Bellows prompted.

"I thought she was with school friends. They were around her age. But they could have just been friends from somewhere else. Trish never really had much of a social group. She didn't easily make friends. I thought at first that it was just because she was somewhere new. Friendships were already established; it's harder to break into the social circles. But I've had foster children who were immediately an accepted part of the crowd. Trish hadn't gone to school before, at least not regularly. So she had that hurdle to get over too. Not understanding how it all worked. Not having that same background as other kids do. The school experience, the popular shows and games. A phone of her own."

"But you thought they were her friends. That she had become part of a group."

"I guess they could have just been smoking together and started talking because they were all in the same place… but I don't think so. The way she moved and looked at them. They were familiar with each other. They weren't girls that she had just met and chatted with casually. They were talking among themselves…" Mrs. Dublin frowned. "You know, facing in, like they shared a secret, rather than just facing out, talking casually because they happened to be in the same place."

Bellows nodded. "Did you know any of the other girls? Have you seen any of them around?"

"I didn't recognize any of them." Mrs. Dublin's eyes closed. "Have I seen them around…? I don't know. I might have seen one or two of them before that, or since. Not together as a group, just… on the street."

"Shopping? Smoking? Or something else."

"Just… walking. Maybe waiting for someone." She opened her eyes and nodded, but was unable to add anything else to the picture.

"And what were your impressions of them? Independent? Girls with a home to go to? Or on their own? Or living rough, on the street?"

"These are really hard questions… we're talking about girls that I might have seen a couple of times; I might not even be remembering properly."

But Micah suspected she was. People cataloged faces better than they thought they did. They remembered them from one place to another and made snap judgments by people's facial expressions, body language, clothing, and other clues. As a forensic artist, she was used to picking through these details consciously, or helping witnesses to think about them. "What was their makeup like?" she asked. "You said that Trish's was grown up, dramatic."

"Well… yes, they were all pretty similar. Bright lipsticks, lots of eye makeup. Like they were actresses or…"

Micah glanced over at Bellows. His lips were pressed tightly shut. Neither of them prompted Mrs. Dublin, waiting for her to come to a conclusion herself.

The older woman shook her head. "No."

"No what?"

"They weren't… streetwalkers."

Bellows nodded. "Okay."

His acknowledgment seemed to irritate her more than if he had argued with her. She became insistent. "They couldn't be. I mean, girls that age, they wear sexy stuff to school, to the store, whatever. It wasn't anything out of the ordinary. No spiked heels or micro miniskirts. Just regular dress. It was a warm day, so they had halter tops and shorts. Just like all of the other kids who were out and about."

Bellows nodded again as if he believed every word she was saying.

"I've been a foster mother for a lot of years, Deputy, and I know what kids dress like. You pick your battles. She didn't look like she was hanging out on a street corner meeting johns. She was just out with her friends, having a smoke."

"Okay. I appreciate your time. And the fact that you called CFS about this back when you saw her. I understand there wasn't anything suspicious to report at the time, but it's been helpful to get a little background, to know what was happening a few months ago."

Mrs. Dublin bit her lip. "Are you going to find her? You'll be able to track her down, won't you?"

He gave a reassuring smile. "One step at a time. If she's still in town, we'll find her."

"I hate to think that something might have happened to her. Trish with a baby…" Mrs. Dublin rolled her eyes. "Heaven help us. If there was one challenge Trish did not need in her life, it was to have another soul dependent on her. If that was the only way for her to give the baby up… well then… it was probably the best thing she could have done for the poor mite."

Micah's stomach clenched in a tight knot. The best thing Trish could have done was to abandon her infant in the wilderness? Totally helpless where she could have died from hypothermia, dehydration, or predation? When there were options for her to have the baby adopted, to relinquish her to foster care, get help with social programs, or rely on the safe-haven laws and abandon her to a doctor, priest, or fire station?

"The girl is seventeen," Bellows said to Micah, watching her face. "She's alone and scared. She probably had the baby unattended, or maybe with another girl to take care of her. She knows what foster care can be like. She doesn't want to deal with a social worker or cop. She just wants to be free."

Micah nodded, her face and neck feeling stretched and tight like she was wearing a mask.

"She wanted to do right," Mrs. Dublin said. "When she was a little girl, things were so hard for her, and she would put on attitude to protect herself, like any kid who's been through what she has. But she wanted so badly to do the right thing, to exceed people's expectations of her. It couldn't have been easy. She was… a lost soul."

"You don't have to convince me of anything," Micah said. "I'm not here to judge her or what she did."

16

Jumping from one interviewee to another had eaten up most of the rest of the day. When they were done, Micah was too exhausted and emotionally overwhelmed to go back and face the demands of work.

So she had Bellows drop her at home, thanking him politely for letting her ride along and be a part of the investigation.

"Sorry it was so hard on you," the deputy said. "It can get to even the most seasoned cop, and you have had to deal with the personal connection too. It's hard to look at a case objectively when you identify with the victim or the perp."

"Where do you go from here?" Micah bypassed the niceties, not wanting to discuss her feelings about the case or the character of Trisha Madro.

"We'll make contact with some of the organizations that help kids caught in the sex trade. See if any of them know her. Reach out to a few of the hookers around her age, particularly in the areas she had been seen. See what we can find out about where she was working and if she's still out there."

"You don't think she would have left town?"

"It's always possible, but these kids don't generally have a lot of resources. It takes money to be independent. She could hitch a ride, try to find some other way to survive when she settled somewhere new, but she'd have to know that the opportunities anywhere else would not be that much better than here."

"A dead end even if she left."

"She could have an out-of-town relative who would agree to house her, help her to find a way to support herself, but from what we've heard so far, she was pretty much alone. No one has mentioned any family. If her own mother is still out there somewhere, it doesn't sound like they kept in touch."

"I wouldn't," Micah agreed.

He looked at her for a moment, then nodded. "Go back to work tomorrow. Work on other files. Leave this to me. If you want, I'll send you a summary at the end of the day, let you know if we have made any progress."

Micah considered. "I don't know. I'll email you tomorrow after I decide how I feel."

"Sure. You've done everything you can from your end. Your job was to help us to identify Sweetie's mom, and you did that. We know who she is now, and we'll work that angle. From what we've heard today, I doubt there was anyone else involved. She made a decision to abandon the child, and did it herself."

"No one said she had a car."

He pursed his lips and tapped the steering wheel, thinking about that. "No. But there are many ways to get wheels, especially if it's only for a few hours. She could have had a friend drive her or have borrowed someone's car. She could have jacked one, even returning it after she was done so that the owner didn't know it had been used in the commission of a crime. She could have rented a car using a fake ID. I suspect she didn't hire an Uber."

"No," Micah agreed. "But you didn't find anything suspicious when you checked out the cars that were parked in the parking lot. No one who'd had their car stolen or said that they hadn't been to Sweetgrass."

"So she may have parked farther away than we thought she could have. Hiked in from farther away or from a location we're not aware of. Pulled onto a shoulder or gravel road where there were no cameras. People have eyes. It's not exactly a secret that those parking lots are monitored. There are big signs up saying that they are."

Micah nodded tiredly. Her brain was fried and it was time to walk away from it and give herself some time to think of something else. The kitten would be happy to see her home. Micah could have something nice to eat and a long soak in the tub. She would shut off her phone and not look at her email, and just take some time to regenerate. Bellows was right. It wasn't easy for her to keep an emotional distance from the case when there were so many parallels to her past.

17

Micah saw Aaron Kwong's head go up when she walked past his door, and expected him to call out to her and stop her from going any farther. He would want a report on what had happened the day before. If they had made any progress and what she had found out. But he didn't call out to her, for which she was grateful. First, she needed to get her coffee, and second, she needed to spend at least half an hour processing what was in her inbox. Maybe an hour. Then she would be ready to face questions from her boss and the others in the team.

She quickly poured herself a mug of coffee in the kitchenette and went to her office. She shut the door, signaling to the others that she was not ready to receive visitors yet. It was only a courtesy; anyone could still interrupt her if it were urgent, but they were pretty good at respecting her space.

Micah sat down at her desk and immediately started with the items in her physical inbox, sorting them into the appropriate folders and, where necessary, adding things to her task list.

But the bulk of information and questions flowing to her came by email, not the physical interoffice distribution. Questions on past cases, current cases, what was coming down the pipeline. Interoffice politics and squabbles. Official and unofficial communications. It was a rat's nest of topics; she was never quite sure what to expect. She went through methodically, archiving anything that didn't appear to pertain to her or was clearly spam. She unsubscribed from a couple of mailing lists that she had managed to get herself added to. The emails she had exchanged with Kwong about taking a few hours to ride along with Deputy Bellows had been copied up the line to Amy Bradshaw, and then to the CEO. Micah doubted that he cared how she spent one day. It wasn't like she was in the habit of disappearing and had a big backlog of cases. She was a steady, reliable employee and although, Amy Bradshaw had made some brief remarks about it not being the best time for Micah to disappear, she had not come right out to say that she was opposed or would not allow it.

There was a knock at the door. Micah swiveled around. Kwong opened the door slightly and poked his head in. "Sorry, Micah, you got a few minutes? I have a meeting in an hour, so I can't put it off."

"Okay. Sure."

He entered and discussed the previous day with her. He didn't know her personal history, so didn't understand why she would be emotionally drawn into the case; he only knew of her interest as part of a case she had developed composites for.

"So the drawings helped identify the girl," Kwong summarized, "and the police have been able to move the case forward. Whether or not they can find her isn't part of our contract."

"No," Micah agreed. "It's just been interesting to see how they proceed after getting the composites."

Kwong nodded. "So you're done with it?" he asked briskly.

"Well... yes. Bellows said that he'd call me with a summary of what he does today on the file. But I'm here. I'm working on the next files," she gestured at the items in her inbox.

"Good, good," Kwong agreed. "So you can close the Sweetgrass Doe— or Madro—file."

"Well... I won't close it until there is a resolution. If they arrest Trisha Madro."

"You can close it now. They won't need anything else from you."

"I don't expect them to. But you know how I like to do new sketches now and then to help breathe new life into a case. Freshen things up, try out a different look, maybe get a bit closer with an age-enhanced picture or a different weight..."

"But they already know who the mother is. So you can close it."

"They won't know for sure until they get her DNA. CFS only *thinks* the composite looks like Trisha Madro. There's no guarantee that it is her until they do a direct DNA test to see if she is the mother of Sweetie." Micah raised her brows, looking at Kwong. He knew that; she shouldn't need to tell him.

"I suppose it will stay open until you have a confirmed DNA match," Kwong finally agreed. "But as far as being on your active list, you can take it off, because you know who it is."

Micah wrinkled her nose. "I don't know who it is until there is a confirmed DNA match. Yes, the pictures of Trish Madro look a lot like our Mama Doe, but someone else could think she looks like another girl tomorrow."

"But you won't be pursuing other identifications."

Micah couldn't help digging in her heels. She would have expected that kind of thing from a non-scientific type, but anyone who understood science and logic should understand that the file was not resolved until it was resolved with hard evidence, and if she wanted to keep working on the file to refine her composite or to do a composite of the baby's father, she would do so.

"It won't be taking time away from other active files."

Kwong studied her, scowling. "You need to listen to what I'm telling you. The file is resolved. Move on."

"I am moving on," Micah returned evenly.

He eyed her for a minute longer, then nodded and headed toward the door.

"But that doesn't mean I'm not going to look at it again," Micah said, as he crossed the threshold.

Kwong paused, his hand on the doorframe, then walked on as if he hadn't heard her.

18

S ara *Thompson-Smith.*

Micah studied the name on her voicemail caller ID and tried to decide what to do. Of course, the polite thing to do was to call Sara back. It wasn't like she didn't want to talk to Sara.

But it was hard sometimes. She and Sara were polar opposites. At least, it felt that way. Sara had gone to the same school as Micah had, from first grade to twelfth. And she had always been one of the beautiful, popular girls. One of the ones who made everything look easy and who always knew the ins and outs of popular culture, fashion, who was friends with who, and all of the other things that were as difficult for Micah as science and math were for Sara.

Opposites.

But Sara had never been one of the mean girls. She had never talked down to Micah or made fun of her. She knew who Micah was, and treated her like a real person. Not like she was invisible or a pariah. It was probably because of Sara's attitude that Micah had survived school without being the brunt of a series of cruel pranks meant to drive her to suicide or dropping out. In later grades, a relationship had developed between the two of them that Micah considered friendship.

They had been partners in some group projects. When Sara was in charge of a group or team, as she often was, she would pick Micah near the beginning. Micah did not enjoy working in a group, but she was okay at it. She was good at explaining complex concepts to the other students. She drew pictures and diagrams and made comparisons to things they were familiar with.

When Sara had a problem with a math concept and could not do her homework, she had often sought Micah out, and Micah would explain each step to her in patient detail, working through each problem with her, until Sara could do it on her own or they had finished all of the questions.

Micah had expected the relationship to end once school was over and they had both graduated, but she continued to run into Sara or to get calls from her and the friendship became part of who they were. They were a wholly unlikely match. Micah hadn't remained friends with anyone else from school. It was a small community, so she still saw people she knew from school, ran into them at the grocery store or the tax preparation firm. Some of them would nod to her and smile and make small talk. Others would act like they had never seen her before.

But it had been a rough week, and Micah wasn't sure she was emotionally ready to have a personal conversation with anyone. She didn't want to have to answer questions about how she was and what she was working on. And how her folks were. And the other things that Sara was sure to say. Micah wanted to just cocoon at home with the kitten, catching up on her reading and not having to socialize.

In the end, she opened the voicemail that Sara had left her. Not the usual breezy greeting and 'call me back.' Sara's voice was low and intense.

"Micah, I need you. Can you call me back?"

No explanation. None of the usual chatter. Something was wrong. Micah didn't know what it was or what she could do about it, but she clearly couldn't go home and soak in the tub for half the night listening to the phone read her latest journals aloud.

She listened to Sara's voicemail twice more, trying to analyze every inflection before she finally called back.

"Micah," Sara's voice was barely recognizable. Much deeper and more gravelly than usual. Micah tried to imagine what was wrong. Had Sara been using drugs without Micah knowing about it? Maybe a closet alcoholic? What had happened? "Thanks so much for calling me back, Mike."

"Of course," Micah agreed She wished she had gone to Sara's house instead of calling so that she could better observe Sara's body language and guess at what was going on. "Do you want me to come over?"

"Could you? I know it's evening and you don't like to go out again. You like your quiet time."

She said it in a way that made Micah feel guilty and selfish for wanting time to herself.

"I'll come over. You're still in the same place?"

"Yes. You've been here before, right? Just ring the bell when you get here. I'll buzz you up."

She hung up. Micah stared at her phone for a few minutes. Sara's behavior was so unusual. Micah couldn't understand what was going on. But what did it matter? She had agreed to go to Sara's apartment, so that was what she was going to do.

Without putting any real thought into it, she grabbed her keys and her purse, made sure that the kitten was occupied away from the door, and headed out to her car. Sara's house was across town, but it didn't take long to get there. She had an apartment in a fourplex, a modern, steel-and-glass kind of place, lots of open space and big windows. Probably cost a small fortune to keep comfortable in the summer sun. But it was later in the year; Sara would be more concerned with keeping it warm. Sunset was early and it was already dark when she got to Sara's house. She double-checked the name beside the button and gave the button a firm push. Not too long, which might be irritating, but long enough that they wouldn't miss it.

The buzzer sounded, and the door lock released without a word from Sara. Normally, she would have spoken to Micah through the speaker to ensure it was her before releasing the door. Micah entered the tiny lobby and went to the right and up the stairs to reach Sara's apartment. Sara was not standing at the door waiting for her. Micah had to knock to gain entrance.

It was Gregory who came to the door.

Never Greg. Always Gregory.

Micah didn't know him well. Enough to nod and say hello, but they'd never really had a conversation that Sara was not a part of.

"Hi," Micah said, when he opened the door and let her in. "Is everything okay?"

Gregory gave a curt nod, unsmiling. Not very reassuring for a guy who was ordinarily laid-back and smiling, always quick to share a joke, serve the drinks, or give Sara a hug and passionate kiss even with someone watching.

Gregory ushered her into the living room. Ivory curtains had been drawn across the black windows to give them some privacy and to make the room cozier. The rest of the room was as Micah remembered it. Same furniture, same artwork. A place that looked like it had been staged by an interior decorator or real estate agent, though Micah knew that Sara had done everything herself.

Sara was sitting on the couch, a velour blanket wrapped around her. Micah gave her a quick, assessing look. She was as gorgeous as ever, her beauty apparently effortless; big, blond curls, flawless peaches and cream complexion, her features just the right proportions. She looked like a movie star. But her eyes were darker than usual, smudges beneath them that almost looked like bruises. She wasn't smiling sunnily like she always was.

"Sara?" Micah hesitated. Normally, she sat in the easy chair across from the couch, leaving Sara alone on the couch or leaving room for Gregory to join her, if he were home. But Micah felt like that wasn't the right approach this time. She looked at the space next to Sara on the couch, glanced over at Gregory for direction, and when he made no sign that he understood what she wanted to know, she sat on the couch next to her friend. "Sara, what is it? Are you okay?"

The smudges looked even more bruise-like close up. Micah put her hand on Sara's shoulder. "What is it?"

Sara took a deep breath in and let it out again. She started at the beginning, with events that had happened months back. Discovering she was pregnant. She and Gregory had been trying for a while. Micah and Sara weren't young kids anymore; it was harder to conceive. Micah nodded, listening without interruption. Things had progressed normally, or they had seemed to. But then… something had gone wrong. The doctors couldn't tell her what it was. Sometimes these things happened, especially with a first pregnancy. They had lost the baby.

There was no reason they couldn't try again. Give her body a few months' rest, and then give it another go. The second time would probably be the charm. Or maybe the third. There was nothing wrong with her; she was in good health, didn't use drugs, alcohol, or tobacco. It would work better the next time.

Micah kept nodding, but she was confused as to why Sara was telling her the story. Surely it was between her and her doctor. There was nothing Micah could do to help. She knew genetics, little about obstetrics. Unless Sara thought there was something wrong with her baby genetically. Maybe the two of them carried some recessive gene and Sara wanted to know if they should try again. Or the baby had a random mutation and Sara didn't believe her doctor when he told her that it wouldn't happen to them a second time.

Sara stopped talking. She dabbed at her eyes with the insides of her wrists, sniffling. Micah didn't know if she should take Sara's hand or say something that would make her feel better. What could she say or do that would make her friend feel better? She had suffered a huge loss. Maybe the doctor didn't think it was anything. Just a fetus that had not made it to term. But to Sara, it was a big thing.

Sara was silent, too overcome to say anything more. Micah waited. Gregory took over. He walked to his wife's side and rubbed her shoulders and stroked her hair. He didn't tell her that everything was okay or that she was being silly over a spontaneously aborted pregnancy.

"Sara wanted to know if you would draw her a picture," Gregory said.

Micah looked at Sara, looking for confirmation and some more details. Sara nodded but didn't speak.

"We want something… a memento of the baby," Gregory explained, his voice rough and full of emotion. "We don't have anything. They… did a procedure. They said that it was just tissue. That they didn't have anything to show us. Nothing to… remember."

Micah nodded. There was a lump in her throat. She had so many questions, but she was afraid to ask any of them. Afraid it would hurt or offend Sara more.

"I know you can do these things," Sara said, voice shaky. "I figure… you can look at us. Gregory and me. And you can… make a picture of what the baby might have looked like, if he hadn't died. It's not exactly what you do. I know that. But… do you think you could? It would… give me something to look at. Something to remember, other than… the procedure room. It was so cold and clinical and… I couldn't mourn my baby. They took him away, and they couldn't give me any kind of comfort. Just 'Try again. Better luck next time.'"

Micah wiped her eyes, trying to keep from breaking down at the pain in Sara's voice. How could someone like Trish abandon her newborn, alone in the cold and dark, when there were others like Sara and Gregory, their hearts breaking over a lost pregnancy?

She nodded and tried to form the words. "You just want me… to look at the two of you. To try to… imagine…?"

Sara and Gregory nodded. It might have been an easier job if they provided her some of the baby's DNA, but then she would have to explain it to EvPro to use their proprietary technology, and baby portraits weren't exactly what they'd hired her to do.

19

M icah looked at the pictures she had produced for Mama Doe, who they now believed was Trisha Madro. She opened the email from Deputy Bellows with the picture of Trisha. She scrutinized the photo for anything that didn't fit the DNA profile. Until they found Trish, they couldn't match her DNA against the profile they'd pulled from the baby and were only going from the social worker's identification. Identification based on a composite picture was by no means certain. They could be completely wrong.

She studied each line and contour of Trisha Madro's face, but she couldn't find anything that would indicate she was not Mama Doe. Everything matched up, from the skin tone to the nose to the unattached earlobes. The age, smoker's lines, and thinness of her face all matched what the epigenome had told her.

Micah picked up her phone and called Deputy Bellows. He answered almost immediately.

"Sheriff's."

"Frank, it's Micah."

Bellows grunted. "So it is. How are you doing?"

"Better. I just wondered whether you'd had any luck tracking Trisha Madro down."

"I didn't send you a summary; you said you'd let me know if you wanted it."

"I know. I wasn't ready until now. If you don't have time, you can drop me an email later."

"Not much to tell you at this point. We've been canvassing, trying to find girls who knew her, resources she might have accessed. There are free clinics, prenatal, housing options for pregnant or new moms, etcetera."

"But no luck?"

"No. Unfortunately, nothing there."

"If it was Trisha, she might not want to access any of those programs while she was using."

"True," he agreed.

"And you couldn't find any other girls—young women—who knew her?"

"They are keeping pretty close-mouthed. We've been checking with homeless, addicts, hookers. I'm sure some of them probably knew her, but we haven't been able to confirm."

"If they thought something might have happened to her, do you think they'd talk to you?"

"Depends on what they thought happened. Did she leave town? Have medical problems following the delivery? If she hiked in and out of the hills after giving birth, she could be pretty sick. But she hasn't shown up in the morgue or hospital."

"Well, that's good…"

"Or is she holed up somewhere with a boyfriend? Just staying out of sight while she recovers and waits for the commotion to die down?"

Micah nodded to herself. "Okay. Well, let me know if you find anything… I appreciate you keeping me informed."

"Sure."

Micah said goodbye and tapped the phone to end the call. She swiveled her chair toward the door, deciding it was time to get her morning coffee, and found VP Amy Bradshaw standing in the doorway. Micah half-rose out of her seat, then stopped, trying to analyze Amy's expression and body language. She was not happy about something.

"Uh… Amy. I didn't know you were there."

"Clearly not." Amy's voice was tight. "What are you doing?"

"I was… talking to the deputy on the Mama Doe case. The mother of the abandoned baby. We ran her DNA and I did composites—"

"Why would you be talking to him?"

"Just seeing what his progress was on finding her. We have a name to go with the face, and it's a pretty good match, but he'll need to get a direct DNA comparison to verify—"

"That's a police matter."

"Well, yes." Obviously. That's why she had been talking to the police about it.

"You were already told, were you not, that your involvement with this file has ceased. You do not need to do anything else at this point. Let the police do their part."

"I told Aaron… until there is a DNA match, the file is still open. I frequently add new pictures to a file down the line. Tweak the hairstyle or accessories, take into account any new information that the police have discovered. There are often things that can be done to keep it fresh, make it more likely that people will see and recognize the subject."

"Which you do not need to do. You've already found the mother. As I said, it's a police matter now."

Micah hesitated. She was getting the feeling that it didn't matter what she said, they were going to keep hammering away at her, telling her to spend her time on the active cases, until she finally broke down and agreed.

Was it a budget thing? They had probably already lost money on the file, testing out new technology. But that would bring them more business in the future. They would make it back easily. But they didn't want Micah spending more time on it when it should be spent elsewhere. What was the point in drawing more pictures when they probably already had the subject? Or talking to the police?

"Sorry," she said finally. "I won't make any more calls on company time."

Amy rolled her eyes and shook her head. "It's not just company time. You've been told to *stay off the case.*"

Her final words were slow and deliberate like each one had a period after it.

"Okay."

Amy's face relaxed. Her shoulders eased down. "Thank you, Micah. I knew we could count on you."

Micah nodded jerkily. She wasn't a liar, but it was clear that no other answer would be accepted. She would have to think about whether she was willing to let the Sweetgrass Hills file go cold. She prided herself on being an honest and forthright person, and the pretense disturbed her.

Amy nodded toward Micah's inbox. "Looks like you've got plenty to do to keep yourself busy," she observed.

"Yes. I'll get to work on the next file."

Amy turned and walked away from the door. Micah got up to get that coffee. She needed it more than ever. As she made her way across the lab, Chastity saw her and made a motion to attract her attention.

"I've got that Lazarus for you, Micah."

Micah gave a quick shake of her head. Amy turned to look at Chastity.

"A Lazarus?" she repeated. "What's that?"

Chastity looked at Micah. She looked back at the vice president. "It's a constructed DNA profile. Let's say that you wanted to know your grandfather's DNA profile so that you could find out more about his genealogy and heritage. But he's dead, and no one is going to exhume the body to get a DNA sample for genealogical research."

Amy nodded, interested.

"So instead, you get the DNA of everyone you can who is related to him. His children and grandchildren, brothers and sisters, whoever you can get a DNA sample from. And then the computer generates as much of his DNA profile as it can based on those relationships."

"You can do that?"

"It's not perfect, and you won't get his full genome, but you can get pretty close if you have a bunch of relatives. You know, if all of his kids have blue eyes, you know that he had blue eyes. You're 'resurrecting' his DNA. Hence the name, Lazarus."

"Fascinating." Chastity blinked a few times. She glanced back at Micah one more time, still a few feet away, waiting for the VP to get out of the way so that she could feel free to get her cup of coffee. Amy gave a forced smile and moved on.

Micah went into the kitchenette without looking at Chastity. She waited a few minutes longer than was necessary for the machine to brew her one cup of coffee, breathing slowly and trying to achieve a meditative state. Once calm, she walked back into the lab. She checked out the position of Aaron Kwong's door—shut, which meant that he was out—made sure that

Amy Bradshaw was really gone and there was no one else from the upper echelons around, then went to Chastity's lab bench.

"What's going on?" Chastity demanded. "You're as white as a sheet. Is Bradshaw getting on your case?"

"She and Aaron have told me to close the Mama Doe file. I was afraid…"

"That I'd say the Lazarus was Papa Doe."

"Yeah. How did you catalog it?"

"It's on the Sweetgrass Doe file."

"Can you move it? Open a new file for me. Call it… Baby Thompson-Smith." Micah borrowed the name from her friend Sara, mentally apologizing to her.

Chastity looked uncertain about the fiction. She didn't like it.

"If they think I'm still working on the file after they asked me to stop, I'm going to be in trouble," Micah told her. "But I don't want to delete the profile. We might need it in the future. I'll hang on to it, see what happens."

"Baby Thompson-Smith?" Chastity repeated, her eyes slits as she considered it. "Who's that?"

"It's no one. I just made it up."

Chastity turned to her computer. Micah pretended to be blowing on her coffee, puffing out her breath and trying to relax. She wasn't sure why everyone was so uptight about the Sweetgrass file, but she didn't intend to attract any more negative attention.

2 0

Micah tried to psych herself up for dinner at her parents' house. She always felt guilty about not wanting to visit. But they had little in common and she often ended up feeling stressed out and awkward, even when she knew they were all trying to make it nice.

She did not doubt that Marianna and Cole loved her. The way they behaved toward her confirmed this fact. She was more ambivalent about her feelings toward them. She was pretty sure that what she felt was love or at least strong loyalty, but she felt like it was too lukewarm. Micah had always had problems with relationships and couldn't help wondering what was wrong with her.

It had been a relief when she had found out some of the details of her origins and realized that she hadn't been born to them and didn't have a genetic connection. At least there was some explanation for why she felt like a foreigner in her own family. But as she got older, her difficulty with them became more of a puzzle than ever. She learned about parent-child bonding and the types of events that could disrupt it, and couldn't find an explanation for her awkwardness with her parents. She had gone to them as an infant, a newborn, and had never had a significant separation or trauma. It was the ideal situation, a newborn put into a loving family of the same ethnicity, no neglect or learning disabilities, no disruptions in her childhood. So why?

She didn't want to leave the cat alone. She should have been home with her. But she knew that was a symptom of her desire to stay home, rather than a cause. The cat was fine when she went to work every day. Meow was happy to see Micah when she got home, but Micah could see no signs that she experienced any distress with Micah leaving her for a few hours. She didn't make any big messes, refuse to use her litterbox, or climb the curtains. Micah would come home and find Meow sleeping peacefully in her corner of the couch. They would have some cuddles, eat, and the cat would snooze on her lap while she did desk work or would tempt her to play for a few minutes with a toy mouse, ball, or the furry thing on the end of a fishing-pole type toy. After playing rambunctiously for a while, Meow would once again lie down for a nap and Micah would get back to drawing or studying.

Micah sighed, said goodbye to the kitten, and left, locking the door behind her.

The street was already dark. She should have headed out a little earlier, but Marianna would never criticize Micah for being late. She would just be happy that Micah had shown up. Cole might glower, but he too would let it go. Micah had begged off too many times before, saying she had work, wasn't feeling well, or was going to bed early. Or she had gotten wrapped up in a project and forgotten she was supposed to be going anywhere until one of them called her. She would never be late or forget about an appointment with someone else, but her parents… that was a different story.

"Oh, you're here," Marianna said cheerfully, giving Micah a big smile. "We were just about to eat. Let me take your coat," Marianna wrangled it off of Micah, "and tell me how your week has been!"

Micah let herself be swept into the dining room. Cole was seated at the table and he raised his hand in a brief wave. "'Bout time you got here."

Micah nodded, smiling wryly at Marianna's flustered admonition, telling Cole to behave himself. She looked over the offerings on the table, decided it was better than usual, and sat down.

"Sorry, I should have left earlier. I hope you didn't wait."

"We've learned not to wait for you," Cole told her.

"Good."

"I never know whether to call you or not," Marianna contributed. "I don't want to distract you if you're on the road, especially if it's icy…" She looked worriedly toward the window, where they could see gentle flakes of snow coming down in the beam of the streetlight. "But I wouldn't want you to miss out just because you lost track of time!"

"You could send me a text. I don't read them while I'm driving, but if I'm working, I'll check."

Marianna wrinkled her nose. "Texting…"

"Then get Dad to text," Micah told her. Cole was a little more comfortable with technology than Marianna was and Micah knew he texted with some of his old work buddies.

They sat down to eat. Marianna said grace. As she was the only member of the family who cared about it, she was the permanent designee.

"So, how has work been?" Marianna inquired, digging into her mashed potatoes with vigor.

Micah looked up, assessing their expressions. "Been putting a lot of work into the Sweetgrass Doe case. But I don't think you want to hear about that."

The two of them exchanged glances.

"It's not that we don't want to hear about it," Marianna waffled. "It's just that…"

"It makes you uncomfortable," Micah summarized. "You're afraid that one day I'm going to track down my biological family."

There was silence around the table. The wall clock ticked loudly. Cole's fork scraped his plate, but Marianna had stopped eating.

"You must have thought about it," Cole said finally. "You work all the time with DNA, matching people up with faces and helping the police to figure out their identities. With the skills that you have, it wouldn't be hard for you to find her. Your birth mom."

"That depends on a lot of things," Micah temporized. "There are a lot of variables. If her DNA isn't in the system, she's moved away from the area, changed her name and doesn't have an electronic footprint, it would be a lot harder." But not necessarily impossible. Micah did possess a lot of skills. "But I'm not searching for her."

"But you must want to know," Marianna said. "They say that adopted children always want to know where they came from, where they inherited different traits. Is it because of us? You think we would be upset by it?"

Micah raised one eyebrow. "Wouldn't you be?"

"You make it sound like we're jealous people. Like… we want to keep you for ourselves."

Micah shrugged. "Isn't that natural? Don't all parents want to keep their children safe? Keep them from possible pain?"

"We're not jealous," Marianna mumbled, putting a big bite of potatoes in her mouth and turning away from Micah slightly as she chewed.

"I know you're not," Micah agreed. "And I've never tried to find her. She abandoned me. She obviously didn't want me to be a part of her life."

"It was just too much for her," Marianna said in an over-emotional voice. "Taking care of a baby is not that easy. And knowing that you need to provide for that child for twenty years… be there for the rest of her life… that's just too much for some people. We don't know why she decided to give you up, because she did it the way she did, but if you listen to people's stories about why they made the choice to give a child up for adoption… it's never an easy choice for them."

Micah thought about Trisha Madro. Was Trisha Sweetie's mother? And if so, where had she gone? How hard had it been for her to leave her baby exposed in the mountains and to run away?

"Abandonment isn't the same as adoption," she told her parents. "Someone who gives her child up for adoption, at least she's made a plan. She does what she can to make sure that the child is taken care of. Someone who abandons her child… that's different. She doesn't know what could happen. She doesn't care if the baby dies. Women who leave their babies in toilets, or garbage cans, or in the mountains, exposed to cold and predators, that's not a loving choice. That's the opposite of taking responsibility for your child's welfare. That's just being selfish."

"You never know what's in someone else's heart," Marianna cautioned. "When you make judgments about someone else like that—"

"Dad agrees with me, don't you, Dad?"

Cole shifted uncomfortably, looking from his daughter to his wife and then staring down at his plate.

"I wouldn't say that all mothers who abandon their children are selfish," he said slowly. "Some of them are mentally ill."

"Oh, and that excuses it."

Even as Micah said it, she felt a pain in her chest for Trisha Madro and the sad life she had lived. If Trisha's traumatic upbringing made her unable to bond with a child, then was it her fault she acted in her own self-interest instead of the infant's? She hadn't chosen to be raised the way she had been.

Who knew what was in her heart? What had she been thinking when she left her baby alone in the cold, dark night?

"Maybe we should change the subject," Marianna said worriedly. "This isn't helping anyone."

Micah shrugged dramatically. "That's what I've been working on this week. You asked. But now… they want me to stop working the file, so I guess I'm on to other things."

"Who doesn't want you to work on it?" Cole asked, eyebrows moving down in a scowl.

"The powers-that-be. I've been told to close the file and not waste my time on it. Even though that's not the way it works. It's like a police file. You don't close it until it's solved."

"Then… you should keep working on it."

Micah smiled in appreciation at the gruff retired cop's viewpoint. "I will," she agreed. "I just won't tell anyone."

The awkward meal over, a couple of hours chalked up to time with her parents, meeting her quota of parent time for the week, Micah said her goodbyes and headed home.

She had never talked openly with her parents about her biological mother, about the possibility of tracking her down either through online registries or DNA. It had always been a forbidden topic, even with her choice of work.

"Families," Micah muttered to herself, shaking her head.

She parked her car and got out, heading up the sidewalk to the front door. She got halfway up the walkway and stopped.

It had been snowing since she had left, just lightly, and her sidewalk was covered with snow.

Only it wasn't even.

There was a clear line of footprints running from the sidewalk to the front door. They had been partially filled in, but were still discernible.

Just one set of footprints. Not someone delivering flyers, walking up her sidewalk and then back again.

She stood there for a few minutes, staring at her house. She looked at the door. It was firmly shut. The windows. No stirring of the curtains. No shadows that shouldn't have been there.

No sign that the house might be occupied, except for that line of footprints.

Micah shivered. She was bundled warmly against the cold front, but the goosebumps that crept up her spine were not from the cold.

She walked back to her car, got in, and locked the doors.

21

Micah stayed in her car, engine running and heater blowing until the police got there. She got out, face warm with embarrassment, and stared at the first cop's feet, unable to meet his eyes.

"I don't want to be accused of making a frivolous call," she said. "I don't normally panic over nothing. But you can see… there are footprints going up to my house, and none coming back. I'm afraid… someone might be in there."

Even though she wasn't looking at his face, she could see the nod of his head peripherally. "Who has a key?"

"No one."

He stood there, not saying anything. Micah shook her head. "No one," she repeated. "I live by myself. No one else has keys."

"Old boyfriend, a neighbor, someone who checks the house while you're out of town?"

"No. None of that."

"Parents? Siblings?"

"No."

"Then how would someone get in?" He looked toward the house. "Doesn't look like the door is broken."

"I didn't give anyone a key."

99

"Do you hide one outside? For emergencies? Did you get the locks changed after you moved in?"

"No, I didn't leave a key outside. I always thought that was an extremely stupid thing to do. And yes, I had the locks changed when I moved in here. Several years ago. I've never had any intruders."

He sucked his lip, considering the information. He called past Micah to his partner. "Colter, check the back for footprints. Don't trample any evidence."

The younger cop, his collar pulled up high to block against the wind, nodded his agreement and went around the side of the house to the back for a look.

The first cop nodded to Micah. "Why don't you get back in your car. Stay warm and out of the way. We'll check this out."

She got back into her car without argument. If the cops managed to flush a burglar out of her house, she didn't want to be in the line of fire when it happened. She couldn't hear what the cop was saying on his radio. She assumed he was talking to his partner around the back, or maybe relaying information back to the dispatcher. He could be asking for backup, though Micah thought that was unlikely given the fact that she wasn't sure there was anyone in the house. It wasn't like she had anything to steal. She lived a somewhat monastic lifestyle and, while she had a laptop and tablet and a TV, so did everyone else, and most of them had bigger and fancier ones than hers.

There was no reason a burglar would single her out. Except maybe that she was at the end of the block. Not as many neighbors to notice anything was going on. She lived by herself, so it was easy to tell whether there was anyone home or not. And her schedule was reasonably predictable, with the occasional Sunday dinner with her parents. Gone for a few hours every second Sunday or so, her house predictably empty.

The cop looked like he was going to approach the house. Micah made one sudden realization and opened the car door.

"Uh, sir? Deputy?"

He looked back at her.

"I forgot to tell you. I have a kitten. So… if you open the door… I don't know. I wouldn't want her to startle you, or for her to get out."

Of course, it couldn't be the highest priority. If they were chasing a burglar, they couldn't be worried about a kitten. But if everything was quiet, she didn't want the door left open for Meow to wander out. She hoped she would have the sense to stay inside and not go out wandering in the snow. But she was just a baby, and she was curious.

"Yes, ma'am," the cop said, nodding gravely.

She felt validated that he hadn't made a face or told her she was being crazy. Maybe it was perfectly normal for pet owners to express their concerns to the police about not letting their animals out or shooting them by mistake.

Micah watched the cop make his way slowly up beside the sidewalk, avoiding trampling the evidence of the previous visitor. His body was tense and he moved slowly like a creeping panther. Micah hadn't seen him draw his weapon, but she could see it glinting at his side as he approached. She kept thinking about his question. What if someone else did have a key? What if there was a perfectly innocent reason for someone to be in her house?

But she knew she hadn't given anyone else a key. And if there had been a problem with water or gas and some city worker had been required to enter, then he would have notified the police, wouldn't he? Or there would be a big truck out in front and several other workers hanging around to let her know what was going on.

The cop got up to the door and paused. He used the radio mounted on his shoulder. Micah waited, holding her breath. She didn't know whether he would enter first, or the cop at the back door, or if he were coordinating so they would both enter at the same time.

He tried the handle and, apparently, there was no need to break in the door. It was not locked, and he opened it, standing back, flattened against the wall, so that if he were shot at from within the house, the intruder would not be able to get a good angle on him.

2 2

Micah was tense, waiting for someone to come racing out of the house, or for the kitten to wander out the door wondering what was going on and why the door was wide open and Micah was not there.

But there was no movement.

After a few moments, the cop moved again, entering the house, swinging the door shut behind him so that the cat wouldn't get out. Micah saw him move across the window. She couldn't see what was going on inside but, a few minutes later, the policeman came back out. He again avoided the sidewalk and approached the car.

"House is clear, ma'am. No sign of any intruder. Any chance that you left the door unlocked?"

"No way," Micah shook her head. "I would never do that. I always lock it."

"You might want to invest in a burglar alarm, then. Give you a bit more security."

"There wasn't any sign that anyone had been in there?"

"You can take a look yourself, let me know if anything is out of place or missing. We didn't see anything obviously suspicious."

"Okay." Micah climbed out of the car. Her legs were shaky and weak. She was relieved, but at the same time, let down. What was going on? She could see the footprints going up to the house. Had he vanished into thin air?

"There wasn't anyone inside? Where did he go?"

"Oh, there are footprints out the back door. Whoever it was entered through the front and exited through the back. Maybe just a homeless person or some curious kid? Doesn't look like anything is damaged. Even the door itself; it doesn't look like the door was forced or damaged. More like it was left unlocked."

"It wasn't left unlocked," Micah insisted.

"Well then, maybe it was picked. That's a possibility."

"Wouldn't you be able to tell?"

"Not necessarily. Some of these guys are pretty sophisticated. They can get in and out just as easily as if they had a key, don't leave any markings around the keyhole. There are automatic picks on the market too…" He trailed off and shrugged. "I can give you some recommendations for locks that wouldn't be so easy to pick."

"Yeah, that would be good." Micah felt angry and vulnerable at the same time. She hated the thought that someone had just walked into her house as if they owned the place. "Would you… are you going to go in with me?"

"Yes ma'am, of course."

He walked up to the house with her. They both avoided the footprints, though why they did, Micah wasn't quite sure. She didn't think they were going to get any evidence teams out there to take pictures of the footprints that were slowly being filled in or take casts, or whatever else they might do on TV. Real life wasn't like that. The cops would file a report indicating that they hadn't found anything, and that would be the end of it.

Micah went inside the house with him. They had tracked snow through the house, but it was all wood floors so that a quick mop would clean it up. The kitten was sitting on the couch, stretching and looking around. She mewed silently at Micah. Micah picked her up and held her close, looking around for any damage, any sign that something had been taken or damaged.

But everything looked as she had left it. Her work was still out in her office, her computer and tablet apparently untouched. Micah looked around. She took a few pictures with her phone, but wasn't sure why she was bothering. If she had 'before' pictures, that would be one thing, but she had nothing to compare it to. Nothing to say that her tablet had been moved an inch to the right or her computer clamshell closed when she had left it open.

The cop watched her without comment. Micah continued to wander around the house, and when she had visited all of the upstairs rooms, she shook her head at him.

"I don't see anything out of place. I don't understand it…"

"Who can predict what people will do?" he asked with a philosophical shrug. "Be glad that nothing was damaged or stolen. Maybe he left when he saw you pull up."

"Maybe," Micah was doubtful. "But his footprints were already filled in quite a bit, so I don't think so."

He went to talk to his partner and they looked around outside for any other clues.

23

On her way to work, Micah was thinking about her strange intruder, trying to make sense of the burglary. But she couldn't make anything fit. Had he walked into her house just to have a look around? Maybe he'd intended to take something, but got spooked by a neighbor and fled?

She'd never had such a thing happen before, or even heard of it happening to anyone else. She participated in her neighborhood Facebook page, and no similar incidents had been reported. It just didn't make any sense.

Maybe it was because she was already nervous that she noticed the car behind her had made the same turn as she had three times in a row. Just someone who was heading into work, the same as she was, who happened to make the same turns as she did.

Or was it?

She hadn't previously noticed anyone on her street who took the same route as she did to work. It seemed like something that would have stuck in her mind. It wasn't the big city; she knew the habits of the people around her. And no one in her area went to work near EvPro.

Maybe he was a visitor or a new move-in. Things didn't remain static over time. It wasn't like he was right on her tail. He was back a comfortable distance. It was only a coincidence that she noticed him taking the same turns as she did. She was nervous about her burglar, so other things were setting off her alarm bells. Things that were totally unrelated.

He didn't make the final turn to EvPro. Micah rolled her eyes and shook her head at her paranoia. Someone following her to work now? Really?

Once she was in the safety of the lab and had shed all of her winter clothing, Micah got herself a large mug of coffee, went to her office, and shut the door. She didn't want any interruptions. She just wanted to focus on her work and not be distracted by other things. Especially not by thoughts of someone violating the sanctity of her house.

Even though she had plenty of regular work to do, Micah spent some time working on her non-work projects too. Visualizing Sara's baby. Taking a stab at making the composite of Sweetie's father into something recognizable.

Since the father's DNA didn't circulate in Sweetie's veins like her mother's did, there was not nearly as much epigenetic data for the father's profile. She was working with only half the DNA and no data as to how old he was or other lifestyle choices that might help her to make the face more recognizable.

Reviewing Sweetie's epigenome could provide a few clues about to her father. Some of those epigenetic switches were passed on to offspring, giving the child a sort of genetic memory of her parents' experiences. Sweetie had a lot of trauma switches, indicators that would normally tell Micah that the subject had been through some very difficult life experiences. She had no way of knowing whether those switches had been turned on by Sweetie's abandonment or were present in the genetic material passed on to her.

Well, some of them Micah could check. She referenced Mama Doe's— Trisha Madro's—DNA and noted that she had a lot of the same switches as the baby. So those traumatic experiences, perhaps Trish's own genetic record of abuse and neglect, had been passed on to her daughter. Did that mean Sweetie would have the same difficulties bonding? The same issues with school and trying to fit in with a family?

Did Micah herself carry similar scars from her biological mother's past? Was that what made her feel different? Or was that only influenced by Micah's lived experience?

She stared at the flat composites of Papa Doe, hoping for inspiration. What made him tick? What kind of relationship had he had with Trisha?

Had they been teenage lovers, seeking solace in each other? Or had he been older? A father figure, an abuser, or a john?

She wished there were some way to identify him. But they wouldn't know who he was until they found Trisha Madro.

Micah looked up in irritation at the knock on her door. She had been closeted in her office for most of the day without any interaction with others, and her boss or coworkers might need to talk to her face-to-face instead of sending her emails she could handle without having to be social.

"Yes?"

The door opened a few inches. It was Veronica Clang.

"Hey, really sorry to disturb you, Micah…" Veronica gave a little shake of her blond bob. A tell that she really didn't feel sorry about the interruption? Or just a nervous gesture because she knew Micah didn't like to be disturbed if her door was closed. "But you might want to turn on the local news."

Micah frowned. The news? She turned back toward her computer and maximized the browser. She typed in the news URL and waited for it to load. There was a live stream, so she clicked on it, waited for it to finish buffering, and then watched the live coverage of a reporter at the Sweetgrass Hills, not far from where the baby had been found.

"There is no word from the police yet as to the identity of the remains," the reporter announced with an inappropriate smile, "but speculation is rampant as to whether this has anything to do with the abandoned baby, known locally as 'Sweetgrass Doe.'"

Micah stared at the screen. Remains?

She glanced back at Veronica. "Thank you," she acknowledged, "I'll keep an eye on this."

Veronica nodded and hurried away again.

Micah watched the TV station play random bits of reports that all added up to nothing.

Eventually, Micah's hand moved to her phone without any conscious thought of what she was going to do once it was in her grasp. She barely took her eyes from her computer to dial.

It took a few more times than usual for Bellows to answer. "Micah. Shall I assume you're watching the news coverage?"

"Yes."

"Phone hasn't stopped ringing since they broke the story. Sorry about that, I like to keep my inside people informed before a discovery makes it to the press."

"Is it…?"

"There won't be any confirmation until the medical examiner has had a chance to examine the body and to send a DNA sample your way, so it can be confirmed, but it looks like… it's Trisha Madro."

"Oh, no."

If Micah hadn't already been sitting, her knees would have given way. She experienced a moment of dizziness as she tried to process the grim news.

"Yeah. Sorry to have to tell you this way."

"What happened? Just preliminary, I know. To be confirmed by the medical examiner."

"She was discovered at the bottom of a crevasse. The position of the body would suggest that she fell. Wandering around in the dark after abandoning the baby…"

Micah's mind flipped through scenarios. Trisha hadn't really meant to abandon Sweetie. She had just put her down while she was looking around. In the dark and cold. In the middle of the night. Maybe it had still been daylight, in the early afternoon, and she thought she would be safe. She was looking for something… she had seen something… Micah tried to fill in the cracks, but couldn't find an explanation that made sense.

Had Trisha been out of her mind? Traumatized by an unattended birth or terrified of being responsible for another human being, had she been so distressed that she hadn't known what she was doing?

"Are you okay, Micah?"

Micah swallowed. "Thanks, Frank. You'll let me know as you hear anything else?"

"Sure. We'll be trying to get everything wrapped up. I know this still isn't direct confirmation that Trisha Madro was the baby's mother, but I can't think of any reason she would be out there if she was not."

"Yes," Micah agreed. There was no chance Trisha Madro had just been a look-alike for the baby's mother and had happened to die so close to her.

"Will you make sure the medical examiner sends a blood sample our way so that we can directly confirm that she's Sweetie's mother? Just to tie up any loose ends?"

"Will do," he agreed. "Sorry to have it end this way."

Micah nodded. "Me too."

But would it have been better to find Trisha Madro out partying somewhere? Or crashed in a warehouse or homeless shelter? Would that have been a more satisfying resolution than finding out she had died near her baby? She had abandoned Sweetie, but her own death suggested that it had not been a cold and callous act.

And now she could do no more harm.

24

Micah did her best to concentrate on her work and finish up what she needed to that day but, in the end, she just ended up going home. If someone had a complaint that she wasn't working as hard as she should be, she could claim that she was sick. The way that her head was pounding and her stomach was twisting, it wouldn't be a lie.

She was looking forward to being home, cuddling with the kitten, and maybe going to bed early or having a nap. She just wanted to shut the whole world out.

It seemed unfair that Sweetie was alone in the world. It was bad enough that she had been abandoned, but now fate had seen her orphaned as well. Unless Micah was able to provide the information needed to track down the father, which seemed unlikely. Having so little of his genome was crippling.

Even though she had already talked to Deputy Bellows, she found herself calling him again in the car.

"Micah," his voice was thin with fatigue. "What can I do for you?"

"How are you?" Micah asked. "You sound terrible."

He chuckled. "Well, that wouldn't be an inaccurate statement. It's been a bear of a day. I'm about done in. How about you?"

"I didn't have to run an investigation and deal with the public and human remains, but I finally gave up," Micah admitted. "I'm on my way home."

"Yep. Sounds good. A hot shower and a beer would be awfully nice about now."

"I can imagine. You didn't find anything else out, did you? The medical examiner won't have had a chance to process the remains yet, but I wondered if there was anything else at the scene that might have helped…"

"Not much, unfortunately. Her clothing was pretty torn up, but that could easily happen with a fall down into a ravine. And there was some evidence that might or might not have had anything to do with Trisha's death. Litter. Don't know how long anything has been sitting there."

"Right. Okay. I just wondered. Thought I would touch base."

"Have a nice night. Take it easy."

"You too, Frank. Have that shower and beer."

"Hot shower and cold beer," he said longingly. "I think I will."

Micah got out of her car slowly, lost in thought. It was over. They knew now what had happened to Sweetie's mother. They might never know why, but they knew what had happened. She had abandoned the baby, and then she had walked off the edge of the earth. Literally.

As much as she didn't want to, Micah couldn't help thinking of her own biological mother. What had happened to her? Had she, like Trisha, met with oblivion? Or was she still out there somewhere, living her own life, not even thinking of the baby she had abandoned?

If she was alive, did she wonder where Micah was? How she had turned out? Would she have been proud of Micah, or disappointed with her personal or professional choices? Micah always sensed that Marianna and Cole were somehow disappointed in her, even if they said that they were proud of her successful career and the way that she helped to put killers behind bars. Would Cole have preferred a cop? A real role in law enforcement instead of just drawing pictures of people? What about Marianna? She didn't seem to mind Micah drawing pictures, but she didn't like her exposure to the underlying crime. Thinking that she was too close to the criminal element. Marianna probably would have preferred it if Micah painted portraits or did caricatures. More of a conventional artist.

Micah looked at the house. Nothing appeared to be out of place. No footprints this time, but there was also no fresh snow to aid her. No sign of whether someone was in the house.

Just to be sure, she decided to check the back as well. Look for any forced doors or windows. She knew there wouldn't be. There hadn't been any forced windows or doors the day before.

Micah walked quietly around the side of the house, her boots clomping too loudly on the sidewalk. She tried not to make any noise, while at the same time pretending to herself that it didn't matter if she did.

She looked around the back yard for anything suspicious or out of place. There was a movement in her peripheral vision, and she turned her head to see what it was. Probably a branch blowing in the wind or being shaken by a bird or squirrel.

A dark shape rushed at her. Micah didn't have any time to focus on it and evaluate whether there was any danger. The blow hit her with the force of a freight train. She felt like she was flipped end over end before she hit the cold, rough ground. The wind was knocked out of her. There was no way she could scream or say anything to stop her attacker.

He was a black shape in the darkness. In the flashes of clarity that interspersed the blur of motion, she tried to understand what was going on. To take a picture with her mind and analyze the man attacking her. He was dressed all in black, including a black knit balaclava that completely obscured his face.

She fought back, kicking and scratching desperately, trying to keep him away from her.

Did he want her purse? To break into her house again? What was in her house that he would care about? It wasn't like she had a collection of precious jewels—she didn't even have a high-def TV.

He kept hitting her. At first, she thought that he had a baseball bat or some kind of truncheon but, as the attack progressed, she realized all he had were his fists. Tight, hard fists that felt like bricks when he hit her. She couldn't imagine anything harder.

She was crying, sounds coming out of her as she got her breath back again. But not calling for help, not saying anything to him that was coherent. She just grunted and cried. What had she done? She didn't understand what the punishment was for, why he was hurting her over and over.

There was a shout, a man's voice, and then suddenly her attacker was gone, running away. A flurry of feet, and he had disappeared into the night. Someone else ran past Micah, in pursuit, then he too was gone.

Micah lay there, panting, trying to process what had just happened. She looked for something familiar to hold on to. Where was she? What had hit her? Her head whirled, a dizzying fast carnival ride, and Micah thought she was a child again, throwing up after riding a carousel.

"Are you okay, ma'am? Just be still. An ambulance is on its way. You'll be alright."

"What happened?" Micah demanded, her tongue thick in her mouth. She could taste blood and wondered whether she had bitten her tongue.

"I'm not sure. Just lay here. We'll take care of everything."

The world tilted and spun. Micah tried to hold on to him to keep from sliding into the darkness.

"It's so… dizzy," she tried to tell him.

"I know. Hang in there. We'll get you help and you'll be as good as new."

"Why did he hit me? Who was that?" Micah tried to sort it all out.

"I can't answer your questions right now. We'll look into it. It's going to take some time."

"I didn't do anything. Why would he hit me?"

"You didn't do anything wrong," he assured her.

"Then why did he hit me?"

"It's okay," he soothed, holding her hand firmly.

Micah closed her eyes, hoping the spinning sensation would ease. Then there were more people there. Asking her questions. Touching her.

"Stop it!" Micah protested. "Get off of me! All of you! Go away!"

The hands stilled and withdrew.

"It's okay, Miss Miller," one voice told her. "We're here to help you. We are going to take care of you."

"No. Don't touch me."

They waited, not touching, looking for instructions from the ones who were in charge. But Micah was in charge. It was her house. Her yard. Her body.

"We're here to help, ma'am. We're just going to evaluate you, make sure it's safe to move you. We'll get you to the hospital and they'll set everything right."

"No."

"What do you want me to do, then?"

Micah couldn't stand the feeling of their hands, dirty and gritty, on her body. "Nothing. Don't touch me."

"No one is going to do anything you don't want."

Micah realized she was shivering. She tried to curl up inside her coat.

"Ma'am, you can't go to sleep out here. You're getting hypothermic. Going into shock."

Micah clenched her fists. She couldn't feel her fingers. She tried to focus on one thing at a time.

"I want to go inside."

"We'll take you to the hospital. They can evaluate you there."

"No. In the house."

"You need to be examined. You took quite a beating. We wouldn't want anything to happen to you if you have internal bleeding or damage to your spine. We need to be sure you're okay."

"Help me in the house."

"I can't move you without a proper examination. We should be putting you into a collar and on a backboard."

Micah shuddered at the thought of being tied down, unable to move at all.

"I can move," she told them.

"Then you'll need to get up and get inside by yourself. If we move you, we could be liable."

Micah pushed herself up with her hands. She felt so heavy. Her head especially felt much too heavy for her body. She felt like she'd been dropped on another planet, where the gravity pulled her down much more than she was used to.

She managed to get up to a sitting position and looked around at them. They were not familiar faces. Everyone stared at her, eyes big, waiting for her to collapse back to the ground. Micah grasped the railing for the back porch area and used it to pull herself to her feet. She hung on to it, her head pounding, stomach heaving, and all of her skin damp and clammy. But she had made it that far on her own. They watched as she started to shuffle toward the back door, leaning on the railing for support. Micah got to the back door and tried the handle, but the door was locked. Micah stared at the handle, unable to juggle her keys out and find the right one.

"Can you help with this?" she demanded. "I think I proved I can get around on my own."

One of the cops stepped forward. "I can help you, ma'am. Do you have your keys?"

She tried to remember if she'd had them in her hand when she went around to the back yard. Or had she already put them into her pocket or purse? Had the intruder stolen her purse? Was that what it had been all about?

"Where's my purse?"

"It's right here, ma'am." Another offered. "Do you want me to see if your keys are inside?"

"In my wallet," Micah told him, "there's a spare key."

The young man checked for her. "Yes, here it is." He held it out to her, then realized he was supposed to be helping her and inserted it into the lock. He opened the door for her.

She had still not purchased a burglar alarm. It was embarrassingly easy to get into her house. No way to alert anyone if there was a problem.

"How did you know?"

"You told me where it was, ma'am. You really do need to get to the hospital. You need to be evaluated."

Micah shook her head, which filled it full of sparklers that popped in front of her eyes in an amazing variety of colors. She closed her eyes, trying to steady herself.

"No, I mean, how did you know I was in trouble?"

"We had increased patrols after your burglary. A car happened to be going by when you walked around the back, and when your lights didn't come on right away..."

Micah groped for the light switch. It had been pure luck that they'd been able to stop the attack. Just luck that they'd had any clue that anything was wrong. Thank goodness for police officers with some common sense.

25

Light filled the room. While it was way brighter than usual, hurting Micah's eyes and making her wince, it felt good to be in familiar surroundings. She was grounded.

There was a small meow and the kitten wandered into the room, looking at her curiously and stopping to stretch out her front legs, to arch her back, and to stretch out her back legs one at a time.

"Don't let her out," Micah murmured. "It's cold out."

There was some discussion about who was going into the house and who was staying out, and after some shuffling, they closed the door to make sure that the kitten could not get out.

"You need to see a doctor," a paramedic with a serious expression and a small black mustache told her. "At least let one of us examine you. And promise that you'll go to a clinic or see a doctor tomorrow. You took a pretty bad beating. I don't think you realize how badly you're hurt. You're still high on adrenaline, and when you come down, you're going to realize how bad it is."

Micah hung on to the counter and tried to make a decision. There were too many people, and she wanted them to all go away. There was no way she wanted all of them touching her and trying to talk to her at the same time. But on the other hand, she didn't exactly want to die in her sleep from a brain hemorrhage, either.

"One person," she said thickly. "Just one, and don't touch me."

He consulted with his partner, murmuring in confidential tones, and then another figure came forward. The paramedic was wrapped up in a thick, dark coat, and Micah didn't realize at first that it was a woman rather than a man.

"I would like to help you," she said in a soft voice. "Now why don't we go to your bedroom, away from the rest of this circus, and I can help you to take off your coat and winter gear and have a closer look at your injuries. How does that sound?"

"Yes," Micah agreed. "Okay."

"Do you want to take my arm?" The woman offered it to Micah.

Micah didn't nod, worried about it aggravating her head more, but she took the proffered arm and let the woman guide her to the bedroom, providing stability and direction.

She sat down on the bed and the paramedic guided her hands to remove her hat, gloves, and bulky winter coat.

"That's right," the woman murmured. "My goodness, you're going to have one heck of a shiner. You should put some ice on that tonight, no matter what else you do or don't go ahead with. You're going to need painkillers, lots of rest, and ice. I'd like you to see someone tomorrow for x-rays. Sometimes people don't realize when they've broken a bone, and you need to get them set in order to heal properly."

"I don't want to go out."

"I understand. But tomorrow. You need to do it."

The paramedic finished getting Micah's winter clothes off and folded them neatly, making a pile on the bed. She had Micah follow her finger, count backward by sevens, and answer various questions to demonstrate her cognitive abilities.

"Do you want me to help you to undress and get into the bath? A nice hot bath might be a good idea, keep you from stiffening up too badly, get rid of those shakes."

"No." Micah was repelled by the idea of someone intruding on her privacy that way. It was as bad as being assaulted in the first place.

"Are you sure? Is there anything else I can do for you? Get you a hot drink? A blanket?"

"No, I'm fine."

"Are you ready to talk to the police? Give them a statement about what happened?"

"I don't know what happened. They know as well as I do."

"I'll send someone in. You'll be okay?"

"Could you… feed the kitten? There's an open can in the fridge. She'll be hungry."

"I would be happy to. Don't worry about it."

"Thanks."

The paramedic left, replaced by a policeman. Micah didn't know whether it was the one who had chased her assailant, the one who had stayed and held her hand, or someone who had arrived since.

"I'm sorry to have to bother you tonight, ma'am. But if you can tell me anything about the assailant, that would be extremely helpful."

"I don't know."

"You hadn't seen him before?"

"He had a mask. I couldn't see his face."

"A mask?"

Micah made a motion over her face. "A balaclava. All black."

"How about his voice? His height and build?"

"He didn't say anything. And I don't know. He just hit me, and kept beating on me. I never got a good look."

"I'm sorry. This must all be very frustrating to you. Do you know of anyone who might want to hurt you?" He looked around the room. "You're recently divorced?"

Micah saw the room through his eyes and was embarrassed. He thought that the sparse furnishings and decorations meant that her husband had taken half of the household items when he had left.

"No, no. No ex. I just don't like… clutter."

"No relationships? Any problems at work? Family problems? Gambling?"

"No. Nothing like that. I can't think of anyone who wanted to hurt me. It must just be random."

"I would agree," he said slowly, "if not for the burglary. To have both a burglary and an assault within days of each other… that's not a coincidence. They are connected somehow."

Micah shook her head slowly, trying not to aggravate her vertigo further. "No. It doesn't make sense. There isn't anyone."

"What do you do for a living?"

"I draw," Micah said. She didn't want to tell him that she drew composites, he would automatically think that meant that she was being attacked because of some picture she had drawn for work. "I draw portraits."

"Oh." Clearly, he didn't see how that could have anything to do with a burglary and assault. Just like Micah didn't see how they could be connected.

"I don't have any enemies, deputy. I don't know of anyone who wants to hurt me. I think… this must just have been a random thing. Maybe a misunderstanding or misidentification."

She wondered fleetingly if it could have something to do with her biological heritage. Maybe she looked so much like her birth mother that someone had mistaken her.

But that didn't make any sense either. She had never been mistaken for someone else. If her biological mother had ever lived in town, she was long gone now. The assault had nothing to do with her.

"I'm just tired," she told the officer. "I'd like to go to bed."

"I'd like you to come into the station to make a statement tomorrow."

"I don't have anything else to say. I don't know who this guy was or why he was here. You already know everything I know."

"Still, it would be helpful…"

"I don't think I'll be going anywhere tomorrow. I'll probably work from here until… I'm feeling a bit better."

"I wouldn't recommend doing too much," he admitted. "But I would like you to make an official statement at the police station. Sometimes people have a better recollection, once they start getting things written down. There might be some detail that you remember once you get going."

"We'll see," Micah said, tiring of his persistence. But she had no intention of following through.

"Good." The cop nodded. "That would be very helpful. I'm sorry that this happened to you. Are you sure you don't want to go to the hospital? Just to get checked out? Make sure there is no permanent damage and that you have the painkillers you need?"

"I'll get something tomorrow if I need it. I just want to sleep now."

26

It was an uncomfortable night. Micah thought more than once that she should have listened to the opinions of the first responders and gone to the hospital. Or at least to a doctor or clinic to get some painkillers. As it was, all she had in the house were over-the-counter pain pills, and none of those were very strong. She didn't generally medicate for pain. She just powered through the occasional headache or twisted ankle, preferring not to take anything.

But the pain from the unexpected attack was not like anything she had experienced before. It hurt to move, but her body was stiffening up and it hurt to stay still. She couldn't get comfortable. She wanted to sleep, but after all of the people left, she found that she couldn't. Her brain didn't want to deal with the attack, but her body was letting her know that it wasn't going to forget that quickly.

Sometime during the night, she managed to drag herself to the bathroom to swallow a few aspirin. Then she lay on the fuzzy bathmat for some indeterminate period, unable to raise the energy to return to her bedroom. The kitten came and meowed over her a few times, nudging her and sniffing her face, and eventually curling up on the bathmat beside Micah, purring and snuggling into Micah's body.

She made it back to her bed sometime around dawn. She knew she wasn't going to be working at the office. She wasn't sure she'd be able to do anything at all. She'd have to call in sick, maybe even explain what had happened. If she did go back to work in a day or two, she would have to explain the bruises then anyway. She wasn't going to be able to walk in without anyone noticing she'd been attacked.

Micah awoke and reached for her phone. It was still in her pocket, and she was still wearing her street clothes, not her pajamas. The phone was nearly out of juice, but Micah at least managed to read the time. She plugged it in and waited for it to charge up a bit. Then she would call in to work.

She felt feverish and unwell. Not just like she had been hurt, but like she was sick with the flu. Everything hurt. She was tired, such a heavy tiredness that she felt weighed down, pinned to the bed.

She clearly should have gone to the hospital. She could barely turn over on the bed to ease the pain on one side of her body, let alone get up to take more painkillers and take care of herself.

And the kitten. She had asked a policeman or paramedic to feed her the night before, but she was going to need to be fed again. It wasn't fair to the kitten that she should go hungry because Micah had been hurt. It wasn't her fault.

Getting herself from the bedroom to the kitchen where the kitten's food and dishes were seemed like an impossible prospect. It was farther away than the bathroom, and Micah wasn't sure how she was going to get herself there again.

The phone was charged enough for her to make a call to Kwong and give him the news that she had been mugged the night before and was too sore to get in. He made appropriately shocked and soothing noises, assuring her that she could rest and they could manage without her for a day.

For a day. Micah wasn't sure whether she'd be able to get back to the office in a week.

But she left it at that. She'd deal with him again the next day, when she was feeling incrementally better. Maybe after she'd taken a painkiller. She lay on her bed, breathing in gasps as if she'd been running instead of just making a phone call. She wanted to go to sleep. But going to sleep wasn't going to help her.

Micah tried to control her breathing and settle herself down again. If she breathed through the pain and was calm, she could make another phone call. She didn't know what she was going to say, but there was no one else to call.

She tapped the speed dial and waited while it rang. Were they home? Or would they be out shopping or running some other errand? Surely at least one of them would be home.

Eventually, the phone was picked up, and she could hear her mother's voice. "Micah? Are you okay? Is something wrong?"

Micah tried to laugh, but it hurt too much. Of course Marianna suspected that something was wrong. Micah never called her during the day. It would take an emergency for her to make a personal call on company time.

"Mom, can you come over? I'm not feeling well. I need help."

"Yes, of course! What's wrong? What happened?"

"There was a burglar," Micah wasn't even sure how to start. She didn't know what to tell them. How to explain about the intruder and the attack.

"Oh, my goodness! Are you hurt? Did you call the police?"

"I talked to the police. But today… I need help with the kitten. And… something for the pain."

"Oh, dear. Oh, dear," Marianna was muttering, doing something noisy in the background, and Micah didn't know how much she had heard.

But it didn't matter. As long as she came over, she could see what Micah needed. They'd work it out.

She heard her father's baritone in the background.

"She's hurt, Cole! She was attacked by a burglar!"

"What?" He snatched the phone from her and spoke into the receiver. "Micah? Is that right? You were attacked?"

"Yes. I'm okay. But… I could use some help."

He swore angrily. "We'll be right there, baby. Hang on."

He hung up. Micah stared at her phone.

She couldn't remember him ever calling her 'baby' or any other pet name before.

As Micah had told the policeman, no one had a key to her house, including her parents, so when they arrived, Micah was going to have to let them in.

She didn't know how she was going to manage that. If she couldn't make it to the kitchen to feed the cat, how was she going to get to the door to unlock it for them?

But she needed to. There was no way for them to get in to help her unless she unlocked the door. Micah crawled painfully out of bed. It was a long way to the door, but it would take her parents at least ten minutes to get there. Maybe longer. Her mother would have to find her purse and her keys and anything else she thought important to bring to take care of Micah. It might even take her half an hour to get all of her things together. If Micah had forty minutes, could she get to the door?

It would have made a funny skit on the TV or stage, the way that Micah inched along the floor, racing at a snail's pace. Every movement hurt. And when she reached the door, she was going to have to find a way to get up to unlock it, and she wasn't sure her spinning head would let her stand upright.

"Micah. Honey. We're here, sweetie. Micah, open your eyes."

Micah pried her eyes open and tried to focus on the blurry shape over her. Marianna. She knew the voice. Everything else seemed hazy, like they had brought the fog inside with them.

"She's awake," Marianna said quietly. "We should get an ambulance, don't you think?"

"See how she is first. She shouldn't have tried to get up."

Micah held her mother's hand. It was warm and silky smooth. Her knuckles were enlarged. How had Micah not noticed that before? Marianna never complained about her health, but she was getting older, things were starting to wear out.

"How did you get in?"

"Your father."

Micah wondered whether he had kicked the door in. It was too cold. The door would have to be fixed right away; the weather had been so wintry the last few days. And Micah didn't want the kitten sneaking out through a door that didn't shut properly.

"Meow…"

"Cole will feed the cat. Don't you worry. The kitten is fine."

"Okay." Micah closed her eyes and rested her head. "Where am I?" She felt beneath her with the other hand. It would seem that she was back on her bed again, though she was sure she had made it at least a few feet down the hall.

"You're in your own bed, dear. Are you okay? Where does it hurt?"

"Everything hurts." Micah moaned a little. She didn't like to show weakness in front of anyone, but Marianna was her mother. If Micah could be human in front of anyone, it was Marianna.

"Oooh," Marianna stroked Micah's long hair. "When did you last take something? I brought painkillers."

"I don't know. Last night. It was dark."

"What did you have?"

"Just aspirin."

Marianna clucked. "You need something stronger than that. You're black and blue, you poor thing!"

Micah normally didn't like anyone, even Marianna, touching her, but she abandoned herself to her mother's ministrations, comforted by her soothing touch and words. Marianna left for a moment to get her a glass of water and some painkillers and, when she returned, helped to prop Micah up a little on pillows so that she could drink the water rather than just dumping it over herself.

"Thank you."

"Your mama will take care of you, honey. I'm glad you called. I can't imagine you just lying here by yourself, in so much pain. You should have had them take you to the hospital last night."

"Didn't want anyone touching me," Micah murmured, closing her eyes.

"Well, sometimes we have to put up with a little bit of discomfort in order to get better. You're a scientist; you know that. People don't heal broken bones or ruptured kidneys just by lying in bed."

"They can," Micah argued.

"They don't," Marianna told her firmly, just as certain. "You need to have a doctor look at you and make sure that everything is okay."

"No. I'm okay."

Marianna *tsked* and shook her head.

Cole returned to the bedroom. "Your kitten is just fine," he told her. "She's lying in a patch of sunshine to sleep off her breakfast."

"Thanks, Dad."

He sat on the edge of the bed, making it rock. Micah tried to keep her seasickness at bay.

"Now, tell me all about what happened. I want to know every detail. Have police reports been made? What have they found out?"

"I had the police here both times. I don't think they've found anything yet; it's too soon."

"Both times?"

"Well, first there was the burglary."

She described the incident to him, from the time she had come up the sidewalk and seen the footprints filling in until the police had checked the house, walked her in, and made sure she was safe for the night.

"Strange." Cole meditated on this. "Doesn't sound like a normal break and enter. If it was, they would have at least taken the laptop and tablet. Your television is crap, no self-respecting burglar would have bothered with that, but the other electronics... easy to fence. Quick money."

"My TV is not crap!"

"Yes, it is," he asserted. "Maybe like he said, they were interrupted by a neighbor returning home. But it's still pretty strange. They could have taken the tablet and computer with them, even if they spooked. But then to show up again last night..."

"I don't know if it was the same person."

"Of course it was. Too much of a coincidence otherwise. Did you get a look at him? Tell me everything you remember."

Micah went through the story slowly, but there wasn't much to tell. Checking out the backyard to be sure the house was secure, getting knocked down and whaled on, and then rescued by the police. The whole thing was over in a space of minutes or even seconds. Micah had not been able to fight back against someone so much heavier than she was, especially after having been taken off-guard.

"I taught you how to fight," Cole pointed out.

"I know. But... I guess I'm out of practice, and I didn't have any time to react. Before I knew there was anyone there, I was on my back and he was punching me."

"You couldn't get any sense of his face or body? You're trained in this, Micah; you know faces and builds."

"I know... but he was dressed in winter gear. Poofy coat, balaclava, gloves. I couldn't see any skin. I couldn't see what his body shape was under the coat."

"You know it was a man."

"Well… I guess so." Micah thought about it. How did she know it had been a man? Had she been able to tell by his body shape? His big hands? Had he said something to her? Grunted? What had given away his sex? "I guess… he was heavy. But he didn't move like he was weighed down. Not bulky. His hands… they were big, hard."

"Yes…?"

"I don't know what else. I'm not sure what else I might have seen or sensed. It all happened so fast."

"But it is over now. It isn't happening fast now. You can think about each thing separately. Analyze it. Picture it in your mind like a movie or slide show that you can slow down."

Micah wished she weren't so dizzy so that she could focus on it better. She tried to do as he had said, slowing it down in her head, taking a look at it like a series of snapshots instead of the high-speed thriller it had been. She tried to imagine what it would be like to draw him. She had seen only the planes of his mask, but they followed the same planes as his face. She couldn't see his mouth and nose under them, but they had been there, out of sight, the elastic knit clinging to them. In ways, it obscured, but in other ways, it couldn't hide the structure of his face.

She saw his eyes for a moment through the holes of the mask. It had been dark, but his irises and the skin of his eyelids had been light.

"He was white," she said. "Blue eyes."

"Good," Cole approved. "Height? You're a tall girl. Was he taller than you? Shorter?"

"My height or taller… I think."

She tried to remember that initial rush of motion before she realized she was being attacked. Had he come at her low? High? Where had he initially hit? It was hard to tell, just picturing it in her mind, what his full height had been. Most of the time, he'd had her on the ground.

"My height. I think."

"Your height, but heavier. Male suspect. Caucasian. Blue eyes. Eyelashes? Eyebrows? Were they dark or fair?"

"I don't know. I'm not sure." Micah shook her head. "And even if they were dark, people often have eyelashes and eyebrows that are darker than their scalp hair."

"True."

"I don't think he said anything. Grunted, maybe, but I don't think he told me anything. He didn't call me by name, or say something in an accent or another language."

"That would be too easy," Cole said, humor in his voice.

"Yeah. It would be nice if he was a one-armed man with an accent. And who wasn't wearing a mask."

"Better yet, if he was a one-armed man and you pulled off his prosthesis," Cole agreed. "Serial numbers."

Micah chuckled, but it hurt the muscles of her stomach, so she stopped. If she'd only been able to pull off his mask. Or she had a surveillance camera that had picked up more details. A lot of people had those now, doorbell and porch cameras. So they knew when someone approached the house. She didn't like to spend money on things that were not necessary, but maybe a burglar alarm and surveillance equipment were not luxuries. Maybe they were a necessity.

"She's tired, Cole," Marianna said. "Those painkillers are starting to kick in. She needs to sleep."

"She might still have more to tell me."

"She'll be too drowsy. She can try to tell you more later. When she's had a chance to sleep."

"The earlier, the better. These cases are often solved based on what can be discovered in the first forty-eight hours. It has already been that long since the burglary. We don't want to wait on this."

"You're going to have to wait for now," Marianna told him firmly. She stroked Micah's hair again. "Go to sleep, sweetie. The questions will still be there when you wake up again. Your father will help to catch this guy."

Micah didn't have the energy to agree or disagree. Drowsiness was taking over. Her eyelids were getting heavier and heavier, and she couldn't hold the picture of her attacker in her mind. The image slid away from her like slippery soap. And as she tried to chase it down mentally, she lost track of consciousness.

2 8

Micah slept and woke several times throughout the day, but mostly she slept. She didn't know how much medication Marianna was giving her, but it was enough that she was not so uncomfortable and could not stay awake for more than a few minutes at a time. She didn't have the energy or desire to tell Marianna to cut down the dose. Maybe after she'd had a day and another night to recover, she would feel better.

She awoke to Marianna straightening the sheets and leaning over her to check her pulse.

"Oh, sorry, honey. I didn't mean to wake you up." But Marianna didn't seem too concerned that she had done so. "How would you like to have a nice warm bath to soak those sore muscles and joints and get out of those clothes? We can get you into some nice comfy jammies, and I'm sure you'll rest better tonight."

"No." Micah clutched her clothes to her as if Marianna might try to rip them off. "No, I'm okay."

"You don't want to keep sleeping in your work clothes. I can get the bath filled and help you into the bathroom, and then you can get undressed yourself. How about that?"

Micah swallowed. She looked at Marianna, remembering her difficult trip to the bathroom the night before, and the occasional trips during the day when Cole had pretty much carried her into the bathroom. "I don't know if I can do that."

"You'll feel better if you can. You're doing much better than you were. You're not in as much pain, are you? And you've had a little bit of nourishment."

Marianna had, of course, made Micah some chicken soup and helped her to eat it. The kitten had been very interested in the whole process and cuddled up in Micah's lap afterward, purring, her tummy full and warm with her own meal.

"I don't know."

"Well, there's no harm in trying. If you decide you can't manage it, then we'll just bring you back to bed."

"Hmm." Micah sat back, closing her eyes and thinking about it. She expected that closing her eyes would make her fall back asleep and she wouldn't need to make the decision, but sleep did not immediately come this time. She thought about how soothing a warm bath would be. Taking the pressure off of her sore joints, easing the flu-like muscle aches. And she could get a look at her body to see how badly she was bruised. So far, she hadn't had a chance to see how much damage there was. She felt like a wimp for being so disabled by a simple fist-fight. She would never again be able to watch a TV show or movie where the protagonist was in a huge fight and then just went on with his business as usual. Hollywood had lied to her.

"Okay," she finally agreed. "You can run a bath and I'll try."

"That's a girl. You wait here while I get it ready, and then I'll help you in there, or Dad will."

Cole had been put through the paces already. A man of his age shouldn't have to be carrying around a fully-grown woman who had two working feet. She was taller than he was. Not heavier, granted, but he still shouldn't have to lug her around like she was a child.

"Just call me. I can get in by myself."

"I'll help you. You don't want to waste all of your strength getting into the bathroom and then not be able to get into the tub."

Micah sighed and waited for her mother to get it ready.

Marianna shook Micah gently to wake her back up again. "We'll get you moving in a minute here," she said. "You've got a couple of ripped nails, and I just want to get them tidied up first, or you're going to snag them on your clothes when you try to undress or get dressed again after."

Micah blinked. She pulled her hand away from Marianna and close to her face to examine the damage. It wasn't like she had a manicure or false nails to worry about. She kept her nails neat and short so that they didn't bother her when she was typing or drawing and, other than keeping them clean and hangnail-free, was not concerned about what they looked like. She didn't bite them or have other bad nail-care habits.

"It will be fine," Marianna said. "I'll just give them a quick clip and smooth them with an emery board."

Micah turned her hand, examining her fingertips, the torn nails, and the matter under her nails. She didn't give her hand back to Marianna right away.

"You need to put the clippings in a bag."

"What?" Marianna looked at her with a frown, clearly wondering what weird OCD behavior this was. She had always thought Micah odd in her personal care. Having to save her fingernail clippings just confirmed how odd she was.

"There are plastic zip-bags in the kitchen. The right-hand counter, second drawer down. You need to save all of the clippings. Especially this one." She indicated the torn nail. Looking at the other hand, she found a couple of torn ones on that side as well. Her body had hurt so much after the assault that she hadn't stopped to take stock of such things. "And these ones. The damaged ones especially. But all of them. Cut them as short as you can."

"They're already short enough," Marianna objected. "You should leave a little bit of white above the tips of your fingers…"

"No. Not this time. I will the rest of the time, but this time, please cut them as short as you can."

Marianna shook her head, but she left the room and went to the kitchen. Micah heard her open and close a few drawers before finding the bags. Marianna returned and, without a word, clipped Micah's nails as short as she could, saving all of the clippings in the bag. She zipped the top and raised her eyebrows at Micah.

"And where would you like these?"

"Just leave them on the side table. I'll take care of them later."

Marianna did so without comment. Micah wondered if she was having visions of a file cabinet in Micah's office with all of her fingernails neatly cataloged in date order. She couldn't help smiling at the image.

Marianna smoothed the rough edges of the nails that had been torn, carefully checking them to make sure they wouldn't snag on Micah's clothes.

"There. That's got it. I've put a set of your jammies in the bathroom. And undies. I'll help you in there and you can have a nice warm bath."

Micah slid her feet off the bed and leaned on Marianna all the way to the bathroom, where her mother sat her down on the closed toilet lid.

"Now, if you need any help, you call me," she instructed. "I don't want you falling down. If it's too slippery or you're too weak, you call me and I'll help you. No need to be modest about it. Okay?"

Micah breathed out, waiting for the vertigo to recede a little more. "Okay, Mom. Promise."

"I'll be close by. If I hear you fall, I'm coming in."

"Okay. And Mom…?"

"Yes?"

"Thank you. Both of you. You've been so good to me."

Marianna smiled and nodded. Then she left, shutting the bathroom door behind her.

29

Micah did manage to get herself into the bathtub, and it was as wonderful as she had hoped it would be. She lay in the warm water, nearly weightless, and closed her eyes, imagining herself in a sensory deprivation tank.

But even though she enjoyed the bath, she couldn't help thinking about the attack. Her mind was more awake than it had been all day, and she worried at the problem, trying to figure out who would want to hurt her, and if she had been targeted as Cole seemed to think. Otherwise, why would anyone come into her house and then leave without taking anything? And come back to beat her up? If the police hadn't been by at just that time to make sure everything was quiet, he could have beaten her to death; she had no doubt. Even with the beating she had sustained in those brief minutes, she would not have been able to get into the house without help. She would have frozen to death outside.

Why would anyone want to hurt or kill her?

For years Micah had helped the police and other agencies to identify some of the world's most violent criminals. EvPro had never made any secret of which cases they had been involved in, putting up pictures and links to every case that was public. And Micah's profile was right there on the website as their forensic artist.

She wasn't hard to find if someone had her name and town. Even if her address wasn't listed, someone only had to ask around the right places.

Any number of criminals could have an interest in avenging themselves on the woman who had given their faces to the police. She'd never thought to hide her identity.

There was a tap on the door. "You still okay in there, sweetie?"

"I'm good, Mom."

"Okay."

Marianna went away again. The water was starting to cool, so Micah turned the hot water faucet on and let it warm up again. She could stay there all night long, until she was wrinkled beyond recognition…

Of course, her body was already nearly unrecognizable. Her skin was mottled with bruises of every description, some light, some dark, all different sizes.

She knew that she would be turning a rainbow of colors over the next few weeks. They would darken for the first few days, and then start to heal and lighten up, to pretty green and yellow shades. They weren't just on her body, but on her face and limbs as well. She was lucky that neither of her eyes was swollen shut, but they were dark, raccoon-like hollows. A good thing she didn't normally wear makeup, because she certainly wouldn't be able to touch her face for some time. She had a fat lip. Cole had used suture tape to pull together a few gashes in her skin. Her attacker must have been wearing a ring or two under the gloves and, even covered, they had snagged her skin or burst it open.

Micah needed to get to the office. Even if it were just for a few minutes. Once they saw the shape she was in, no one would object to her missing a few days. She needed to talk to Chastity. She would need to get permission to log in to the company servers remotely, which she normally wasn't supposed to do. But they would understand and be happy to have her still working even if she couldn't be at the office.

She could take long baths and naps and work for an hour or two at a time throughout the day. She might not put in the number of hours that she normally would, but it would help her to keep up and stay on top of the urgent cases. Long-cold cases could wait until she had recovered a little.

Micah closed her eyes and, despite her resolution not to fall asleep in the tub, she woke up shivering some time later, the water and her skin cooling quickly. She drained some of the water and again filled it with hot water, resolving that it would be the last refill. Then she would get up and get into bed.

———

She should have known that Cole and Marianna would object to her going into the office the next day. They had slept over, even though Micah didn't have a spare bedroom or even a pull-out couch. Marianna had slept on the bed beside Micah. Cole had slept on the couch. Not particularly comfortable for either one of them, Micah suspected, since she had been very restless and had wakened Marianna numerous times. It was like being a child with the flu again, having to wake her mother every time she threw up to make sure she knew about it. Why that had been important, Micah wasn't sure. She should have just let her mother sleep. But that wasn't an option when Marianna was lying in bed beside her and Micah was used to being able to flop around with the whole bed to herself.

"You can't go in looking like this," Marianna insisted. "You need to stay home for a few days before you even consider going into the office. You don't have the strength and your body needs to heal. You can't just push through something like this."

"I agree with your mother," Cole said, sounding like it was the last thing he wanted to do. "You need your rest. Work can wait. No one is going to expect you to go in looking like that."

"Well, they're not going to know that I look like that unless I go in. Then they'll tell me to go home and won't be getting after me to come back right away."

Marianna rolled her eyes dramatically. "Take a picture of yourself and message it in. You kids do that all the time. You don't need to go in."

"I have some things I need to do. People I need to talk to and see. Just for a few minutes, and then I can come back home."

"It's not a good idea," Marianna insisted. "And you can't drive yourself. You can't get behind the wheel like that."

"Good thing I have a couple of people who are able to drive visiting me, then," Micah said dryly.

"There's no need for you to be sarcastic. You know it's not a good idea, Micah. Listen to us."

"It will just be for a few minutes. You can go with me. Wait in the car. Make sure that I am only a few minutes. But I need to go."

"Why? What's so important?"

"I just need to," Micah said, not wanting to discuss the details with them. "It won't take long."

"Don't harass the girl," Cole put in. "You know how she gets when you try to tell her what to do."

Micah had an unfortunate reputation for being stubborn. She wasn't quite sure where it came from. Her parents were far more stubborn than she was. She only dug in her heels in self-defense.

But maybe that reputation would help her to get what she wanted. Marianna wouldn't want to fight with her all day about something that meant so little.

Marianna shook her head, still rolling her eyes. "You know this is not a good idea."

"I know, Mom."

"If you're going to do it, you need to make sure you have something to eat this morning. Some good hearty oatmeal to give you the strength you need. One of us will drive you and you can't stay for a long time. You have to promise me that it will be less than an hour."

"Yes, Mom. It will be less than an hour."

"And oatmeal?"

"I hate oatmeal. I'll eat something else. A whole-grain cereal that isn't all ground up into unidentifiable mush."

"What do you have in the kitchen? I will make it for you."

"I can cook something myself."

"No, you can't. If you are going into the office, you need to conserve your energy."

"Fine. I have some kasha. There are instructions on the box."

"Good. You just worry about getting yourself dressed. Then rest until it is ready."

"Okay, Mom."

Marianna walked out of the room. "Do you put something on this kasha?" she called back. "Sugar or maple syrup?"

"Maybe some fruit. No sugar."

Cole followed Marianna out of the room. "You still drink coffee, right?"

"Yes, Dad. There's coffee."

"Good thing," Cole muttered. He was often grumpy in the mornings, and probably more so after sleeping on the couch. Although Micah hadn't forced him to. He could have gone home and slept in his own bed. He was the one who had said they would stay over. He would feel better after a cup of coffee. Or two or three. Micah wondered how many he had drunk in a day when he had been on the job. She knew that Marianna watched his caffeine intake now.

Micah looked around. She rolled over on the bed so that she could reach the door, and pushed it shut. She didn't want to put on her usual work attire, but she needed something other than the flowered flannel jammies that Marianna had lain out for her the night before. She sat on the bed and reached for her dresser and managed to get out some yoga pants and a bra and t-shirt. Not that she did yoga, but they were comfy when she was just knocking around the house alone.

She grabbed her purse and slid the plastic bag of fingernails into it. Best to have that out of sight before Marianna had a chance to wonder about what she was doing with it.

By the time the kasha was cooked—a little overcooked, unfortunately—Micah was ready for her foray into work. She ate what she could of the kasha. Marianna had made far too much, and neither she nor Cole wanted any. Marianna put the leftovers into a bowl in the fridge.

"Now you have something to heat up in the microwave for tomorrow's breakfast. Quick and easy."

"Thanks." Micah looked at the two of them. "Now… which one of you is driving?"

"I'll take you in," Cole offered.

Marianna looked surprised. "I was going to do that."

"You still look like you need more sleep. Why don't you lie down for a while? I'll take her in."

"I'm sure I got just as much sleep as you did. I'm perfectly capable of taking her into the office."

"I'm doing it," Cole said firmly.

Marianna sighed. "Fine. I supposed I'll clean up here. Play with the kitten so she gets some exercise. I can find something else to do."

"Just have a nap, Mom," Micah advised, not comfortable with the idea of Marianna poking around the house looking for something to do. "Dad's right. You've been so busy taking care of me. You need a rest."

Marianna shook her head and muttered about how she was perfectly capable of taking care of herself and didn't need to be told what to do. Micah picked up her purse, slipped on a pair of shoes, and nodded to Cole. "I'm ready."

As they reached the front door, Cole looked back. "Be sure to lock the door after us," he told Marianna.

"You aren't going to be that long."

"Micah has keys and can let us in when we get back. I don't want you here with the door unlocked."

He waited until he heard Marianna slide the bolt. Micah walked slowly toward his car. "Do you think she's in any danger? The burglar got in without a key before." She frowned at the door, looking back at it. "And so did you, come to think of it."

"You need better locks and better security." He didn't say anything else until they were both in the car, Micah securely buckled in. "I don't think there's any danger of him returning to finish the job. Not with the police having been here twice already. Too dangerous to make a third attempt. But there's no point in being sloppy. We need to upgrade your security, make sure that you have an alarm hardwired to a live security center. You can't afford to take chances."

Micah thought about it as he drove to the office.

The unsub wouldn't make a third attempt.

Her mother would be perfectly safe there during the day. They wouldn't be gone for long.

30

Micah was anxious after talking about her security, even more focused on her visit to EvPro being a short one. She entered the building, went past the main security desk without anyone stopping her, and headed for the lab. Once there, she looked around for Chastity, hoping to talk to her without anyone else listening in.

Veronica was there as well, but she'd be the one handling the evidence, so that was okay. As long as Kwong and the higher-ups weren't around to put a stop to Micah using company resources. She motioned to Veronica and Chastity. Both were wide-eyed at her appearance.

"Oh, my goodness," Veronica said, her mouth dropping wide open. "Aaron said that you reported being mugged, but I never thought… oh, my goodness… you look terrible."

"It looks worse than it is," Micah lied. "Listen, I need a favor."

Veronica couldn't drag her eyes from Micah's face. "Oh, my goodness," she repeated faintly.

Micah unzipped her purse and pulled out the plastic bag. She laid it on the lab bench. "I might have scratched him. Can you retrieve any tissue and run it? Then Chastity can run the profile for me?" She glanced aside at Chastity.

Veronica looked down at the fingernail clippings. "Shouldn't the police be doing this?"

"Uh… probably. But you know how long it will take them to run it and then they won't share the information with me. As the victim, I'd be barred from getting any information, even if they decided to give EvPro a contract."

"But… what are you going to do with it? Even if we do a profile, you're not going to be able to give it to the police. Chain of custody and all. It's compromised as evidence in a trial."

"But I'll know who it is," Micah said. "I can do a composite. If I see him again, I'll know him. I can give the police a drawing, tell them that I realized I saw more than I remembered that night."

"That's…" Veronica's eyes were wide. "That would be a lie." She knew that Micah was a rule-follower and never lied as a social nicety or to cover for herself or for someone else's mistake.

Micah met her eyes. "I need this."

Veronica hesitated, then nodded. "Okay."

They both looked at Chastity. "Is this going to be a problem?" Micah asked.

Chastity matched Micah's gaze without flinching. "Is *what* going to be a problem?"

Micah studied her, trying to discern whether she really didn't know what Micah wanted her to do, or whether she was agreeing to look the other way.

"You'll do it?"

"I just process what I'm given." Chastity shrugged. "If it's in my in tray, it will get done."

"Thanks."

"How do you want this labeled, then?" Veronica asked, pulling the bag toward her.

"Uh… yes." Micah thought about it, trying to figure out what would be the least suspicious way to label the sample so that it wasn't pulled out by Kwong or somebody else with questions. "Can you post it as an unsub for Michael Morse? I'll call him and give him a heads-up in case someone asks."

Veronica frowned, looking at her. She knew that Michael was a software consultant, not a client. But clients and consultants shared the third-party identifier database, so the same number could be used in either the supplier or purchaser field.

"Put it under Michael Morse," Micah repeated.

Veronica nodded, grabbing her intake form and writing Michael's accounting code at the top. Micah looked at the two women, breathing out slowly. "Thank you."

"You don't know who it was?" Chastity asked.

"No. And it's weird… because I don't think it was a random attack. I'm worried that it might be someone who is already in the system. Someone I did a composite for. Someone I put behind bars."

"If you put him behind bars, then what is he doing out?" Veronica asked.

They both just looked at her. Veronica rolled her eyes and nodded. "Okay, just because someone gets sent to prison doesn't mean they stay there. Sorry. I guess I always think of our unsubs as being lifers. People that have done such horrible things, that once it goes to trial, they're never getting out."

"Even people serving life sentences get released, get put on some work program, or escape. This guy… if the police hadn't been by to check on things, he could have killed me."

Veronica stared at Micah's bruised face, nodding gravely.

"If he's someone we've processed before, it will be flagged by the system," Chastity advised. "Hopefully, we'll know who it is right away. I'll let you know."

Micah nodded. She leaned on the counter, exhaustion dragging her down. She still needed to get permission to access the company server on her laptop to work from home. And she needed to grab whatever was urgent from her physical inbox.

She sighed. "You're going to need my profile to eliminate," she told Chastity. "You're bound to get some of my skin and blood cells from those clippings too." She raised her brows at Veronica. "Can you get me a collection kit?"

"I'll just eliminate the double-X," Chastity said. "No need to worry about it, unless your mugger was a woman."

"No. But… you're still going to need my profile."

Chastity shook her head. "No. It's fine. It will be easy to tell which DNA profile is yours, because you're a woman."

Micah swallowed, looking at Chastity, then glancing over at Veronica. "I need a collection kit."

Veronica blinked, then reached under her lab bench to pull out a sealed collection kit with a swab inside. She handed it across to Micah.

"You're not?" Chastity demanded, frown lines forming between her eyes.

Micah had never needed to share her medical history with the EvPro team. She didn't want her details to become water cooler gossip. But she worried that Chastity was going to come to incorrect conclusions and start rumors. The two had never been close and Chastity often acted like the two of them were in competition. That was all Chastity needed, some rumors to spread about Micah's sexuality.

"I have AIS," Micah told her stonily. "I have X and Y chromosomes."

"Androgen Insensitivity Syndrome?" Veronica said, a little too loudly.

Micah looked around, making sure that they were still alone. "Yes. And that's private medical information, so if you share it with anyone, you're in breach of the law." She looked at both of them to make sure they understood.

"So you are genetically male," Chastity said. Her eyes were curious, sweeping Micah's body as if she were looking for some sign that she was transgender, or that Micah was making a joke.

"Women with AIS don't respond to testosterone," she said quietly, though it was something Chastity, a DNA expert, should be fully versed in. "An AIS body doesn't develop male characteristics. It instead converts androgens to estrogen. It has a male genotype, but a female phenotype."

Chastity nodded. "Do you have complete or partial?" she asked curiously.

Micah was not prepared to deal with the questions. She was exhausted and wanted to sit down or have a nap. "You don't need to know that for the profile." She indicated the test swab in her hand. "You only need this."

"Right. Of course," Chastity agreed, professionalism reasserting itself. "If you'll have Veronica process that, I'll eliminate your profile and see what is left."

"Thanks. Let me know when it's done. I'm going to do some work from home." Micah gestured toward her office. "I need to sit down for a minute. I'll do this," she indicated the test kit again, "and talk to someone in IT. I'll have it to you in a few minutes," she informed Veronica.

"Yeah, sure. Sounds good." Veronica dropped her eyes to examine the nail clippings. "I'll get right on this."

31

Micah was asleep by the time Cole got her home. He shook her arm gently.

"We're home. Let's get you inside."

Micah groaned. "What?"

"Let's go into the house. You can go straight to bed when you get in. I told you that it was going to be too much for you."

Micah fumbled for her door handle, made sure she had a grip on her purse, and tried to get out. Cole reached over and released her seatbelt. Micah looked at it, juggled her purse so that the belt could retract, and tried once more to exit. This time, the various parts of her body worked together and she was able to stand up and start shuffling her way up the sidewalk.

She was badly in need of more painkillers. She had thought that maybe she'd be able to start weaning herself off, but it was way too early for that. She was going to need them for at least a few more days. And of course, Cole and Marianna had both been right; it had been too soon to venture into the office. Micah had known that. But she had to get her attacker's DNA processed if she had managed to scratch him during their fight.

She needed to know who he was. How to recognize him if he showed up at her door posing as a salesman or walked a dog down her street looking for another opportunity to get close to her. And she wanted to know if he was someone she recognized or had put in prison.

Her work had always seemed theoretical before. It was practical, because they helped to catch perps and put them behind bars, but it was still several degrees removed from her. She never saw the criminals, rarely saw the police officers or other parties who had contracted for her work. She sat in her office where it was safe and drew faces. At the end of the day, she went home and didn't worry about how she could destroy someone's plans, completely changing the direction of his life.

But now it wasn't theoretical. Now someone was targeting her. It had to be someone she had drawn.

Cole walked at Micah's side, and when her energy started to flag and she slowed, uncertain she could make it to the door, he put his arm around her and had her lean on his shoulder, steadying her and helping her to get the rest of the way.

"Thanks," Micah breathed. "I never knew my sidewalk was so long."

She had to dig her keys out when she got to the door because Marianna didn't meet them at the door and it was locked. Micah didn't want to ring the doorbell and wake her if she was asleep.

Cole unlocked the door for her and pushed it open. Micah hesitated, not stepping in straight away.

"You okay, Micah?"

"Yeah. Just... just anxious."

He looked around her. "Is there anything out of place? Is something wrong?"

His questions just made her more nervous. What if the man had returned while she and Cole were gone? They had left Marianna there alone, defenseless.

But the door wouldn't still be locked if he had broken in. It would be unlocked, like the last time.

"No. Just nervous after what happened. I'm sure it's fine."

"Let's go in, then."

Micah lifted her feet over the threshold, one at a time. She had never noticed how high it was, either. Her body was not cooperating with her. She thought she had a glimpse of what it would feel like to have mobility challenges or to get old and start to lose control of her functions.

It wasn't a very nice feeling.

The house was quiet. Cole followed her in and shut and locked the door, muttering again about the lock. He took her arm once more and helped her down the long hall to her bedroom.

Marianna was asleep on the bed, and roused when she felt Micah lie down on the bed, letting out a prolonged sigh. Micah was relieved to see that she was okay. No burglars. No attacker. She had just needed a nap.

"Micah! Are you okay?"

"I'm fine, Mom," Micah mumbled. "But I could use a drink and some more painkillers."

"I'll get you some. You rest here. I'll be right back."

Marianna hurried out of the room. Micah's eyes met Cole's. "Where exactly does she think I'm going to go?"

He chuckled. In a few minutes, Marianna was back and helped Micah to sit up to drink the water and swallow the pills. Micah sank back down into her pillows, closing her eyes and waiting for the drugs to take effect.

———

She slept a lot longer than she thought she would. She had been waking every couple of hours the day before and thought that would continue, with her being able to stay awake a little longer each time and gradually gaining in strength and stamina so that she could start to do some work.

But instead, she slept the day away and, when she awoke again, the room was getting dark. Micah flailed, disoriented, feeling like the world was tilting on its side.

"Mom?"

Marianna hurried in. "Micah. Hey, that was a long sleep."

"Mom?"

Marianna sat on the side of the bed, tilting the world even farther, and Micah grabbed her and held on, trying to prevent herself from falling off.

"It's okay," Marianna assured her. "You're alright. Did you have a dream? Cole said that you might dream about the attack. But you're safe, sweetie. Everything is okay."

"No…" Micah squeezed her mother's hand. "No, I wasn't dreaming. I don't think so. I just… didn't know where I was at first." She looked around the room, and it gradually became more familiar to her. Not her childhood room at her parents' house. But her own bedroom at her own house. She was at home.

Everything was where it was supposed to be. Micah had never realized that the layout of her bedroom was the opposite of the one she had grown up in. It had never mattered to her before. Now she found it disorienting and unfamiliar.

"Do you want another pill?"

Micah moved her body slowly, feeling the deep bruises, the strained muscles and swollen joints. "Yeah. I guess."

Marianna had left a glass and the pills on the side table, so she had them close at hand and didn't have to leave this time. She smoothed Micah's dark hair, studying her with concern. "There. Are you okay now?"

"Yeah. Just felt weird when I woke up."

"Do you need anything? You should try to eat again. Do you think you could manage some soup and crackers or toast?"

"Mmm." Micah tried to sit up. Marianna helped her, readjusting pillows and helping Micah to lift herself the best she could. Eventually, Micah was sitting up most of the way. Her head spun. "Maybe a little toast. Just one slice. No soup."

"You need to get enough nourishment if you want to heal fast."

"Not too much. Nauseated."

"Okay. Do you want your father to come sit with you while I make it?"

"Umm… okay." Micah would never have predicted that she would be afraid to be alone or would want one of her parents there to keep her company just because the other was leaving the room. She felt like a feverish child, fussy and hanging on to a teddy bear. Like when she'd had tonsillitis.

"Cole!" Marianna headed to the kitchen, explaining to Cole on the way that he needed to sit with Micah.

He sat down on the bed. "How are you feeling?"

"Like I just slept the whole day away."

"Well," he shrugged, "you did."

"And I feel like… like I'm sick. Nauseated and disoriented. My head is spinning."

"If that lasts too long, you'll want to go to the doctor and make sure you don't have an infection. But it's probably just the painkillers. They can make you woozy."

"Oh." Micah nodded. It made her feel a bit better to have an explanation for the way her head was feeling. Just a side effect of the medication. She would get over it. "Yeah, that makes sense."

"Mom is going to make you some food?"

"Just toast."

"Well, she should be able to manage that." His eyes twinkled, and Micah realized for the first time that he knew she wasn't a good cook. In all her years, she'd never heard him criticize her mother's cooking. He always ate it without complaint, as if it were exactly what he wanted. She smiled.

Micah heard buzzing and looked around, trying to identify it. She thought at first that it might be a fly against the window, but it was too cold outside for insect life. Then she thought it might be the cat, cuddling up to her and purring, but she didn't see any sign of Meow.

Cole caught her searching gaze. "It's your phone," he said. "Do you want it?"

"Oh! Yes, please. Where is it?"

He picked her purse up and poked around in it gingerly before coming out with her phone and passing it to her. Micah squinted at the screen, trying to control the movement of her eyes, but the vertigo kept her from being able to focus properly, her eyes moving from side to side, trying to control the spinning of the world around her.

"Dad…?"

He took it from her and looked at the screen. "You have some text messages. The last one says, 'Evidence processed and passed on to Chastity for sequencing.'"

"Oh, good." Micah put her hand over her stomach. "That's good."

"Don't they know that you can't work right now? They shouldn't be sending you messages; they should just be letting you sleep."

"No, this is something I asked for. I wanted them to get this for me."

"You can't do work right now," he warned. "You can't even see straight."

"I'll be better once I have a bite to eat. And maybe I'll tell Mom to lower the dose of the painkillers a little bit."

"You'll be in too much pain."

"I need to be able to see and type. And draw."

"Too fast. You're going to have to wait for your body to start to heal. Right now, you need sleep, not work."

"Can I have the phone back?"

Cole handed it over.

"I need to make a call."

He looked at her, eyebrows raised. "You want me to put the number in for you?"

"No, it's in my contacts list. I can just tell it to call."

"These newfangled phones. It's crazy what they can do." He sat there, not moving.

"Why don't you go see how Mom is doing," Micah suggested. "I'll only be a minute."

"Oh!" He finally seemed to get it. "Well, just tell me to get out of the way, then. Is this a work call or a personal one?"

Micah let out a laugh. Did he think she had a boyfriend on the side? Someone she wasn't telling him about? "Work."

"Okay. Just give us a shout when you're off. It shouldn't take too long to finish making toast."

"I hope not."

He left the room, pulling the door just behind him. Micah told her phone which contact to call, and put it to her ear, waiting for it to ring through.

Michael Morse's voice sounded in her ear.

"Michael here. Oh, Micah. How are you doing?"

"Well... actually not too good," she admitted. "I was attacked the other day, in my yard, and I'm feeling pretty rough."

"You were attacked?" he repeated, his voice jumping to a higher register. "You're kidding! Are you okay?"

"Just bruised. Nothing serious," Micah assured him, knowing he would be thinking about the assault of his girlfriend, Ash. Micah's assault, brutal as it was, had at least not included rape or left her in a coma. Ash was recovering, but Micah knew it would be a long time before Ash could put it behind her.

"What can I do to help?" Michael was anxious for more information. "What exactly happened? Who attacked you?"

"I don't know. But you're already helping me to find out."

He was silent for a moment. Then a cautious reply. "And how am I helping you find out?"

"I'm having our lab process some DNA evidence. See if I can put a face on this guy. But since I can't process my own evidence, I had to put it into the system under someone else's name."

As someone who had been known to... push the boundaries of what might be considered legal with his cutting-edge virtual reality software, and who was willing to go above and beyond to help solve the crimes against

Ash and even Lace, a woman he had never even met, Michael had seemed the natural choice for Micah.

"Oh, I see!" Michael's laugh carried over the line. "So you put it under my name."

"Yeah, I needed someone who was already on the system so it wouldn't raise any red flags. I'll pay the bill, of course. But I didn't want you wondering who this unsub was that you supposedly contacted us about."

"It's all starting to come back to me now. I think I definitely remember giving EvPro some…"

"Fingernail clippings."

"Some fingernail clippings to process for me. Yes, definitely." He chuckled to himself. "No problem, Micah. Your secret is safe with me. I'm delighted to help."

"Thanks so much, Michael. You're a lifesaver."

3 2

She was afraid that she would be awake or restless all night after having slept so much of the day, but she wasn't. She slept soundly, not tossing and turning like she had the previous night. Micah didn't ask Marianna what she had given her. Marianna obviously knew what she was doing.

Cole still slept on the couch, refusing to go home to his own bed. "I've got the security company coming tomorrow. After you have new doors, locks, and a proper alarm, I might feel safe leaving you to fend for yourself. Maybe. But not before that. I'm not leaving my little girl, or both of my girls, alone and unprotected while I go home to sleep in comfort."

"We would be okay," Micah protested, but not too strongly, because the truth was, she didn't want to talk Cole out of it. She knew that she should try to get him to go home to sleep so that he would have an easier night, but she wanted him to stay.

"Not a chance." Cole made a motion to dismiss any further argument. "We'll all sleep here tonight. After the security has been upgraded... we'll see."

For the first time since Micah had moved out on her own, she didn't want to be the only one in the house when she went to bed. Sometimes a person needed family close by.

In the morning, she awoke feeling more clear-headed, the spinning sensation gone. Her body was healing, or it was adjusting to the medication.

Or maybe Marianna had changed up the medications to see if it would help with the side effects. Micah rubbed her eyes, careful of the bruises on her face. She looked down at her clothes and saw that she still had on the yoga pants and t-shirt that she had donned to go to the office.

"Mom?"

Marianna stirred beside her. "Micah? What is it?"

"I'm going to have a bath. You don't need to get up."

"Are you sure? I can run the bath for you, make sure that you can get in safely…"

"No. Go back to sleep. I'm just going to relax in the hot water."

"Okay." Marianna's eyes closed and she let out a long sigh. "You call me if you need anything. I'm right here. I'll hear you."

"Go back to sleep."

Marianna didn't say anything else. Micah sat on the bed while she got out a change of clothing, glad that her dresser was so close in the small room. Then she toddled into the bathroom and sat down on the toilet while she filled the tub for herself.

"You're looking a lot better today," Cole observed. "Bright-eyed. More like yourself."

Micah nodded. She was able to sit on the couch in the living room instead of staying in bed all day. Even though she didn't have much strength or stamina, she still felt more human sitting on the couch. She watched the workmen who were upgrading the security at Cole's instruction. The kitten had been locked away in the bathroom, crying piteously, to make sure that she could not get away while they were upgrading the doors and frames. Micah had a quilt tucked around her to keep her warm, though the weather had warmed up to a balmy fall day, melting a good deal of the snow and turning everything a muddy brown.

"I'm feeling a lot better. Still pretty sore, but not so sick and… icky."

"That's good. But don't get the idea that you can go right back to work. You still need time to heal and recover."

"I know. But I can do a little today."

"No work," he said sternly.

"Dad…"

"Nope. No work."

"What am I going to do, then?"

"Read a good book. Watch daytime TV and see what you've been missing all these years. Have a nap."

"I'm not watching TV."

He laughed. "Only kid that ever had to be told to put her homework away and go watch TV."

Micah shrugged. "I enjoyed the homework more."

"And then you laid awake all night because your brain wouldn't shut off. You needed some downtime before bed so that you could relax and go to sleep."

"Yeah, well, what you didn't know was that I had schoolbooks hidden under my blanket."

"Oh, didn't I?"

Micah couldn't help giggling. She had never guessed that her father knew what she was up to, flashlight in hand, long after he and Marianna had gone to bed or when he was on night shift.

"I want to draw," she decided. "Could you bring me a couple of things from my office?" She gestured toward the spare room so he wouldn't think she wanted him to go all the way to EvPro to fetch her something.

"What do you want?"

"In the second drawer of my desk, there's a red pencil box. And on the bookshelves, there is a sketchpad with a black cover and a label that says #14."

He nodded and went to find them.

When Marianna returned with several grocery bags half an hour later, she scowled at the sight of the sketchbook in Micah's lap.

"You are not supposed to be working. Cole, didn't I tell you to keep an eye on her and make sure she didn't do too much?"

"She's not working."

"She's drawing. That's work." Marianna drew closer to get a look at Micah's picture to prove that she was working instead of relaxing.

Micah let her see the rough sketch of the baby in several different positions as she explored various ideas.

"You see? Is that Baby Sweetgrass?" Marianna demanded.

"No. It's a picture for a friend."

"A friend?" Marianna shook her head at the idea. "Who?"

"You remember Sara Thompson from school?"

"Sara? Yes, I remember her." Marianna's scowl smoothed out. "You're drawing a picture for her? I didn't know she had a baby."

Micah pressed her lips together, trying to decide whether she was allowed to tell Marianna what had happened. She didn't want Marianna approaching Sara at the store to ask her how her baby was.

"Mom, it's confidential, okay?"

"Confidential? What's confidential?"

"Sara. She lost a baby. She wants… something to remember him by."

"Oh." Marianna's face crinkled up. "Oh, the poor girl. I didn't know!"

"No, and I don't think they're telling anyone, so you can't bring it up. But I just want you to know… so you don't ask her any awkward questions."

"No, no, you're right to tell me. I don't want to cause her any pain." Marianna sat down on the couch, resting her grocery bags on the floor and taking a long look at Micah's sketches. "I like this one."

She indicated a close-up of a baby's face; one tiny fist balled up next to the sleeping face. Very peaceful. Sara's baby, born asleep.

Micah nodded, a lump in her throat. "Thanks. I really like that one too."

Marianna reached over and rubbed Micah's back briefly. She didn't normally like a back rub, but she appreciated her mother's emotional support, and her touch soothed sore muscles and bruises. She put her hand on Marianna's arm.

"Love you, Mom."

"You too, honey." Marianna sat there for a moment, then stood, picking the grocery bags up again. "I'd better get these things put away."

Micah didn't ask Marianna what she had purchased. Micah had plenty of staples on her kitchen shelves and fresh produce in the fridge, but Marianna's and Cole's eating habits were quite different from hers, and they probably felt like she had nothing to eat.

Her parents stayed at her house one more night but, in the morning, Micah informed them that they would be sleeping in their own bed that night.

"I'm doing a lot better now. I can get around to get the things I need. I promise I'll call if I need anything in the night, but I don't think I will. I've been sleeping through and you guys deserve to be back in your bed tonight."

"Can I still come back in the morning to check on you?" Marianna demanded.

"Yes," Micah agreed. "Sure."

They had been there when she needed them, and she didn't want to cut them off too abruptly. She would try to taper off their involvement over the next few days. And maybe it was time to start inviting them over to dinner now and then. Marianna might enjoy a break from cooking, and Cole a change in cuisine now and then.

They had been there for her and she realized that they meant a lot more to her than she had previously thought. She could live with having them around now and then without acting like it was cutting into her precious time.

Marianna looked at Cole to see what he thought of the matter. He had said that once the security was upgraded, he would feel better about leaving her there alone. Cole considered for a long moment and then nodded.

"I'm sure Micah needs her space. She's safer now. That security alarm goes directly to a staffed security center. They can send the police at the first sign of trouble."

"And we can check in on her in the morning."

"We'll come in the morning," Cole agreed. "Just to see if there's anything else we can help with."

Micah nodded and, eventually, they both agreed with her. That still left them the rest of the day to get their fill of her. Then when they started to get tired, they could go home and sleep.

***

She managed to sneak online a couple of times on her computer to monitor her inbox and check for DNA results from Morse's unsub. As long as she was quick and left other browser tabs open, neither parent could catch her at it. Sort of like the old days, reading her school textbooks under the covers after they had gone to bed.

She was anxious to get the results and the first chance to look at her attacker's face. Hopefully, it would match someone already in the system, and they could find a way to put the police onto him without admitting that they had drawn outside the lines. She could say she had drawn a sketch from her recovered memories of the attack, that she hadn't even remembered how she had pulled off the balaclava. And one of the others in the lab could recognize it for who it really was. They would work it out one way or another.

It wasn't until after her parents left for the day that the DNA sequencing and computer-generated phenotype finally showed up on the server. Micah pulled a blanket around her shoulders, shifted the kitten, asleep in her lap, and clicked on the results.

34

Micah first saw the flat, computer-generated phenotype. Male. Handsome, well-proportioned features, clean-shaven with generic brown hair. The computer, while it did a good job, couldn't predict his hairstyle, facial hair, or many other features. And Micah would have to look at the epigenome for information like age and other details. She had a pretty good idea of height and weight from direct experience, and she knew that he was strong. She would give him good muscles as she tried out different looks. Hopefully, she would be able to tease a few more details out of the epigenome as well and to make some predictions from the totality of the information.

She scrolled down through the data on range of skin tones, hair and eye color, racial heritage—mainly white European—and a few other details.

At the bottom of the profile, there was an alert that there was a profile match in the EvPro database. She would tell the IT guys that they should move matches in the database to the top of the file rather than burying it at the bottom where people might not see it. If there was a profile match, then that should be the first thing the recipient should see.

Micah was relieved that there was a match in the system. She clicked on the hyperlink to see the identity of her attacker.

Baby Thompson-Smith.

The pseudonym that Micah had created for the Lazarus profile of Sweetie's father.

Micah sat there in the silence of her house, staring at the screen.

The man who had attacked her was not someone she had put behind bars and who was trying to get revenge on her. He was the abandoned baby's father.

She tried to wrap her mind around it. Why would he attack Micah? Did he somehow know that she was behind the identification of Trisha Madro, and was afraid that she would also be able to identify him? Was he afraid he might somehow be blamed for the baby's abandonment?

Or the mother's death.

Micah tapped her keys lightly, not hard enough to push down, just enough to make a light clicking as she thought.

If he was Micah's attacker, then he was a violent man. He could have killed Micah.

And he could have killed Trisha Madro.

It was getting late and Micah was exhausted. She had planned to go to bed immediately after her parents left, and had just checked the server one more time to reassure herself so she could go to sleep and rest easy.

She hadn't planned to stay up later working on the new profile. And she hadn't intended to call anyone.

But that had all changed. Micah couldn't just go to sleep and forget about it until morning. Who knew how much could happen before then? What if Sweetie's father had been watching the house, waiting until her parents were gone and Micah was alone once more? He could be out there, planning his course of action.

She called the number she had previously been able to reach Bellows at, and a brisk female voice answered.

"Sheriff's Department."

"Oh. I was looking for Deputy Bellows. I thought this would go to him directly."

"Deputy Bellows is not on duty right now. How may I direct your call?"

"I was calling regarding one of his cases. The Sweetgrass Hills baby."

"He'll be in during the day tomorrow and you can go over it with him then."

"It's kind of an emergency."

"You didn't call an emergency line. Deputy Bellows is currently off duty. We don't route calls to off-duty officers."

"I don't think he would mind you making one exception."

"Everybody thinks they are an exception. Our officers need to sleep if they are going to be able to perform their functions. Do you need an emergency responder?"

"I don't know."

"What seems to be the problem?"

"I was attacked the other day; there should be a file on your system."

"Uh-huh. Yes?"

"I'm afraid that… the man who attacked me might be back, watching my house."

There was rapid-fire keyboard clicking in the background. "I will have an officer dispatched to your house," she said immediately. "Is this your correct address?" She read it off.

"Yes. But I don't know…"

"Did you see someone hanging around your house? What made you think the man who attacked you might be there?"

"I didn't see him. But I just found out… that he has something to do with a case that I'm working on for law enforcement. On Sweetie's case. That's why I wanted to talk to Deputy Bellows."

"A case you are working on for law enforcement," the woman repeated. "Does that mean that you are a law enforcement officer?"

"No. I work with DNA. I'm a contractor. With EvPro."

It was not a big city, and many people knew about EvPro, especially if they were in law enforcement.

"You work with DNA? And what does that have to do with this man who attacked you?"

"The man who attacked me is connected with the abandoned baby case."

The woman sighed audibly. "A car has been sent to your house. You can explain it to them when they arrive, and they can decide on any further steps to be pursued. Do you want me to stay on the line until they get there?"

Micah looked out the window. She couldn't see anything, but it wouldn't take long before the police arrived.

"Uh, no, I think it will be okay. Thank you."

The woman said goodbye and terminated the call. Micah watched the street in front of the house, waiting for the police. She felt silly about them being sent there on an emergency basis when she didn't know if her attacker was anywhere close. But he could be and, even with the new security measures, Micah didn't feel safe.

She wanted Deputy Frank Bellows. He was the one who knew the case and she needed to tell him the developments. She would have to keep telling the story, first to the officers who showed up and then again to Bellows. Not until the next day, because the duty officer wouldn't forward the call to him.

Micah supposed that was the woman's job, but it was still irritating. She wished she had asked Bellows for his cell number or home number in case anything came up.

She hadn't expected to find anything out about Sweetie's father after hours. That was a complete shock.

3 5

A squad car pulled up in front of the house, lights flashing but siren off. Micah went to the door and turned the locks to open them. She shivered with the cold when she opened the door for them. It had warmed up significantly, but she'd been snuggling under a warm quilt and her body didn't like the shock of the chilly air. The two officers took their time getting out of the car and approaching the house. Micah wished they would hurry up so she could close the door. The kitten was sleeping on the couch and didn't look interested in getting any closer to the cold breeze.

"You have a prowler, ma'am?" one of the cops asked.

"I'm not sure. I've had two incidents, and… my parents just went home and I'm alone, and I'm worried that he might try to attack me again."

"Two incidents?"

She was surprised that he hadn't brushed up on her case on the way there. "A burglary and an assault, on two different days."

"And you saw him tonight, or you didn't?"

"I didn't."

He rolled his eyes. "We'll take a look around. Close and lock your door and we'll knock after we've cleared the area."

They had pulled up with their lights on. If Micah had been a felon lurking about outside, she would have taken off at the first sign of trouble.

But she obeyed their instruction and sat inside, waiting for them to make sure she was safe. It wasn't long before they were knocking at the door.

"Don't see anyone out here, or any sign anyone has been lurking around," the first cop said, shrugging. He had unzipped his jacket and eased his heavy duty belt up on his belly before releasing it again.

"I didn't know if he would be around… I'd really like to talk to Deputy Bellows, though," Micah said, rubbing her eyes tiredly. "He's going to want this new information."

"You'll have to try to get him in the morning. If it's not an emergency, they're not going to wake him up. And it's not an emergency," he told her firmly.

"What if this guy comes after me again? You wouldn't know anything was wrong until it was too late."

He looked around. "Looks like you've beefed up security measures. I'd say you're safe. Don't open your door to anyone."

"He's attacked me before."

"Do you have a description, ma'am?"

"Well… actually, I do." Micah picked up her laptop and brought up the computer composite. "Dark hair, brown eyes. I don't know his age yet, so keep in mind he could be older than this."

The cop looked at her screen for a long moment. "What program is that?"

"It's what I do at EvPro. Composite drawings. I'm not done with this one yet; this is just the initial computer prediction."

"And does he look anything like that?"

"I haven't seen him. But yes, he looks substantially like this."

She tried to ignore the nagging doubts in the back of her head. She knew that a person could greatly change his appearance so that he didn't look anything like his genotype said. Micah did not look like her genotype, even though she hadn't deliberately changed her appearance.

The cop eyed the picture doubtfully. "You don't recognize him?"

Micah analyzed the man in the picture. She manipulated pictures and studied the human face every day. She cataloged people by their features, noting their heritage, their dominant and recessive genes, unexpected surprises. Faces were one of her favorite things.

But she didn't know the man. Not yet. At least if she saw him on the street, she would know him and be warned.

"Pass that on to Bellows in the morning," the cop eventually told her. "Things look secure here for the night. You should be safe. You should call the officers who handled your assault case as well; give them that picture if they don't already have it."

"Okay."

"Sorry, ma'am. Not much else we can do."

"I know. Thanks for coming by."

The night was a lot harder than Micah had expected. She thought she would be able to sleep through like she had when her mother had been there, but even though Marianna left her with the drugs and dosage instructions, Micah's body pulsed with pain and her brain wouldn't stop running on a hamster wheel. Spinning and spinning and getting nowhere.

She awoke in the morning after a long, restless night to a loud knock on her door. She stumbled to her feet, realizing that she had slept late, and her parents were already there.

She didn't check the new door cam, having left her electronics in the bedroom without remembering to look at them. She unlocked the locks and yanked the door open.

And it wasn't Cole and Marianna.

For a moment, Micah stood there, frozen, like the proverbial deer in the headlights. It wasn't her parents. It was Deputy Bellows. And Micah was in her pajamas, hair mussed from sleep, eyes blurry, and covered with bruises.

"Oh. Frank. Come in."

She shivered in the cold outside air and shut the door behind him. She ushered him into the living room, trying to think of what to do. "Do you want coffee? And I need just a few minutes… to wash up."

"Sure. I didn't mean to get you out of bed. Should have realized with the tough time you've had the last few days."

"It's a ridiculous time to be in bed still," Micah criticized herself, face warming. "I don't know what you must think."

"I think that you're recovering from a pretty nasty beating, and it's probably lucky that you're even home, let alone out of bed."

"Well…" Micah tried to shake off his observation. But what was she going to say? It wasn't that bad? She was just being lazy? He knew that wasn't true. He'd seen assault victims before.

"Go wash up. And if you don't mind me in your kitchen, I can make the coffee."

"No, you're a guest."

"I'm perfectly capable. Go freshen up and let me get the caffeine going."

"Oh… okay. Thanks. It's just through there."

She was sure she didn't need to direct him through the open doorway to the kitchen, but did anyway, for lack of something else to say or do.

Bellows nodded. "Do you need anything else?"

"No. Coffee. Lots of nice, piping hot coffee."

He grinned. "Good. That I can manage."

Micah retreated to her room and shut the door. She sat on her bed for a minute to catch her breath and gather her thoughts.

"You start," Bellows said. "I want to hear what happened to you. You look just awful."

"I know," Micah said. She'd looked in the mirror before joining him in the kitchen, and the bruises had set in nice and dark. She looked like someone from a zombie walk. "The thing is, I think it might be related."

"Related to what?"

"Related to the case. To Sweetie."

He raised his eyebrows. "How could that be?" He considered. "You think that someone we interviewed attacked you? Or leaked the information to the person who did?"

"I don't know how he got the information. But somehow, he did. Maybe it was because of the people we interviewed or he knew that I had done the composites of Trisha. I was with you, so I guess people would know I had something to do with the case."

"But why would he come after you? What good would that do? You're the artist, not an investigator. Getting you out of the way would not do much to stop the investigation. Not to be rude, but you're not vital to the case."

"I don't know. I don't know what he knows or suspects, or if he's just fighting back against me because I'm not… as able to defend myself against an attack. Going after you might… present more difficulties."

"It wouldn't be that hard if he had a weapon."

"Maybe he doesn't have one. Or doesn't think he can use one. I don't know. He didn't… I thought when he started hitting me at first that he had a baseball bat, but he didn't have anything, just his hands. His fists. He hit me really hard."

"He may pride himself in his ability to hurt someone with his hands. He might justify himself that if he uses his hands he's not breaking the rules. You never know what kind of twisted ideas these guys can have. They have their own morality systems, and they won't look anything like yours or mine. They can't. They have to make themselves righteous in their own eyes."

"Or they just don't believe in anything."

"In my experience… everybody believes in something. Maybe it's fate or the universe. Maybe it's nature or genetics. But everybody believes something. And you build your morality system on top of that."

Micah shrugged stiffly. "I don't know. Maybe."

"So, what makes you think that the guy who attacked you is related to the case?"

"I'll get to that. I want to tell you the rest first, see what you think."

"Okay."

"When he first came, when he burgled the house… he just came in and looked around. He didn't take anything. Or move anything. Everything seemed to be completely untouched."

"So you interrupted him."

"I don't think so. His footprints were partially snowed in. That means he had left before I got there. Before anyone got there."

"Someone could still have spooked him, though. A dog walker. Neighbor returning from the store. A helicopter flying overhead. For someone with a guilty conscience, any little noise could mean discovery."

"I think he was looking for something. And he didn't find it here, because it isn't here. I think it has to do with work, but he was hoping that I would have brought it home with me."

"That's speculation. Anything to base it on?"

"No… just that he didn't touch anything. Or anything he did touch, he put back in exactly the same spot. If it were a regular burglar, someone after valuables, he would have taken it. Money, gold, electronics… my dad says the TV is garbage, but everything else is worth something. I don't have much cash or jewelry around the house, but it was all still there. The tablet and the computer, still there. If it were just someone looking for quick cash, he wouldn't have left all of that behind, even if he was spooked."

"Maybe. But jumping to it being related to work is too much. Too big a jump."

"Okay. When he attacked me, he didn't try to… molest me. He didn't threaten me, or try to take my purse or my watch. He just hit me. Over and over again. He didn't say anything. He didn't do anything except hit me."

"Again, his fists. Not his voice. I think this guy is seriously obsessed with hurting people with his own hands. If he was trying to hurt you so badly or kill you, why not use a weapon?"

"I don't know. But he didn't seem to have any other goal. It wasn't theft. It wasn't to take advantage of me. It was just to hurt me."

"Some people operate that way."

"For the next part, I have to teach you something about DNA."

"Okay." Bellows nodded. "I think I've been a good student so far. What do I need to know?"

"Well… you know that everyone is a product of the two DNA donors, the mother and the father."

"Yes, it seems to me we covered this in biology…" he said with a chuckle.

"We know the full DNA profile of Sweetie's mother because she also had her mother's full DNA in her blood."

"Right."

"And we have Sweetie's full DNA because we have her blood sample."

"Of course."

"So half of that DNA sample is from her mother, and half of it is from her father."

"And since you have her mother's DNA, you know which half is which," Bellows said promptly.

"Yes. And the difference, then, is the father's DNA."

"Okay. But it's only half of his DNA, am I right? So you don't have enough to identify him?"

"We would have enough to identify him if he was in the system. He wasn't."

"Right."

"I thought that maybe it would be enough to do a composite of the father. Not a very good one, because we would have to guess a lot. But… it would at least be a starting point."

Bellows agreed. "I guess something is better than nothing. You would know that he was white because the baby doesn't appear to be mixed race. And maybe you would know a few things like eye color."

Micah nodded. "Some traits are dominant, so if Sweetie had that trait, and she didn't get it from her mother, then she got it from her father. And because it is dominant, he has to show it too. And some traits are recessive and for her to show that trait, she would have to inherit the recessive gene from both her mother and her father. There are some things that we can figure out, but it wouldn't be as good a picture as what I could produce with full genome and epigenome."

"So what did you come up with? Do you have a picture for me?"

"Getting there."

"Sorry. Go on."

"When the officers rescued me from the attack, I didn't realize that I had evidence on me that could help solve the case. I didn't realize until a day or two later that… my fingernails were torn from scratching him. I didn't know whether I had gotten any of his skin or just his clothing, so I… took it in to EvPro."

Bellows frowned. "You should have had the police come back to process the evidence."

"I know," Micah admitted. She was glad to be coming clean to him. She hated the dishonesty of having EvPro process the evidence and then telling the police that she had remembered the unsub's face or gotten the information from somewhere else. "But I knew that even if the police did come out to collect it, it would still take months for you to process."

"This isn't a good idea."

"Stay with me. I'm not done."

He eyed her, took a sip of his cooling coffee, and nodded for her to go on. "Okay. Continue."

"Our processing is much faster than yours. My team prioritized it. The DNA profiles were separated and the unsub's was sequenced and run through our databases. Then through the initial computer-generated phenotyping."

"Already? That is quick."

"Very. Top of the line equipment and proprietary technology. We process thousands of samples a year from all over the country. All over the world."

"So you have a picture for me of the man who attacked you, and you think that he might be related to the Sweetie Doe case. That's why you wanted to talk to me."

"One more step."

"Okay," Bellows was getting impatient, his tone taking on an edge. "Take me through the last step, then."

"When the computer sequences the genome, it automatically runs the genome against our database to see if we already have a match. I was worried that it could be someone who I had drawn a composite of, that they were out of prison and wanted revenge."

"Uh-huh. And you came up with a match, I gather?"

"It came up with a match. The Lazarus."

Bellows looked at her blankly. "Is that some code name or serial killer name I'm unfamiliar with?"

Micah realized she had not given him all of the information he needed. "When we create a DNA profile for someone using information from relatives, we call that a Lazarus. In this case, Sweetie Doe's father."

"Sweetie Doe's father," Bellows repeated slowly, trying to chain it all together. "His DNA profile was—" Bellows sat bolt upright, splashing his coffee. "Sweetie Doe's father is the man who attacked you?"

Micah nodded, pleased with his reaction in spite of the mess. "Yes. Exactly."

Bellows's mouth was a round O. He stared at Micah. "So now you have the full DNA profile for Sweetie's father, and that means you can do a picture. And we have something to match if we can track him down. And..." his words slowed and became reflective, "it means that he's still around town and that he knows he is the baby's father."

Micah thought about it. Why else would he be attacking her? If he didn't know he was Sweetie's father, then they wouldn't have triggered his attacks by working on the file. He would have been as oblivious as anyone else. Particularly since they had not released Trisha Madro's name. There was no one saying, 'Hey, weren't you Trisha's boyfriend?' There was no one accusing him of being the baby's father. The only ones who knew that were probably Trisha and the father himself.

"Did you have any leads on Trisha? Someone she was seeing a few months ago? Friends and acquaintances that might have some insights?"

Bellows sat back in his chair and sighed. "Things have not gotten any easier. If anything, they are even more difficult."

"Why?"

"Because Trisha was likely a sex worker. So identifying a boyfriend or the father of the baby becomes very difficult."

"But she knew. She told him. Otherwise, he wouldn't have known the baby was his."

Bellows made a helpless gesture, palms up. "I wish I could say I was close to finding out who that was."

"You must have found out if she worked with a pimp. And whether any of the other girls were friends with her. That could help."

"These girls are virtual prisoners. Some of them are literally prisoners. But even the ones who are not physically restrained, they're still held prisoner by the men further up the food chain. It's not necessarily like you're thinking, with one pimp running a handful of girls, taking care of them and making sure no one interferes for a large cut of the money. Instead, we're talking about… organized crime. Sex trafficking. The girls are assets. They're sold and traded, trafficked across the country sometimes."

"But Trisha wasn't trafficked across the country; she was kept here."

Bellows nodded. "Yes. She was. This is where she was in foster care, and this is where she died. For some period of time in between, the last year or more, she was in the grips of these… lowlifes."

"You know that for sure?"

"From what I've been able to sort out… yes. You remember how Mrs. Dublin said that when Trisha saw her and recognized her, the other girls closed in around her, and she was hidden from sight? And then she never saw Trisha again, even though she looked for her a few times?"

Micah tried to swallow the lump in her throat, understanding. "They weren't protecting her. They were protecting the organization. Making sure that no one could connect with Trisha, that she couldn't talk to anyone she knew from the past. Hide her and get her out of the neighborhood to make sure no one could rescue her."

"Yeah."

"Do you know which organization had her? Are there different cartels here in town? I don't understand how a group like that could operate here, let alone more than one."

"They are part of larger organizations. They may not be based here in town. They may run out of Billings or even out of state. I have some intelligence on which one Trisha may have worked for, but they don't have membership lists or org charts. We don't have someone we can go out and arrest because he is involved in the trafficking. Investigations into trafficking run for years. You don't bring down an organization over one victim."

Micah rubbed her forehead. It was just one conversation, but she was already feeling fatigued. Was she ever going to put in a full day of work again? She felt like her body was falling apart.

"But the father is out there somewhere and he knows that we found the baby."

"And he knows that we've found Trisha," Bellows said, "because we couldn't keep it out of the media that we found human remains in the mountains. The media isn't stupid; they've already connected it up with the Sweetgrass Doe case."

Micah shook her head. "Too bad you couldn't keep that a secret."

"What do you have on your attacker? Do you have a picture for me?"

"I'll work on it today. I just have what the computer spit out, and I can do much better than that. Once I factor in age and weight and any other details I can remember or get from the genome and epigenome, I'll have something much closer to how he looks now."

"Okay. I'm going to leave you alone to do that. Are you okay? Here by yourself?"

"My parents are supposed to be coming; they should arrive any time. But I think I'm going to need to lie down for a nap for a little while. Then I'll get right on to Papa Doe."

"Take care of yourself. Remember, this isn't a race. I know that all of the TV shows will tell you that the first forty-eight hours are the most important, but we're long past that now. From now on, it's a plod, not a sprint. So spend what time you need to to get it right."

Micah stood up, leaning on the table. "Thanks. I'll try to get you something today, but if my body doesn't cooperate, I won't worry too much if it takes an extra day."

"I'm not letting this case get cold. We're still actively investigating it. We're going to find out what happened to Trisha and the baby."

"You don't know whether it was an accident or homicide? Trisha's death?"

"No finding yet. It's pretty hard to tell from a body whether someone fell or was given a little push. She might have been wandering around in the dark, disoriented or unwell. Or she might have met the father out there, and…"

"He's violent," Micah said. "We know he's violent."

Bellows nodded grimly. He moved toward the door. "If the father had something to do with it, yes. We're making that assumption, but we don't have the evidence to support it yet. Just our suspicions."

"He wouldn't attack me if he didn't have something to do with Trisha's death, would he?"

"No… I can't think of a reason he would."

Micah spent most of the day, at least when she wasn't sleeping, working on the composite of Sweetie's father, who she had dubbed Mr. X. She closed her eyes and tried to picture him, his height, weight, the contours of his face beneath the mask. And she scoured all of the information she could find in his genetic and epigenetic code.

The methylation clues put Mr. X at around fifty-five, so she aged the composite accordingly. The default for EvPro's computer program was twenty-five, so aging made a significant difference. She added silver to his hair, especially around the temples. A cleft chin. She experimented with glasses but, in the end, went without them. He hadn't been wearing glasses when he'd attacked her. Contacts, maybe.

She looked for diet and lifestyle indicators. Mr. X didn't appear to be a smoker or a heavy drinker. His diet and the trace elements in his environment were right for someone living in Montana, but they already knew that. It looked like he had grown up in the geographic region. There were no malnutrition indicators like there had been with Trisha. Quite the opposite, it would appear that he'd had a rich diet, and he had no major stress indicators. He was likely upper-middle class or higher. She knew from their encounter that he was vital and muscular.

When she finished, she had a very different picture from what she'd had when she had initially visualized Trisha and her boyfriend, the father of her baby. She had pictured a skinny kid, another foster child, addict, or bad boy. The type of person who would have circulated in the same social circles as Trisha. But what she had was the opposite. A middle-aged white guy, big, tough, and privileged. The kind of guy who would be running a sex trafficking ring? Or was he a john, one of her clients? How had he known that he was the father of the baby?

Micah lay down again to rest and to meditate on the possibilities. He was the father, and somehow he knew it. Maybe Trisha had a paternity test done while she was still pregnant. It would be unusual, but not impossible. Both amniocentesis and maternal blood testing were available.

And then when the baby had been born… what? Trisha had decided she couldn't take care of her and had taken her to the Sweetgrass Hills to abandon her there, figuring that the chances she would die of exposure would be higher there than if she abandoned her in town. Had she wanted her to die, then? Why else leave her out there?

After abandoning Sweetie there, leaving her under that bush where she would be found the next day… then what? Trisha lost the way back to her car? She was disoriented or feverish and fell into the chasm by accident? Or had she run into Mr. X there and he had chased or pushed her to her death?

That would suggest that she had either gone there with him, or he had followed her. He must have kept a close eye on her, just as he had on the investigation. He knew that Micah was involved in the case and had wanted her out of the way, perhaps so that she couldn't produce the composite of him. If he'd been that concerned about Micah being involved in the investigation, then she had no doubt that he'd been keeping track of Trisha. Maybe using electronic surveillance, and maybe using human spies who kept him informed on what she was doing. And so he had followed her out there, into the Sweetgrass Hills, to get rid of a problem that might lead back to him.

Micah jolted awake with a jerk. Her heart was pounding hard and fast, like someone had just knocked on the front door and she was in danger. Who knew how long it would be before Mr. X showed up at her door again. She fumbled on the nightstand, knocking things off.

"Micah?" Marianna materialized next to her. "It's okay, honey. What are you looking for?"

Micah continued to feel blindly for it, swiping pills and the glass to the floor with a crash, growing more desperate. "My phone!"

"It's plugged in. The battery was getting low. Here. Just stop for a minute."

Micah stopped flailing and waited while Marianna reached around the lamp to where the phone was connected to a charger. She pulled it off and handed it to Micah.

"There you go. Do you need a hand?"

"I can manage to make a phone call by myself," Micah snapped.

Marianna withdrew and let her have the room to herself. Micah didn't look at the floor to see what kind of devastation she had caused. She could clean up anything broken later. She needed to get ahold of Bellows.

"Micah," he greeted after a couple of rings. "How are you feeling?"

"Where is Sweetie?"

"Mmm, what?"

"Sweetie. The baby. Where is she? You have to make sure she is safe."

There were a few seconds of silence. "Did you just wake up?"

"Yes."

"Ah." He said it as if that explained the phone call. "Give yourself a few more minutes to finish waking up. Sweetie is fine. She's safe with her foster family. You don't need to worry about her."

"He killed Trisha and he tried to kill me. He's trying to wipe out all evidence that he fathered that baby."

It took a couple of beats before Bellows followed that premise to its obvious conclusion. "And you're afraid that he's going to go after the baby herself."

"Of course. Wouldn't you? He knows that she can be used to establish his paternity. He might not know about the Lazarus or that we already got his DNA from his attack on me, but he knows about paternity tests. Her DNA establishes his guilt."

"His guilt in what?"

"I don't know. In having sex with a minor. Engaging a prostitute. If he's part of the organization, then in his role in the sex trafficking."

"Yes," Bellows said slowly. "But what if he is not part of the organization? What if all he did was hire her services? He can say that he thought she was eighteen. That the only thing he's guilty of is a minor prostitution charge. That's not worth killing people over."

Micah thought about that. She sat up in bed and rubbed her forehead with her free hand. She had still been disoriented when she called him, he'd been right about that. But she'd been absolutely sure that Sweetie was in danger.

"Then there's something else. He's a high-powered politician or something like that. He has a reputation that he's trying to protect."

"That's a possibility," Bellows agreed. There was a pause. "How are you doing?"

"I'm mostly okay. Still sleeping a lot." Micah realized what it was he had been careful not to ask. "I do have a picture for you."

"Excellent. Do you have a scanner, or do you want me to come over and pick it up?"

"I have a good scanner. I'll email it to you."

"How does the picture look?"

"Pretty good. I'll do a few variations over the next few days, but it should be recognizable. I have the age and everything pinned down, so unless he's had a lot of plastic surgery or other modifications, it should be accurate."

"I'll be watching for it. And… I'll check in with the social worker. Get her to contact the foster mom to make sure she hasn't had anyone lurking around there or anything she's concerned about. But it's going to be a lot harder for our unsub to track down an anonymous baby in foster care than it was for him to trace you. Babies don't have an electronic footprint, and everyone on this case is well aware of the need for confidentiality. He won't be able to find her."

"But you're going to check anyway. Just in case."

"Yes."

Micah let her breath out. "Good, thanks."

38

Micah was awakened the next day by the ringing of her phone. She rubbed her eyes and looked over at it, trying to decide whether she needed to answer it. She sat up so that she could see the caller ID and groaned.

Amy Bradshaw.

She couldn't very well duck calls from a vice president of the company.

She didn't know whether Amy knew she was at home, recovering from her injuries, or whether she thought she was just calling Micah at work. Her work extension twinned to her cell phone so she could answer it wherever she was and people didn't have to try to track her down by calling multiple numbers.

Micah groaned aloud, then reached for her phone and answered it. "Micah here."

"Micah," Amy sounded like she looked. Cool and professional, never smiling unless it was socially requisite. "I'm glad I caught you. I really hate to interfere with any of my teams, but I have heard that you are still working on the Sweetgrass Hills abandonment case. I thought we had talked about that."

"Uh, yes, we did."

"But it looks like you've still been working on it."

Micah tried to figure out what Amy might have seen or heard. She'd been careful not to post anything to the server that might alert someone to the fact that she was still active on the Sweetgrass Doe case. The DNA profile and pictures had been saved to pseudonym files. She didn't think she had touched anything on the Sweetgrass Doe file that would give her away.

"Where did you hear that?"

"I hear things. They trickle in here. So is it true? You're still treating the file as active?"

"You may have seen some activity on it because of the mother being discovered," Micah suggested. "There were human remains found in the Sweetgrass Hills, and preliminary identification shows that it was Trisha Madro, Sweetie's mother. But that didn't come from me, that was the police on their own. I didn't have anything to do with it."

"You didn't."

"No."

"You're still all buddy-buddy with the cop though, aren't you? The one in charge of the case?"

"Uh, Frank Bellows. I wouldn't say that we're buddies. We've talked."

"And you went with him on interviews, which is totally outside of what we do here."

"I haven't since you talked to me."

"You haven't talked to him?"

Micah winced and tried to answer the question honestly, but without getting herself into deeper trouble. "I've talked to him. He wanted to know how I was doing after the assault. But no, I haven't been doing any more interviews with him."

"He must have other people to interview."

"After finding Trisha's remains… I expect so. But I haven't been privy to that."

"You don't know where they are in their investigation?"

Micah shifted, trying to find a more comfortable position. Her muscles and joints were sore. She hadn't taken any painkillers since the previous evening, and her body was letting her know it.

"I'm sure Deputy Bellows could fill you in if you gave him a call."

"I see. Well, then. How are you coming on the annual report information?"

"I haven't had a lot of time to work on it. I didn't think it was a high priority."

"It isn't rush, but it is important. We can't get new investors and funding or new customers without having something to show them about how we are doing. We need evidence that shows we are making a difference to law enforcement and the way these cases are being solved. And that we are at the forefront of the technology."

"Yeah, of course. I'll take another look at it today."

"Can you get me something by close of day?"

She just wanted some statistics on the number of cases they had closed in the past year using Forensic DNA Composites, where the technology was going and how they were staying ahead of it, and a representative case study where investors could read a summary of a particular 'solved' case and feel good about themselves. It normally would not have been a big deal, but Micah had to ration her energy like she never had before.

"Yes, I can get you something. It might not be final, though. Is first draft sufficient?"

"That will give Graphic Design a chance to see how much space it is going to take up and what kind of images we are going to need."

"Great. I'll have something preliminary to you before the end of the day."

"Thank you, Micah. And one more word on the Sweetgrass Doe file."

"Yes."

"If I find out that you have been working the file after you were told not to… there will be consequences. So don't let me down."

"Okay," Micah said, drawing the word out. She couldn't claim that Amy hadn't made herself clear the first time. But Micah had continued to work the file, and if they brought down the hammer, it was too late for her to change her decision. She had already broken the directive, and she might not be able to cover her tracks.

"Good," Amy said, and terminated the call.

39

After a shower and some coffee, Micah logged in to the work server and had a look around. She checked the Sweetgrass Doe file to make sure she hadn't left any electronic fingerprints that she hadn't remembered. It might be too late to be worrying about it, but if there were any damage she could mitigate, it was best to do it right away.

Everything looked clean and untouched, so she left it that way and went on with her other work. She could work on some additional composites of Mr. X later. For the moment, she had the annual report to work on, and other files were piling up. She didn't want to get too far behind in her work.

But on the other hand, she still didn't have the stamina needed to get through her day like she usually would. She needed to pick and choose what to tackle.

The priority for the day wasn't hard to pick since Amy had just told her what it was. Get the first draft of the annual report for her team done. Micah pulled a report from the server on the number of files that had been opened that year and which had been solved. That was the easy part. She needed to pick a representative case as well as to summarize the improvements in the technology.

She was excited to include the findings of Trisha's full genome within Sweetie's blood sample. That had never been done as a practical exercise before. The way that Micah had been using epigenetic data to enhance the composites would be a big part of the report. She could do so much more than she had been able to two years before. And as far as she knew, no one was using the epigenome as extensively as she was. EvPro's competitors were just starting to look at epigenetic data on an experimental basis. None of them had an extensive trait database already built up like EvPro.

Micah alternately napped and worked on the report throughout the day. As evening drew near and she knew Amy would be looking for it in her inbox, Micah pulled up the previous year's annual report, wanting to make sure she had not neglected any facets she should have covered and to eyeball how much space she had used the previous year. She didn't have to do exactly the same thing every year, but she wanted to keep it consistent. Someone reading through several years' annual reports should be able to follow their progress naturally and to see how their solve rate had grown with the advancing technology.

The report did not have a clickable table of contents, so she scrolled through it a page at a time to find her report. It was near the front, which was good; that showed her team was valued, and what they were doing with Forensic DNA analysis was one of the draws for outside investors and clients.

Micah clicked from the previous year's annual report to her current draft several times, looking for the parallels and tweaking the layout so that they progressed the same way.

A stray key press backed the report up a page, and Micah reached for the laptop's touchpad to click it down again, but then stopped.

There was a report from the president, a picture of him smiling reservedly at the camera beside his report. And at the bottom of the page were profile pictures of each member of the board, evenly spaced, with their names below.

Micah had probably seen their faces a dozen times before, but she had never really paid any attention to them. They were not people she dealt with personally. No one who would ever come to the lab or her office for a conversation. She didn't even know how many of them lived locally and how many were across the country or around the world.

But this time, one of them seemed to jump right off the page at her.

Brown hair and eyes. About fifty-five years old. Cleft chin. The other facial features in the phenotype she had just been working on.

It was Mr. X.

4 0

Micah's first reaction was to slam the laptop lid shut, as if he might jump right off the page into her bedroom. She sat there on her bed, heart racing.

It was silly. While it was possible to establish a possible identification from a composite drawing, it was impossible to get a confirmed ID. That's just what she kept telling Bellows and everyone else about Trisha. Even though she looked like Micah's drawing, that didn't mean that she was actually Sweetie Doe's mother. Not until it was confirmed through direct DNA comparison or some other method. It didn't work that way.

She couldn't be *sure* that the man in the picture was her Papa Doe or Mr. X. It could just be coincidental. It could be Micah seeing things. Part of her concussion. Or it could be PTSD. Micah's mind could easily be playing tricks on her. She'd let herself get too tired and now she was going to see Mr. X everywhere.

For a long time, she just sat there, with her eyes closed, thinking through these issues. Eventually, once she had herself mostly convinced that it was just her mind playing tricks, she opened her computer again, typed in the password, and looked at the thumbnail again. It was so small; it was impossible to tell if it really matched her Mr. X or not. She enlarged it on the screen and studied the face point by point. All of the right features were there. She had not been wrong about that. But that didn't make him her attacker. There might be a hundred people with those same features. In Montana? Maybe they were related. He could be a brother or a cousin. The traits could be common in one particular community if it were very insular. There was no guarantee that the man was her Mr. X.

Micah looked at the name beneath the picture. Kirk Haynes. It was a vaguely familiar name. She'd heard of most of the board members before. As well as being on the board of EvPro, a lot of them were active in the community, with charitable connections and a lot of aid given to social causes. EvPro was not a charity, but was connected with law enforcement and ensuring predators were put behind bars. There was a lot of crossover with the victim support groups.

And if Kirk Haynes were involved with a young prostitute? Either as a john or as part of the organization trafficking her, what would that do to his reputation? He would no longer be trusted by those in the community. He would be kicked off any of those boards and foundations. EvPro's business would take a big hit if it became known that they had a predator on the board.

All of those requests to drop the Sweetie Doe case and just let the police handle it… They had come from up the corporate ladder. They weren't concerned with Micah wasting resources on a losing proposition. Someone wanted to stop her from finding anything out. Did Kwong or Amy Bradshaw know that Haynes was involved? Or were they just passing along the pressure they were receiving from above? How deep did the corruption run?

When she thought about Haynes possibly having access to proprietary EvPro data, Micah felt sick. Had he had his finger in other files? Had he previously derailed police investigations with false information? If he had other people acting for him in EvPro, he could have them change key details in a phenotype or in another type of evidence. He could have caused all kinds of damage.

Micah thought about who she could call, trying to gather her energy. She couldn't call anyone at EvPro, having no idea how far the corruption had spread. She would end up being like one of those heroines on TV who called the killer when she thought she had solved the mystery. That was out.

She knew that Bellows would not be able to take her word for it that

Haynes was Mr. X—nor should he—but he had to know that Haynes was a viable suspect and they could investigate him, looking deeper into his background to see if there were anything suspicious on his record. They could follow him around and get a sample of his DNA from a cigarette or cup and test it against Micah's attacker. They could prove he was the father of Sweetgrass Doe. They might not be able to get him for the murder of Trisha Madro, but it was a good start.

Micah kept her computer open and dialed Bellows.

"Sheriff's Department. How may I direct your call?"

Micah's heart sank. "I need Deputy Bellows, please."

"Deputy Bellows isn't on duty at the moment. Can I take a message or help you with something?"

"I really need to reach him. It's…" Micah wanted desperately to say that it was an emergency, but was it? And if she said it was an emergency, the dispatcher was going to send police over to her house, and then she would have to explain the whole story again, and they would say that it was not an emergency and she was abusing the system. Why did things have to be so complicated?

"The message will reach him when he gets back on duty."

"But… isn't there any way to reach him at home or on his cell? He's going to want to hear about this right away."

"I'm sorry, ma'am. No. We have policies. Callers are not given officers' numbers or transferred to them when they are not on duty. I'm sure you can understand how important that is for them. They need to be able to do their jobs when they are on shift and spend time with their families or getting the rest they need when they are not. Making them respond to calls at all hours is not the way to maintain a healthy police force."

"But, don't you think you could help me… you could pass a message on to him, and then he could decide whether it was important enough to call me back."

"No, I'm sorry. Do you have a message you would like me to pass on to him when he gets back on duty?"

"When is he on again?"

"I'm sorry, I can't divulge officers' duty schedules. It's against our policies—"

"Of course it is," Micah muttered. What if Bellows was on vacation for a couple of weeks? If he was gone, she would have to talk to whoever was covering for him on the file. But if he was around, and would be back in a few hours, she would just wait.

Either way, she wasn't going to give the dispatcher all of the details over the phone. She would have to wait and talk to Bellows or his alternate in person. At least over the phone.

"Is he in tomorrow?"

"I can't divulge that, ma'am," the dispatcher said patiently.

"I need to know when he is in again so I can reach him."

"If you leave a message, I will have him call you back when he's on duty next."

Micah rolled her eyes and shook her head in exasperation. Obviously, the dispatcher could not see her. She would never have been so rude if the woman were in the room with her.

"Fine. Will you please have him call Micah. It's urgent. He has my number."

"I would be happy to pass that on, ma'am. M-I-C-A-H?"

"Yes. Thanks."

"Will he know what it's about?"

"Yes. The Sweetgrass Hills abandonment file. He knows. That's the only thing I'm working with him on."

"Thank you, ma'am. Is there anything else I can help you with today?"

"No." Micah gave her grudging thanks and then hung up the call.

She assessed her options.

It wasn't like Haynes was going to come after her during the night. He might have before, but that was before Micah had upgraded her security. She wouldn't be going out or opening the door to anyone, and he wouldn't be coming in. He couldn't get past all of Cole's new roadblocks. Micah didn't even know what they all were. Cole had explained, but she had been too tired and could only remember the essentials. How to arm and disarm the system. The password to let the security company know that everything was okay if they got an alarm.

So she might as well go to sleep. She couldn't do anything else until the morning.

Micah put her computer to the side and turned off the lamp, but sleep did not come easily. She kept looking at her phone, hoping that Bellows would call or text her. But there was no sign of a response from him.

Eventually, she decided to get back up. It was too early to be going to sleep. She would just be restless until it was a decent bedtime hour—no point in getting all frustrated that she couldn't get to sleep.

Maybe she was overtired. She really wanted to go to sleep but, while her brain was exhausted, her body was telling her 'no way.' She turned on the lamp, took a couple of painkillers that Marianna had left, and turned her attention to her phone.

She saw that while she had been talking to the police dispatcher, Sara had called her. She hadn't left a voicemail. Micah remembered how despondent she had been when she had called Micah the last time. How Gregory had hovered nearby, worried about her state of mind and what she might do, but trying to give Sara the space and time she needed.

Micah tapped the number to return the call.

It rang a few times before she heard Sara's 'hello?'

"Sara, it's Micah. How are you doing?"

"I'm okay," Sara lied. Her voice was faint, as if she were fading away into nothing. She needed Micah. Needed what only she could do.

"I'm sorry I didn't get back to you. I had… an accident. I've been recovering, and haven't had much energy to do anything."

"Oh. I see."

"But I have worked on your picture, Sara. I didn't forget about it."

"How is it coming along?"

"I just need to put some final touches on it. When should I bring it by?"

There was no answer. Micah waited. She pulled her phone away from her ear and looked at the screen. Nothing. It was back to her icons. The call had terminated. Micah tapped back on the recent numbers, but the list was empty.

"What the...?"

Micah frowned. She went to her contact list. It too was blank. How could her numbers have just disappeared? Her phone was malfunctioning, or maybe there was something wrong with the service she was on. Micah pressed the home button and looked at the screen. Most of her icons were gone; it was just the base icons for the operating system. She tapped on the app store and looked at it. Her email address was gone, the app indicating that she hadn't entered her account information yet.

Micah knew Sara's number if she thought about it hard enough. She went to the phone keypad and tapped it in. Nothing happened. Micah watched the screen. The 'connecting' message disappeared, and instead, the status changed to 'no service.'

No service? Micah glanced at the top row of tiny icons. The one indicating provider signal was gone. How could she not have any service?

Micah shook her head and pressed the power button, holding it in until the phone started it's shut-down procedure, and eventually the screen went blank. Micah pressed it again, and in a few more seconds saw the device splash screen pop up, and then it ran through its usual start-up sequence. Micah often had to go get a coffee to wait after it rebooted from a software update. It was so slow.

Micah put the phone down, rubbed her eyes, and let out a deep breath.

She was getting closer. She would give Bellows the information about Kirk Haynes when he got back on duty. He would follow up and make an arrest in due time. She would be able to recover from her beating and go back to work, continuing as if nothing had happened. Except maybe she would make sure that her phone number and address were not publicly listed anywhere. And she would talk to EvPro about not putting her name on the website. And she would make an effort to spend more time with her parents, knowing how important it had been for her to have them close after she was hurt. They really would do anything for her.

She opened her eyes and looked at the phone screen, hoping that after her brief meditation period, it would have finished booting up. But it was still showing no service bars.

Micah searched her nightstand for paperclips but had to go down the hall to her office to find any, setting her computer on the desk to recharge at the same time. She popped out the SIM drawer and made sure the card was seated correctly. Then she closed it again.

She stared at the phone, all back to its factory defaults, with no service. What the heck was going on?

Then the lights went out.

4 2

Micah froze.

She waited for a few seconds, expecting it to come right back on again. Power blinks were not unusual. Weather conditions, old lines, wind and snow—there was always some challenge to keeping the town's power running consistently. Even a squirrel or a bird happening to arc a line.

But it didn't come back up again. Micah looked down at her phone, the screen glowing. She swiped it to enable the flashlight mode and shone it around the room, making sure everything was still where it was supposed to be and she didn't get disoriented as to where she was in the room.

It was probably not a good idea to leave the flashlight on for long; it would run down the battery, and if the power didn't come up for a few hours, she would have no way to charge it.

Although what good was it to her in factory-new mode with no service?

She could play solitaire to keep herself busy for a while, that was about it.

Micah tiptoed toward the door of her office. The kitten mewed from the other side of the house, disconcerted by the lights going off and the rest of the humming appliances in the house going quiet.

"It's okay, Meow. Just the power."

Not that the kitten could understand her. The words were more for Micah herself than for the kitten.

She looked down the hallway toward the living room. Nothing was out of place. No intruders. Had she thought there would be intruders? The whole Sweetgrass Doe case had her on edge. But she had a good security system. She would be able to talk to Deputy Bellows about Kirk Haynes in the morning. The best thing for her to do while the power was off was simply to pile the blankets on and go to sleep. Everything would be back to normal again in the morning.

Micah turned back to her bedroom. A sliver of light made its way past her blinds to the bed. Micah turned toward the window, wondering if it was a full moon. It was very bright. She slid a couple of fingers through the slats of the blinds to peer out, first at the sky, which was overcast, with no sign of the moon and the stars, and then across the street, taking in the streetlights and the other houses across the street.

The lights were all on.

Only Micah's house was blacked out.

Anxiety rising in her chest, Micah stepped back to the light switch and flicked it on and off a couple of times.

Unsurprisingly, that did not solve the problem.

"Must be a tripped breaker," Micah said aloud.

Whatever squirrel had caused the power to blink, it had also tripped one of the breakers, and that was why the lights were not coming back on again as they had for everyone else. All she needed to do was to go to the breaker box and make sure all of the switches were flipped.

Still using her phone as a flashlight, Micah made her way through the kitchen to the basement, where the breaker box was hidden in a dark, spidery corner. She had always thought she would develop the basement sooner or later. It would give her a nice place to entertain a visitor with a movie or a game. Maybe a freezer, so she had more space to put up the summer produce she got at the farmer's market when the prices were so good. But she had never gotten around to doing anything with the unfinished basement.

She opened the door to the breaker box and ran her eyes down the row of switches. They were all facing the same direction. She ran her fingers down, searching for one that was not snugly in place. Maybe it had popped out, but hadn't flipped all the way back to the off position. They all seemed to be perfectly aligned.

Micah flipped them left and then right one at a time. The lights did not come back on. The house did not hum back into life.

"What's wrong?" she muttered to herself.

It had to be something to do with the security system. The men who had installed it had crossed a wire somewhere and it had shorted out the whole electrical system. She should have vetted them instead of just allowing Cole to get whoever he felt like. He'd probably hired a couple of old buddies who didn't know much more about electrical wiring than Micah did.

"This was supposed to make things better, not worse."

She looked at her phone face again. As if it would work better in the basement than on the main floor. But service bars had not magically appeared on the screen.

Did one have anything to do with the other? It seemed bizarre that her company phone would suddenly stop working. Everything disappearing like that… it didn't make any sense. She'd have to go into EvPro in the morning and have IT take a look at it. Maybe they'd had an employee quit without returning his phone, and they had bricked it to prevent him from using any of the EvPro client contacts or other proprietary information. But they had slipped up or down a line when looking up which phone was his, accidentally bricking Micah's instead of the rogue ex-employee's.

That was probably what had happened.

43

Micah headed back up the stairs.

Her first idea was probably still the best. Sleep until morning. See if it straightened itself out. If it did not, she could drive to the electric company's office to make a complaint, and then drive to EvPro to have them look at her phone. Or, she could head to the nearest coffee shop and make phone calls to both the electrical company and the EvPro IT department. She could have good coffee and a relaxing morning while she waited for them to straighten everything out for her. She could use the coffee shop's Wi-Fi so that she could still log in to EvPro to do her work. It wasn't her fault that she hadn't been able to get the annual report information to Amy Bradshaw before her power had gone out. That was out of her control.

Micah tripped as she reached the top of the stairs. She realized from the dark shape that darted away from her and its squeal of protest that it was the cat.

"Sorry," she apologized. "But I can't see in the dark. Don't stand in front of me, or I'm going to trip over you."

There was a noise in the darkness. Micah tried to identify it. What had the cat gotten into?

She stood still, listening, straining her ears.

Footsteps?

Her heart raced, and she tried to soothe herself. There was no one else in the house. She had a new security system. Top of the line. No one could get in.

Except that the power was off. So the system was down. She didn't know if there was any emergency power backup, but how could there be? She couldn't hear a generator, and none of the lights had come back on. Her house was completely blacked out.

But the doors were still secure. There were new locks. Cole hadn't said that they couldn't be defeated, but he said that they were better, that she would be safer with them. Was any door or lock impenetrable?

Micah looked down at her phone again. It was useless. If someone had been able to enter her home, Micah's only choice was to run. They would know she was there; she couldn't hide. She needed to get away and to get to somewhere she could call for help. But with the condition she was in, even just going down the stairs and climbing up them again had fatigued her, and she didn't know how she was going to get any farther.

———

Micah shut off her phone screen and light. She stayed as low as she could and crept along the wall, listening for any movement in the house. She was sure her mind was playing tricks on her. She thought that Mr. X was Kirk Haynes, so suddenly she thought that everyone was after her. She was paranoid. Even if Mr. X was Kirk Haynes, why would he or his minions be coming after her? How would he know that she had produced a composite picture of him that was a close enough match to be recognizable?

She was sure she heard footsteps. Slow and furtive.

Then there was another yowl from the cat, and a startled, whispered curse.

There *was* someone else in the house. There could be no doubt in Micah's mind. She froze where she was, looking for a hiding place or escape route. Even though the adrenaline was being pumped through her veins by her pounding heart, she knew she didn't have the energy to run. If she snuck out the back door, they would hear her and come after her. And this time, there would be no police officers just happening to drive by on patrol to make sure she was okay. Kirk Haynes would be free to finish the job he had started. And then he would be free of suspicion.

He wouldn't be, though. The thought was satisfying. Even if he took

Micah out, she had sent a picture to Deputy Bellows already. And she had saved a copy of it on the Baby Thompson-Smith file. If something happened to her, someone else in the company would need to clean up those files, and they would see his picture. They would, sooner or later, be able to match Haynes's DNA to the baby's in a paternity test, and that would prove…

What?

It would prove that he was the baby's father, but that wouldn't prove that he'd had anything to do with Trisha's death and the baby's abandonment. There would be shadows of doubt that dogged him for the rest of his career, but proof? That would be up to the police, and Micah had no idea whether they would be able to get it.

Could they prove that he was the one who had attacked her?

She had ruined the chain of evidence as far as his DNA under her nails went. She had not let the police take and preserve the evidence, she had handled it herself.

She couldn't let him get away with it all.

4 4

"Computer here," a voice whispered. It was as audible to Micah as if he'd been in the room with her.

She could hear them touching her things. Anger welled up in her. He hurt her. He broke into her house. And he touched her things. He would do the same thing to her computer as he had done to her phone, wiping it completely if he couldn't find the information he was looking for.

She couldn't stand it when people touched her stuff.

Micah found herself creeping closer to her office. She didn't have a clue what she was going to do when she got there. It was as if her body were acting of its own accord. She should be taking the opportunity to get past them to the front door. Even if she could only get a few steps, she could at least raise the alarm, attract some attention. Not like when she was in the back yard, hidden by the tall fence and the darkness. In front, at least she had a chance.

"Is it on there?"

Micah crept ever so quietly to the doorway and peeked in.

Two men. One of them had to be Kirk Haynes. He had the right body size and shape. The other man was smaller, shorter than Micah, with a slight build. Like a gangly teenager.

Light beamed from Micah's laptop screen, silhouetting them.

The slim man hunched over, tapping the keys, studying the screen. He was already past the password lock. He must have had the higher-order IT EvPro password to log in. He had complete access to her laptop.

"Should we just grab it and go?" the little man questioned nervously. He looked over his shoulder. Micah didn't move. He was less likely to see her peering past the doorframe if she stayed still, his eyes dazzled by the bright screen. If she moved, he might see her.

"I want to know what she's done with it."

"Where is she?"

"She can't get far," Haynes said dismissively, as if it were of no importance. "She can't do us any harm."

Micah's blood was like ice in her veins. She suppressed a shiver. How much did Haynes know about her condition? Was he relying on the fact that with her physical injuries, she wouldn't be able to run?

She started to inch backward, ears straining, every muscle tense, doing her best to avoid making any sound that they might hear.

She had always been opposed to violence. She had never even considered owning a gun. Even non-lethal weapons like pepper spray or a taser had been out of the question. But for the first time, she wished she had listened to her father so she had something in the house. She was a sitting duck and Haynes was utterly confident that she had no chance of getting away from them, even while they were busy looking at her computer. They had their backs to the door, and if she'd had a gun or taser, she could have taken them down.

At least one of them.

Maybe.

Micah continued to back down the hall toward the front door. That was her best bet. If she could get out the front, she could yell and attract attention. In the front, there was a chance that someone would see what was going on and come to her aid.

She let out her breath when she got to the living room, and stood there for a moment, just breathing in and out and trying to regulate her breathing and slow her pounding heart. She was closer to the door than they were. Even though she didn't have any energy, she at least had a chance of getting out the door before they did.

In and out. In and out. She breathed slowly, trying to convince herself that she was not really in any danger.

Pretty hard to do with intruders in the house. But they hadn't tracked her down, yelled at her, or threatened her. They had just walked into the office and checked out her computer. How dangerous was that?

"Where did she send it?" Haynes's voice cut through the darkness, above a whisper this time, frustrated and not caring if anybody heard him. "And where is it saved? We need to get rid of every trace. This has to be stopped now."

There was a softer answer from the smaller man. Micah couldn't hear him clearly. Some plea to keep his voice down and not do anything that he was going to regret later. If they were there to clean up the trail they had already left, they needed to take care not to leave a worse mess than they started with.

Did that mean not killing Micah?

Or just not leaving any physical evidence behind when they did?

Newly energized by her anxiety, Micah turned and started walking toward the door, facing forward this time and taking long, deliberate steps instead of the tiny, careful shuffle. A few long strides and she would be out of the house. She would be safe.

Or safer.

Micah thought fleetingly that she should get a coat on before she left. It was cold out. She always dressed properly before she left the house. She recognized that it was a ridiculous impulse, but that didn't stop it from entering her head.

She gave her head a quick shake as if to banish it from her mind, and took the last step toward the door, reaching out to grab the handle.

45

A hand went over Micah's mouth and jerked her backward into a body waiting in the little alcove inside the door. He was strong and pulled her to him, squeezing her tightly and overwhelming any attempt by Micah to fight back against him.

"I've got her, boss."

Micah gave another mighty attempt to pull free of him without any success. She could barely even wiggle.

She heard footsteps down the hallway. Not tiptoeing this time, not trying to keep quiet at all. She was turned and pushed into the living room and saw Kirk Haynes come around the corner to see her.

"Micah Miller," he said in a flat tone. "I don't think we've had the pleasure before."

Micah tried to free her head and her mouth. The man who was holding her apparently decided there was no danger in allowing this and released her mouth.

"We have met once before," Micah pointed out. "But you didn't stop to introduce yourself then."

He chuckled quietly. "I stand corrected." He walked closer to them. Micah couldn't see him well in the dim living room, lit only by the street-lights outside. She could see the lines of his face, his nose, his forehead. She couldn't see into the dark hollows of his eyes. "Well, I'm not sure I can say I am happy to make your acquaintance now. I haven't ever been… unmasked before."

She remembered the balaclava that he had worn when he'd attacked her. He'd thought that keeping her from seeing his face would keep her from seeing his face. But his own skin cells had betrayed him. Somewhere on his body, she wasn't even sure where, there was a scratch she had inflicted while trying to fight him off. And that had been all it took.

"You're not going to get away with this." Her voice was shaky, near tears. She hated the way that it made her sound vulnerable and afraid, when she was equally angry and outraged. Emotion was strangling her and she could barely get the words out. "You might have up until now, but it's over."

"Oh, it is, is it?" He was so close to her now that she could feel his breath on her face. It was pleasantly minty and warm, but to Micah it was like breathing in the exhalations of a coyote. She turned her face to try to get unpolluted air. "You may have made better progress than anyone else, but you don't have me trapped. I am the one who has you."

"The sheriff's department has your picture. You are not going to get away with this."

"The sheriff's department isn't going to get very far with it. In fact, it's going to stop right where it started."

"What?"

"Deputy Bellows. Sadly, the picture never made it past his desk."

"Frank?" Micah gasped. It was inconceivable that he had been involved in the conspiracy. He couldn't be part of Kirk's organization. But what else was she supposed to think? She had sent him a picture of the killer, and he had turned around and put Kirk onto Micah.

Kirk laughed again. "Frank," he repeated, in a quiet, satisfied tone.

"No. He was… he was working the case. He let me go with him to do interviews. He wouldn't have done that if he was working for you."

"Keep your friends close and your enemies closer. Take care of her," Kirk told the man holding Micah. "We need to get out of here."

The hand went back to her mouth, this time squeezing up to cut off her ability to breathe through her nose as well. Micah fought harder than she thought she had strength for, but he kept his hand there, held her still, and everything went black.

4 6

Micah awoke slowly and groggily. Her body hurt all over. Her mind took her back to immediately after the assault when she was trying to sort out all of the sensory inputs, her body seized so strongly with pain that she couldn't focus.

She groaned and tried to move, to test out which part of her body hurt the most and to establish herself somewhere in space. She was disoriented and unanchored, floating somewhere in the universe, but not sure where.

Every movement was excruciating. Micah kept her eyes closed and let the pain wash her away again.

She had several more partial awakenings, growing a little more alert each time, but it seemed like a long time had passed before she was able to raise enough consciousness to force her eyes open.

It was dark. It must still be night. Or several days and nights had passed, Micah wasn't sure. She squinted, waiting for her night vision to give her some clue of where she was. She didn't think she was at home anymore, but couldn't be sure.

She was lying somewhere, uncomfortable and cold, her body pulsing with pain. She wanted to go back to sleep and recede into the darkness once more, but she knew that she was in danger. She couldn't remember why, but she remembered the feeling, and it was growing stronger, trying to assert itself amid all of the other messages her body was sending her. The danger was more important than the pain. It was important for her to figure out where she was and how to escape the danger.

There was a noise nearby. Micah froze. She turned her head, trying to find her way free of the darkness to see what had caused it.

She was cold. The only light in the room seemed to be the moon outside, which was dimming and brightening as clouds went past. She blinked away tears of pain and tried to focus. There was another shape nearby. It could have been a pile of clothes, or it might have been something else.

"Is…" Micah licked dry lips. "Is someone there?"

"Micah?"

Micah tried to place the voice, while at the same time trying to bring him into focus, straining her eyes in the dimness. "Frank?"

Relief flooded through her. Frank was there. He would help her.

The shape moved, shifting around and eventually turning in her direction. She could see his pale face in the moonlight. She filled in the details from her memory, trying to make him more real.

"Frank? Where are we?"

He didn't answer right away. Micah closed her eyes to try to steady herself, then opened them again because it was too dark.

"It's some cabin or shack," he said, his voice sounding rough and gravelly. "I assume we're in the Sweetgrass Hills, but I don't know where. And I assume… no one else knows where."

"What happened?" Micah tried to remember how she had gotten there. "I… there was someone in my house…"

"A break-in?"

"Yes. All that new security that my dad put in…"

"If someone is determined, they'll find a way."

"They cut off my power."

"You don't have a backup?"

"I guess not."

Micah tried to move but found that she could not. It wasn't just her tired, sore body. Something was wrong with her. She strained her muscles. It was some time before she realized that she was bound.

"Are you okay?" Frank asked. "Are you hurt?"

"I hurt all over… but I don't know… I don't know if I'm hurt."

They were both silent for a while. "Why did they bring us here? What are they going to do?" Micah asked.

"I have come to the conclusion… that they plan to leave us here."

"To die?"

"I think so."

"Why? I don't understand."

"I guess he thinks we got a lot closer to him than we did."

"Oh." Micah's consciousness drifted for a while. "Do you know who he is?"

"Papa Doe? No. I just had the picture you sent me. But I guess… he found out about that, somehow. There must be a leak, someone on the inside."

"He's on the board of EvPro."

"You know who he is?" Bellows's voice was incredulous.

"His name is Kirk Haynes and he's on the board at EvPro… and has a lot of other charitable and community connections." Micah tried to process everything that had happened, what Kirk had said to her at her house. "He told me you were the leak. Or he implied it."

Frank cleared his throat, a loud, harsh sound. "Me? Never. I want to catch him and put him behind bars for the rest of his life. Getting that girl pregnant and then killing her and trying to kill the baby? No matter what else he's done, good or bad, he deserves to go to prison for the rest of his life for that."

"Yeah." Micah rested again for a while. She wasn't feeling the cold anymore. The cabin seemed to be getting lighter, or her eyes were adjusting to the dimness. She could hear Frank's breathing rasping evenly a few feet away from her, and thought that he had fallen back asleep too.

"Micah."

She tried to rouse herself from her stupor. "Mm… what?"

"Micah, we need to try to get out of here."

She shifted around. "How?"

"I don't know. Don't let yourself fall back asleep. We need to figure this out."

Micah tried to wriggle into a sitting position. She blinked, looking around. It was getting lighter. She must have been there all night. She could see the interior of the cabin just faintly. It was small. An old-fashioned wood-burning stove in the corner. Unlit and probably unused for many years. Covered with a thick layer of dust, like everything else in the cabin. She probably wouldn't have called it a cabin, but a shack. The kind of place that a hunter or fisherman might sleep overnight once or twice a year, but not the sort of place that someone would have lived year-round. There was a bed with a metal bedframe in the corner, but she and Frank were both on the dirt floor like a couple of discarded sacks of potatoes.

There were a few canned goods on shelves nailed to the walls. There was no insulation, just plank walls that didn't do anything to keep the cold out. It was no wonder she was so sore. What was surprising was that she was no longer cold.

"You don't feel cold when you get hypothermia," she told Frank.

He blinked at her. "I know."

"How are you feeling? Are you still cold?"

"Numb."

"I'm not cold anymore."

Frank attempted to sit up as she had done, using his bound feet to push the floor away until he was pressed up against the wall. He studied Micah.

"We don't have a lot of time, then. You're going to get confused and not be able to think straight. Keep talking to me."

Micah felt better being able to see their bonds. They were both bound up with duct tape. It wasn't as strong as rope or chain, so maybe they had some hope of getting themselves free.

"Is there anything sharp we can rub the tape against?" Micah asked, looking around. There was the stove. She didn't see any sharp edges, but it was metal. Maybe there was a spur on one of the legs that could cut through the tape.

Nails were protruding from the wall where they had been hammered from the outside of the shack but had missed the studs or crossbars. She might be able to reach one of those.

Frank watched her. "You have more movement than I do. Or maybe I'm just not as flexible."

"Women tend to be more flexible than men," Micah agreed.

And she was younger than he was and not as heavy. But she didn't say that. With his hands bound behind his back like they were, he could hardly move a muscle. His shoulders must have been aching. He'd been there for longer than she had. Hadn't he? Or maybe he'd been tied up in the trunk of

Haynes's car when he had gone to Micah's house to try to find what evidence she had so he could destroy it.

"What if they burned my house down?" she asked Frank worriedly, as she tried to rub against one of the nails, wincing whenever she poked it into her arms.

"Houses can be replaced. At least he didn't burn it down with you in it."

But what about the kitten?

"What's wrong with this guy? He can beat me up, but he can't kill anyone outright? What's up with abandoning people in the hills to die?"

"I don't know. Maybe something traumatic in his past. Or he doesn't like to get his hands dirty, and tells himself that if he didn't see us die, he didn't have anything to do with it."

"Maybe it's all about alibis. He can go somewhere else and not be here when we die."

"We're not going to die, though. So he's going to have to deal with that."

"Yeah," Micah agreed. She stabbed herself again with a nail but continued to work at it. It didn't matter if she poked herself a hundred times with a sharp nail, that wasn't as bad as what was going to happen to her if she didn't get out of the cabin. It would be years before anyone came across their bones. They would need a forensic artist to reconstruct their faces.

"What are you smiling at?" Bellows demanded.

"I don't even know," Micah said, trying to blank her expression. The hypothermia must have been setting in. Her thoughts were definitely not appropriate.

"Are you having any luck there?"

"I think so. I can feel it making holes in the tape, and hitting fibers. It is going to give sooner or later." She tried to pull her wrists apart and could feel it ripping some more. "Duct tape. Did he really think we wouldn't be able to get out of duct tape?"

"I thought duct tape works for everything," Bellows said in good humor. Cheered by the fact that Micah was making progress, she supposed.

"How many corpses have you found with duct tape on their wrists?" she challenged.

He looked at her and didn't answer.

Inappropriate.

Micah kept working on the tape. "I'm going to get it off. It's going to work. And then we'll walk out of here."

"How are we going to know which direction to go? Do you know the mountains?"

"We'll go downhill. And then we'll walk a straight line until we get to a road. And then we'll keep following the road until we find someone to help us."

He nodded. "Okay. She's got a plan."

Micah pulled on the tape and felt it pulling free. "I've got it. I've got it!"

It took some more pulling and wriggling but, eventually, Micah got one arm out, and then, using numb fingers, pulled the rest of the tape off of her wrists. She used her thumbnail to try to free the end of the tape on her ankles.

Frank wriggled, trying to see. "Can you get it? If you can't get your feet, you can try to get my hands free, and then I can help."

She looked at him, analyzing his position. "That's going to be harder. Just wait. I'll get this."

He was quiet, letting her work on it.

Eventually, Micah managed to get a corner of the duct tape free, gripped it, and started to unwind it. "Are you sure he's not coming back?"

"Sure? No. I just figure… he left the baby out here to die. He left Trisha out here, or else pushed her down the ravine. What are the odds he's going to come back to face us directly?"

"No. I guess not."

"We'll get out of here. You're going to get us out."

4 7

Micah turned her attention to Bellows's bonds. She ignored the blood on her hands and wrists. That wasn't important. The only thing that was important was getting them out of there. They had to escape before it was too late. Micah's brain functions were already being affected, fuzzy and jumping from one thing to another and going in the wrong direction.

She would have to trust Bellows to keep her on track and not let her lie down in the snow and die.

"We're going to get home," she repeated. She scratched away at the duct tape, trying to lift one of the corners. "Are you married?"

"Yes," Bellows said slowly, as if he weren't quite sure. "Yes, though… you know how things go."

"Umm… no. What do you mean?"

"We're separated… talking about whether to stay together."

"Do you want to?"

"Yes. Very much. But life is very stressful for a cop's wife. It really isn't something you would wish on anyone. Always wondering if your husband is going to be okay. Whether tonight will be the night that he runs into some crazy with a gun." Bellows paused. "Or some crazy who decides to tie him up with duct tape and dump him in a remote cabin."

"Do you really think she worries about that?"

He snorted. "No."

They were both quiet. Micah finally managed to get the end of the duct tape unstuck and started to pull. Unlike with her nearly-hairless arms, already numb, Bellows's thick, hairy arms caused him considerable pain as they pulled the tape free. He yelped and flinched away, trying to protect them, but he forced himself to sit still and let Micah finish her job. Luckily, his legs were taped around his pants instead of directly to his skin. Free of the bonds, Bellows rubbed his arms, trying to warm himself up.

"You're too cold," he reminded her. "Warm your hands up under your armpits and run on the spot for a few minutes."

"We'd better get our exercise outside. I'll warm up while we hike away from here."

"Oh. Yeah. Okay. But you should still warm up your fingers like I said."

Micah tucked her fingers under her armpits, but it didn't feel any different. They approached the door cautiously.

"He had at least two guys with him," Micah whispered, thinking for the first time that she'd better lower her voice in case they were overheard. "One of them was guarding my door. I just about got out, and he grabbed me."

Bellows tried to peer through the grimy windows, but couldn't get an angle on the door. He pressed his ear to the door and listened, but couldn't hear anyone out there.

"We're just going to have to chance it," he said with a shrug. "I'm going to burst through there fast, make a run for it, and we'll see if anyone comes after me. You stay here, watch for a minute and make sure the coast is clear before you come out."

"Okay."

Micah feared that running out of the cabin would just get Bellows shot in the back, but he was the professional, so she'd have to rely on his judgment. Maybe he'd zigzag like a rabbit, and no one would be able to get a bead on him.

Bellows waited by the door for a moment, breathing slowly and planning his escape, and then he opened the door and bolted.

Micah watched from the doorway. He dashed across the clearing in front of the shack and into the trees. He didn't zig or zag. There was no pursuit. No gunshots. Micah waited until he was out of sight, hidden behind a tree, before running after him.

Despite the fact that Bellows was overweight, he was in good shape and had moved quickly across the clearing. In contrast, Micah felt as if she could barely move. She'd been convalescing for days, but her body felt like she was right back at the beginning again. As if they had beaten her again before dumping her. Her movements were slow and sluggish and she wanted nothing more than just to lie down and go back to sleep.

Bellows stepped out from behind the tree and watched her progress. When she got close enough, he walked up to her and took her by the arm.

"You're in pretty bad shape," he observed.

"I'm not normally…"

"No, I didn't mean you're out of shape, I mean… you're not doing very well. Are you going to be able to make it down the mountain?"

Micah looked around. There was no way to tell how far they were from civilization or how long it would take them to hike out of there. She didn't want to take another step.

"It's the only way out of here. I'm going to have to."

"We'll go slowly. Take breaks."

"I don't know if we should take breaks. I don't want to freeze. I want to take breaks, but I don't want to."

He nodded as if he understood. Micah wondered if she was babbling and he was humoring her.

They looked at the shack on the other side of the clearing. There was no sign of anyone else. No guard had been left to watch them.

"I left the door open," Micah noted. "I guess I should go back and shut it, so if they come back to check, they don't know that we're gone…"

"That's just using extra energy. If they come to check on us, they're not going to judge that by whether the door is open or not. They're going to go inside."

"Yeah. Of course."

Micah leaned on a tree, trying to get her breath back after her hobble-sprint escape.

"You okay?" Bellows checked.

Micah wiped her forehead with her arm. She felt like she had a fever, in spite of the cold weather. "There's a road," she observed, pointing it out. "I didn't think about there being a road, but I guess that's how they got us here."

"You think we should take the road down?"

"It's going to be easier than bushwhacking."

"Let's get going, then." Bellows struck off toward the road. Micah knew that the longer they stayed there staring at the road and trying to figure out the best plan of action, the more the inertia was going to set in and she wouldn't be able to get started. She followed Bellows, trying to avoid thinking of the journey ahead of them. Who knew how long it would take them to get down the mountain and to civilization. They didn't have any food or water and Micah was already hypothermic.

Bellows waited for her at the road. When she caught up, they walked side-by-side. It was only gravel, but it was still easier to get through than the weeds and undergrowth a few feet away.

They set off. Micah knew they were going at a snail's pace, Bellows slowing his speed to match hers.

"Maybe you should go ahead and send help back."

"I'm not separating."

"You might have to, eventually. Maybe you should get a head start now, you'll get to help a lot faster than I will."

"No. We're staying together."

"Okay."

They walked on.

"How are your feet?"

Micah looked down at her feet, numb from the cold. It wasn't until then that she realized she wasn't wearing any shoes. She had been in her bedroom, not planning to go anywhere, and Kirk and his men had not bothered to put any on her when they had transported her to the cabin.

"They're okay. I can't feel them."

"We'll try to stick to smoother areas. I don't want them getting all ripped up."

Micah's feet felt like something separate from her, something that didn't even concern her. "What matters is that we get away. If my feet get cut up… that's not really important."

She was so dreadfully tired. She didn't know how she was going to keep walking for the hours she was going to need to. But she kept going.

As they walked down the road, the sky growing lighter, Micah became more aware of their surroundings.

"What if they come back? We're right here on the road. It's the only way in or out, so they're going to see us."

Bellows looked at her in dismay. It was so much easier walking down the road than it would be to cut through the bush, even if the road did switch back and forth as it went down the mountain. But there hadn't been any roads branching off to the side. Just the main road they were on.

"We'll keep our eyes and ears open, and if a car comes, we'll get off the road," he told her. "We'll hear them before they see us."

Micah sighed with relief and nodded. "We'd better walk near the edge, then."

They adjusted their positions. Micah felt Bellows grab her arm and realized she'd been about to totter off of the road into the ditch.

"Sorry," she apologized. She tried to focus on keeping herself upright.

It seemed like an eternity, just walking down the road, keeping their eyes and ears peeled for any sign of vehicles. It was a beautiful, crisp, clear day, new frost clinging to each stalk of grass and tree branch. Birds were singing. The sky turned a bright blue. Micah's thoughts turned again to her kitten and her hopes that Kirk hadn't burned her house down when he'd been unable to find the evidence he needed. She hated people touching her things and she had gotten attached to the kitten.

"Micah! Car!"

Micah practically fell over trying to follow Bellows's example and get off the road quickly. She was glad that he wasn't like a TV show cop, waving down the car and explaining that he was a police officer and they needed to take him to safety or let him use their phone. He was just as intent on getting out of sight as she was.

They watched the car zip by on the road without even slowing. There wasn't much to see, as they were keeping their heads as low as they could to avoid being seen. A dark colored sedan, moving at a pretty good clip. Micah didn't like driving on gravel roads and always crept along them, not wanting to chip her paintwork. But Kirk or whoever was driving was more concerned with reaching the shack quickly than he was about protecting his car or even staying in control.

"Was that him?" Micah asked, gasping for breath. "Did you see?"

"No, I didn't see. But I think we can be pretty confident that it wasn't just a random tourist."

"No. I guess not."

"Maybe this would be a good time to take a break."

Micah giggled, maybe a little hysterical. Bellows took one of her hands in between his and tried to warm it. But his hands probably weren't much warmer than Micah's. She couldn't feel them, so she didn't know for sure.

They stayed hidden for a few minutes, ears pricked.

"How long does it take for them to figure out that we're gone?" Micah asked, anxious for something to happen.

"They know by now. They're probably looking for us, checking out the woods."

"It won't be hard to find us."

He looked at her, biting his lip. He didn't argue and tell her otherwise.

"Maybe we should get moving again," Micah suggested.

Bellows nodded grimly. "Yeah," he agreed.

"Through the woods this time. We can't wait for them to come down the road looking for us."

"Your feet…"

"They won't freeze if we keep moving. Walking forces circulation through them. They'll only freeze if we stop."

Bellows raised his eyebrows. But he had to know that their only chance to escape was to go through the woods and make their way down the mountain in as straight a route as possible. Staying on the road would just make it easier for the thugs to find them, and they were going to be returning from the cabin before very long.

Without any further discussion, Bellows got to his feet, doing his best to stay low, below the level of the road. He held his hand out for Micah and got her moving. They made their way into the woods. Bellows looked around, seeming disoriented.

"Just go down," Micah reminded him. "Down is the way to civilization."

4 8

Micah kept stumbling along. It was not easy going over the rough ground through loose snow. If it had been trampled down a bit, it would have been easier. She had Bellows walk ahead of her so she could step in his footprints and not have to break trail. He kept looking back and talking to her so that he could be sure she was with him and hadn't fallen down or decided to take a nap in the snow, which was a very tempting prospect. It would have been so much easier just to lie down and go to sleep.

She kept listening for any sound from pursuers and, a couple of times, they heard voices or a car engine. Neither said anything about what was going to happen if they got caught. They couldn't cover their trail and Micah couldn't go any faster. But Kirk and his henchmen didn't seem to have found their tracks yet. Maybe they had decided that sooner or later their quarry would have to make their way to the road and were keeping a lookout for them there.

Micah tried not to think about how much time had passed or to calculate how much longer she could keep going, which felt like not at all. They had crossed the road, which switched back and forth several times, and the sun was getting high in the sky.

"Why do you think he did it?" Micah asked, trying to focus on a problem other than her physical pains. "Just to protect his reputation?"

"High-powered political types are very sensitive about things that could damage their reputations or make them look bad in some way. They'll do just about anything to protect themselves. In some ways… their rep is more important than even their lives. Certainly more important than anyone else's."

Micah thought about this, shaking her head. "I can't imagine being that concerned about what people think of me."

Bellows chuckled. "Your parents raised you right, then. Most of the people in the world—or at least America—are very concerned about how other people see them, about not stepping out of line in fashion, goals, leisure activities, anything. Keeping up with the Joneses doesn't even begin to describe it. They are so sensitive to how people look at them, it's devastating to be publicly shamed or bullied."

"Yeah. I've seen that. But I'd rather be different and be happy with myself than the other way around."

"There's a lot of self-hate in the world. No one can succeed in being everything society thinks they should be."

"Even if you do what the Joneses think you should, there's still the Smiths across the street," Micah contributed. "And they think you should be something else."

"Exactly."

Micah thought about it, stepping carefully into Bellows's tracks. "Do you think it's the way I was raised, or innate?"

"You're the expert on genes. You tell me. Nature or nurture?"

"My parents care a lot more about appearances than I ever have, so I think it must be nature. They can probably influence it to an extent, but I definitely have a preference for non-conformity."

They kept going. A cloud covered the sun and it was suddenly a lot darker in the thick woods. Micah looked at her wrist, wanting to know what time it was. And when was sunset? What were they going to do if it got dark and they weren't any closer to safety?

"You haven't said much about your parents," Bellows said, keeping Micah engaged. "You must have had a better experience than Trish."

"They're very good. Very loving. My experience was more like Sweetie's than Trisha's. It's a lot easier for a kid who lands in their permanent family as an infant than one who gets bounced around when she's older than five."

When they next reached the highway, Bellows stopped Micah. The slope was not as steep as it had been, and the highway was wide and paved, with the sound of traffic in the distance.

"It's time. We need to try to get help now."

"What if we flag down the bad guys?"

"Harder for them to do anything on the highway. We'll pray for good luck."

Micah looked at him. He closed his eyes briefly, looking grim, before opening them again and looking either direction.

"Any idea which way to town?"

Micah had been watching the progress of the sun. "Right, I think. We'll know after the first car. Even if it's going the wrong way… if we can get a ride anywhere, we should take it. Get as far away from Kirk as we can."

They walked on the side of the highway, waiting. When a car came toward them, Bellows stepped out in the middle of the lane and held up his hands, motioning them to stop with such authority that the car slowed to a stop instead of honking and swerving around them. Still, the driver was cautious, only rolling his window down an inch to talk to Bellows.

"Deputy Bellows, sheriff's department," Bellows identified himself briskly. "We're in a desperate situation here. Can we get a ride into town?"

The young man's eyes went from Bellows over to Micah. They must have both looked a sight. Walking all day without proper clothing, fearing discovery any minute. Micah wanted to turn away from his gaze, but she forced herself to stay still. Let him see her blue, cut-up feet. Her feverish eyes. She was probably as white as a ghost. It would be obvious to him, even without Bellows's words, that they were in dire circumstances.

The driver hit the switch to unlock the power locks.

"Thank you!" Bellows told him sincerely, and went around to the passenger side to help Micah in. "You take the front," he offered.

Micah shook her head. "I'd rather not be sitting next to a stranger."

He considered for a moment, then opened the back door for her and made sure that she was able to lift her foot high enough to get in, and then gave her a little boost to get her into the seat when her legs couldn't manage the shift in her weight. He pulled the seatbelt across her and clicked it into place, then shut the door. He got into the front seat beside the helpful stranger. As they pulled out, he looked behind them, as if expecting the goons to burst out of the trees at any moment, or to come racing down the highway in pursuit. Everything stayed quiet.

"Do you have any water?" Bellows asked the driver.

The young man indicated a small cooler in the back seat, and Bellows reached back to pull out a couple of bottles of water. He cracked the seal on the first and passed it to Micah and kept the other for himself. Micah dribbled the water into her mouth. She didn't feel thirsty. She didn't feel cold. She just felt foggy. And tired. And sore.

49

W hen she next awoke, Bellows was trying to pry her out of the car. She put her hands up to stop him and looked around, disoriented.

"What is it? Where are we?"

"Hospital. A couple of officers will meet us here. Can you get out? You weren't waking up for me… and I really didn't want you to. You need rest."

Micah looked toward the emergency doors of the hospital. "No… I just want to go home. No hospital."

"I'm going to have to insist. This is not one of those cases where you can decide for yourself. You have hypothermia and are more than likely dehydrated and exhausted. You could lie down and never wake up again. Come on. I'll carry you."

"I'm too heavy for you," Micah countered, swinging her feet out the door and pausing to steady herself.

"You look like you could blow away in a strong wind."

"That's an illusion. I'm tall, so it looks like I'm a waif, but I'm not."

He offered his arm, and Micah took it, glad to have something to hold on to. She didn't want to be carried in, but she wasn't going to crawl, either. Her legs barely supported her, wobbling and shaking like a kitten's.

Closer to the entrance was a fleet of wheelchairs with the hospital's name stenciled across them, and Bellows guided her into one of them.

"I don't need a wheelchair," Micah protested. But she slid into the seat anyway, her exhausted body too tired and sore to continue all the way to the emergency room triage and chairs.

Bellows lifted her feet into the footrests, released the wheel brake, and pushed her through the big automatic doors. He knew his way around the hospital and, even though he didn't have his identification on him, he was able to talk Micah to the front of the triage line, listing all of the issues that could stop her heart in the next five minutes. While Micah had always ended up waiting for hours in the emergency room before, she was on a gurney almost immediately, with a monitor pinched to her finger and an IV inserted into her arm. Despite her dehydration, the nurse managed to get the IV in the first time and smiled grim satisfaction as she taped it into place.

"This is the fastest way to get fluids into you. And we're going to give you some warming blankets, so you'll be nice and toasty soon."

"Thank you."

"Is there someone I can call for you? Spouse? Next of kin?"

"My mom. Actually, my dad." It was probably best if he took the call and then broke the news to Micah's mother. She gave the nurse Cole's phone number.

"Good. I'll make sure they know that you're here and that you're being well taken care of. Someone will be in shortly to clean up your feet and to see what aftercare they will need." The nurse shook her head. "I'm not sure I understand what was going on out there... but it's not a good time of year to get lost in the woods."

"No," Micah agreed. "Summer would have been much easier."

Although, then there were biting insects to worry about, poison ivy, nettles, and large predators. At least in the winter, most of those were not a problem. It was a good thing they'd managed to get picked up before nightfall. Micah would not have wanted to deal with coyotes or wolves on her trail, smelling fresh blood.

The nurse continued to make notes on Micah's chart about the various treatments she was being given and Micah's answers to various questions. Some of the questions, Micah thought, were not so much necessary for her treatment, as to make sure that she was coherent and knew where she was.

She didn't know how long it was, dozing and being woken every now and then by nurses or interns for treatment, before her parents got there.

They had probably been in the waiting room for some time before they were allowed to see Micah.

Marianna's eyes were rimmed with red, and she put her arms around Micah, giving her the best hug she could manage while Micah was in the bed. "Oh, sweetie! We were so worried about you! When we got to the house and you were gone, you can't imagine how afraid we were for you! We've had every police force in the region out looking for you." A couple of tears slid down her face as she beamed at Micah. "I'm so glad to see you—to see that you're okay."

"I'm fine, Mom. Or I will be, anyway. No permanent damage."

"What happened? You'll have to tell us everything."

Micah wasn't sure she wanted to tell them everything. She didn't want them to be any more upset than they already were. She looked at Cole.

"How did you… when did you get to the house?" She hadn't been expecting them that morning. She'd told them that she was on the mend and didn't need them to stop by. But they must have anyway.

"I got an alert from the security company on my phone. They said that the power to your system had been cut and they were not able to reach you on the phone to confirm that you were okay. By the time we got there, the police were already there ahead of us. But none of us had any idea what had happened to you or where you had gone."

"Is the kitten okay?"

He laughed. Marianna leaned close to Micah again, kissing her on the forehead. "Your kitten is fine. She's wondering what happened to you, but she was still inside, and she's been fed, and you don't need to worry about it. We'll look after her until you're home again."

"And they didn't burn it down?" Micah knew it wasn't logical. Obviously, if the kitten was safe inside, they had not burned it, but she'd worried about it all day and needed to hear their reassurance.

"No, they didn't burn your house down," Cole assured her.

50

"So, what happened?" Marianna asked, "Can you tell us?"

There was the sound of footsteps, and Micah looked up warily, needing to assure herself that it wasn't Kirk or one of his men. Instead, it was Bellows. He still looked much the same as he had all day, but his cheeks were pink and he was smiling. Much better than the grave expression he had been wearing all day as they both wondered whether they were going to survive the ordeal.

"Mind if I come in?" he queried. "These must be your folks. Am I intruding?"

"No, come in," Micah told him, motioning to a guest chair. "Sit down. Dad can get more chairs."

Cole looked around.

"This is Deputy Frank Bellows," Micah introduced him. "He and I were together. I don't think I could have made it out without him."

"And I know I wouldn't have made it out without Micah," Bellows said. "I'd still be tied up in that shack. Or... worse." He cut himself off from saying that he would be dead, having regard for her mother's look of anxiety. "But now we're both safe."

"What happened?" Cole asked, standing beside her rather than looking for more chairs. "I don't understand where you were and what happened. Someone kidnapped you?"

Micah nodded. "They cut the power and I guess jammed the phone after remotely wiping it. There were too many of them for me to escape. At least three. Probably another one waiting at the back door." Tears came to her eyes and she felt the illogical need to apologize. "I'm sorry, Dad. I did my best…"

"Of course you did! I don't expect you to be able to fight off four men! Probably armed, too. No, you didn't do anything wrong, baby. Don't think that."

"They wanted to destroy the evidence. And I guess… that included me and Frank too. We knew too much. I had figured out his identity. He wanted to stop us before we could get any farther and expose him."

"Who?"

Micah looked over at Bellows to make sure that it was okay to give them that information. He wouldn't want anything to leak out. They needed to be able to arrest Kirk Haynes before he knew what was happening. Bellows shrugged.

"Kirk Haynes," Micah told Cole. "He's—"

"I know who Haynes is. He's an unbearable twit. But a criminal? We never had any reason to suspect him when I was on the force."

"We don't know all of what he's involved in," Bellows said. "But it looks like at the minimum, he was involved in the sex trade. With someone as high-powered as he is, I expect it goes much deeper than that. He probably has his fingers in a lot of pies."

"I never would have pegged him as a gangster. He seemed harmless. It just goes to show that you can't judge a book by its cover. So how was Micah involved with this? One of her drawings?"

Micah nodded. "He's the man who attacked me. And who probably…" Another glance at Bellows and another nod. "He probably killed Sweetgrass Doe's mother as well."

Marianna shook her head, pale and waxen. She swore quietly. Marianna never swore.

"He was Sweetie's father. I was the one who uncovered the connection, and I drew a composite based on his DNA. I sent it to Frank…"

"And it was apparently intercepted," Bellows agreed. "We've got a mole… When he saw the picture, he told Haynes, and Haynes took action… destroying all evidence of the picture and managing to kidnap me." Bellows looked embarrassed by this. As if an experienced cop shouldn't have been kidnapped. But as with Micah, with the element of surprise and overwhelming force, it hadn't been that hard. It wasn't like TV where the cop knew kung fu and could whip all of their butts as they attacked one at a time. There were several of them, and they had weapons and the ability to catch him by surprise when he was alone.

"And me," Micah offered. "And they were checking my computer to see where I had saved it and who I had sent it to so that they could cover it up."

"Looks like they took your laptop with them," Cole said apologetically. "It wasn't in your office."

"Yeah, I figured."

"So that evidence is gone," Bellows said. "And what about all of the information on the EvPro servers? He'll have wiped that too."

"He'd have to find it first."

Bellows raised an eyebrow.

"I didn't put it under his name," Micah offered.

"But as a John Doe? Papa Doe?"

Micah shook her head. "I used... the name of a friend of mine. He wouldn't know unless he looked through one file at a time, or wiped all of my recent files from the server."

Bellows's eyes glittered. "That was very smart of you. What name was that?"

Micah was suddenly uneasy. She remembered Kirk's claim that Bellows was working with him and had made sure that the picture didn't get any farther. Was he telling the truth, or was Bellows when he said there was another spy within the sheriff's department?

He was the one who had helped her to escape from Kirk. He had been held captive just as she had. There was no doubt of that. But that didn't mean he hadn't been working for Haynes, just that Kirk Haynes had no longer considered him useful. And he might consider Bellows useful once more if he solved a problem for him.

Micah looked at her parents. She tried to warn them with her eyes not to use any names.

"I'm so tired," she said, and it wasn't a lie. "I can't even think straight anymore."

Cole studied Micah's face. He motioned to Bellows. "Why don't we go for a coffee? Marianna can sit with Micah."

Deputy Bellows considered, then rose to his feet, adjusting his duty belt over his paunch. "I could use a coffee," he admitted. "And a piece of pie."

Cole laughed. "Yes, you probably could," he admitted. "How about you, Micah? Do you want me to bring you something up from the cafeteria?"

As Micah's body started to recover from its cold, exhausted state, she was starting to feel hunger pangs. "Well… maybe some fruit?" she suggested.

Cole cocked his head at her. "Some fruit," he repeated. "I'm thinking that there's something else you want."

Micah's face heated. She looked away from him, embarrassed. "Well… hospital cafeterias almost always have… Jell-O."

"Nothing wrong with Jell-O."

"It's not exactly healthy."

"You need a little treat now and then. You eat perfectly all the time. Jell-O isn't bad for you. It's a hospital. It's *healthy* Jell-O."

Micah laughed. She shrugged, trying not to look embarrassed about it.

"Color preference?" Cole asked, as if it were perfectly normal.

"Well… not green."

"Orange or red are okay?"

Micah nodded, not meeting Bellows's amused look. She wasn't sure why she cared if he thought her tastes were juvenile or peculiar. "Yes."

"Alright. We'll see you later, honey, get some rest."

The two men left. Marianna sat down and held Micah's hand. "Are you okay, dear?"

"Fine. Why?"

"You seem like something is bothering you. Did you not want your father to take the deputy away—oh! Are the two of you…?"

"No, there's nothing between us. He's married. I did want Dad to take him. Something… doesn't feel right. Frank was really good to me and helped me to get out of there safely, but…"

"But something isn't right," Marianna repeated.

"Yeah."

"Maybe you should get some sleep. Your brain can't function properly when you are exhausted. It will all make sense when you wake back up."

Micah rubbed her eyes. "I don't think I'd better go to sleep yet. Do you have my… can I borrow your phone?"

"Of course." Marianna started digging around in her purse. "I don't know if you're supposed to use one in here, they always give you such dire warnings about cell phones and sensitive medical equipment. If you have someone you want me to call to let them know that you're safe…"

"No, I need to talk to her directly." Micah glanced around the curtained area, but she didn't see any warnings about cell phones, so when Marianna found hers and handed it over, Micah immediately called the EvPro main number.

Who could she trust? Not Amy Bradshaw or Aaron Kwong, who had told her to get off of the Sweetgrass Doe case. Either of them could be taking directions from Kirk Haynes or someone in his employ. Veronica Clang and Mr. Hawkins were too low on the totem pole to agree to do anything against company policy without considerable pressure. IT would ask a lot of questions and report anything they heard to management.

That left one person. She had to put her trust in the person who liked her the least.

"Chastity Pollard, please."

She waited for the receptionist to put her through, then waited while Chastity's phone rang for a long time. Finally, Chastity picked up.

"Chastity Pollard."

"Chastity, it's Micah."

"Micah? How are you feeling? Are you okay?"

"Pretty rotten," Micah admitted. "But I'm safe."

There was silence from Chastity, then an uncertain "Okay…"

Had the employees not even been told that she had been kidnapped?

"Chastity, I know I've asked you for a couple of favors lately. I just have one more…"

There was a sigh from the other woman. "Micah, we've all been told to stay off of the Sweetie Doe file, so if you have more requests to do with that… I can't."

Micah glanced around, making sure that there was no one listening in on the conversation. Who knew how many thugs Haynes might have around. And with only curtains for privacy, there was no way of knowing who might be nearby listening in.

"Do you know why you've been told to stay off of it?"

Chastity didn't answer immediately. "No," she said finally. "They said some nonsense about not putting resources into a cold file, but it's not cold. And we put resources into cold files all the time. That's our thing. Reviving a case when there were no more leads. Finding new information."

"Somebody… in the company… is involved in the case."

"What does that mean?"

"It means that someone on the board is Mama Doe's killer."

"What?" Chastity's voice squeaked. "How can you know that? If you do know something, you need to let the police know."

"I did. But the police have a leak, and it just about got me killed. We need to preserve the evidence, Chastity. Because he is going to try to wipe it out, if he hasn't already."

"If he hasn't already?"

Micah could hear Chastity typing quickly. She could picture the familiar wrinkle between Chastity's brows and the frown on her face as she checked the file system to make sure that everything was still where it should be.

"The Sweetie Doe file is still here… it looks like everything is where it should be. Baby and Mama."

"Good. Can you… make a backup? I know the company has its own servers and cloud backup and all of that, but we need to know it's safe somewhere else. Download it to your computer. Make a copy on a portable drive. Half of Sweetie's DNA is his, and if they wipe it out, and do something to her… there won't be any evidence to convict him."

"Okay," Chastity murmured. She muttered beneath her breath as she did what she was asked, letting Micah know that she was still there and working on it. It was a few minutes before she gave her attention back to Micah, her words clear once more. "What about Papa Doe? We did the Lazarus and your fingernail samples."

"Yeah. That's what I was most concerned about. It's under Baby Thompson-Smith. He won't know that, but if he does what Bellows said and just wipes out all of my recent files, he'll destroy it."

"Mmm-hm." Chastity tapped away, looking up the file. Micah waited while she had a look through the files or started them copying to her USB drive. Chastity swore suddenly. "This is him? This picture?" Her voice had gone all squeaky again.

"Yes. I just uploaded it—"

"He's here! He's in with Aaron right now!"

51

Micah's stomach clenched. Marianna hovered near her worriedly. "What is it, Micah, what's wrong?"

Micah waved her mother away. "What's he doing talking with Aaron? He's never come by the lab before."

"No. Why would a member of the board be slumming around with us?"

"Are you close enough to listen in on them?"

"*You* could hear him if you were here."

Micah's office was on the opposite side of the lab from Kwong's. And she often had her door closed.

"What's he saying?"

"I don't know. I wasn't listening until now. I thought he was just… I don't know… arguing about financial analysis or something." Chastity swore again as she listened. "He's talking about your job. Says you're on suspension. He needs to see all of your files, secure them for an internal investigation."

"You need to get them downloaded!"

"I am. They're copying right now."

"Aaron won't give them to him, will he? He'll know it's a load of crap. I'm not suspended."

"You've been behaving erratically," Chastity whispered into the phone.

"You sustained a head injury. He doesn't know which files might be in jeopardy. He needs everything."

Micah closed her eyes, moaning. Chastity had to get the files copied and transferred to a safe location. It was a struggle to keep her mouth shut and not try to hurry Chastity along.

"Okay." Chastity's voice was calm once more. She cleared her throat. "That's the first step. But I've got to get the backup off the premises before they figure out that I copied the files. Which could be any minute."

There were, of course, security logs to show who had accessed files when. Full audits of every action, because they had to be able to show law enforcement the chain of custody and that no one had been able to access the files who shouldn't have.

"Can you get it out?"

Micah tried to think of the best way to get a USB drive out of the building. Put it in an envelope to be couriered or mailed out? Try to walk through security with it? They weren't usually searched too carefully, but if the alarm were raised, no one would be able to get out of the lab without having everything carefully searched. Not just a quick stroll through the metal detector and x-ray, but a hand search, pat down, and whatever else they thought necessary. Chastity, like everyone else, had consented to this possible violation of civil rights when she had signed her employment agreement.

"Just give me a minute." Chastity was moving around as she spoke on the phone, and Micah pictured her slipping the USB drive into her purse and hoping it would avoid detection. "Sheesh, he sounds like he's going to blow a gasket in there. Whatever you did, Micah, you've pushed this guy into nuclear meltdown mode."

"Can you do it? Sneak out of there?"

"*Sneaking* is not going to be possible. Stay on the line, but don't talk."

Micah opened her mouth to ask Chastity what she was doing, but then closed it and obeyed. She could hear the yelling as Chastity clearly got closer to Kwong's office and the screaming director. Then the yelling suddenly stopped.

"Aaron," Chastity's voice was faint, farther away than it had been. "I don't mean to interrupt, but… I have to go home. I'm not feeling well."

You had to admire the woman. Who else would have dared walk right into the argument and boldly let them know that she was leaving?

Micah couldn't hear Aaron Kwong's words, but his tone was exasperated.

"Sorry," Chastity said once more. "Female trouble, and… I might have to go to the emergency room, I've never had this kind of—"

"Just go!" Kirk Haynes roared.

"I'm sorry," Chastity said again.

Then she was walking away from the men's voices, and Micah could hear a little hitch in her breathing as she walked, as if she were sobbing or out of breath. Or… laughing?

"Chastity? Are you there?"

There was no answer. Micah assumed that the phone was still in Chastity's pocket. She now had permission to leave, and no one would think her sudden departure suspicious. Haynes himself had told her to go home. She had only to get through the security screening.

"Afternoon, miss," the security guard on duty greeted. "Earlier than usual."

"I'm not feeling very well," Chastity confessed. "I'm hoping if I lie down for a while…"

"That's too bad," the guard commiserated.

Micah could hear Chastity putting various items into the bin on the conveyor belt, including the phone, still broadcasting live to Micah's hospital bed.

There was the buzz of a walkie-talkie and bursts of static. Micah waited, anxious for Chastity to get through security and to freedom.

"Uh, Miss Pollard. Looks like there's problem. You copied some files from the server?"

Crap.

They were already onto her.

Micah wanted to throw the phone across the room.

"Yes," Chastity agreed. "Micah Miller asked me to get them for her. I put them on a USB drive and left them in her desk. It's all locked up. No one is going to walk off with them."

"It's in her desk?" The guard relayed this information over his radio.

"In the locked drawer," Chastity said helpfully. "I made sure it was secure."

"You have the key to this drawer?"

"Micah has one, and I have one at my desk. It's in my drawer with the rest."

Micah happened to know that despite the woman's good work habits, her desk drawers looked like a garbage dump. Or the results of an explosion at an office supply store. Haynes and Kwong would need an hour to go through everything for the nonexistent key.

"Mmm," Chastity groaned, which Micah assumed was accompanied by painfully holding her pelvic region. "Can we finish up here? I'm really not feeling good…"

"Sorry, Miss Pollard." The guard relayed the last few details over his radio. "I'll get you through as quickly as I can. Would you turn out your pockets, please?"

"Women's clothes don't have pockets." Chastity's voice was growing irritated. "I just have my purse, and I put everything else in the bin. Can we get on with it?"

"Step through the gate, please, and hold up your arms… turn around…"

"What's all this? You guys think I'm selling company secrets?"

"Just a precaution. Extra security today."

"Is that it? Am I done?"

"I'm just going to do a quick pat-down, if you would put your hands on the wall, please?"

Micah listened in disbelief as the guard gave Chastity instructions and checked to make sure she didn't have the USB drive hidden somewhere on her body. How far were they going to go with the search? Was there any hope that Chastity would be able to get the drive out with her?

Chastity sounded calm, but irritated, repeating several times that she wasn't feeling well and wanted to get home.

Micah could hear the conveyor belt as it ran the phone she was eavesdropping on and the rest of Chastity's possessions through the x-ray.

"You're going to search my purse?" Chastity demanded a moment later. "You just x-rayed it. Exactly what do you think I'm hiding?"

"Just a precaution, miss. Please, I'm doing my best to get you out of here, but I need to make sure you're not taking anything out with you."

"Maybe I have it in my shoes. Do you want me to take my shoes off for you?"

"Just let me search your purse, please."

Micah could hear the various zippers sliding open. How could Chastity be so certain that he wasn't going to find the drive? Haynes would do anything to stop her.

She tried to analyze the other noises coming through the phone, but couldn't be sure what the guard was doing as he looked through Chastity's purse and personal items. Finally, she heard the zippers again.

"Thank you for your patience, miss. That will be all."

"About time," Chastity told him crossly. She picked up her things and walked out. She didn't take out her phone and talk to Micah right away. When she got into her car in the company lot, Micah heard the phone cut out and then cut back in again as her car's Bluetooth picked it up.

"Be off the lot in a minute," Chastity said quietly, her voice still calm.

Micah didn't know if she should answer or not, so she stayed silent. Eventually, Chastity spoke again. "Okay, we're clear."

"You got it out?" Micah demanded.

Chastity chuckled. "Sure."

"How?"

"I'll show you when I get there. What's your address?"

Micah started to give it to her, then realized that Chastity was going to drive to her house. Her brain still wasn't operating at peak capacity. "I'm at the hospital."

"Oh, are you? Okay, I'll go to the hospital. What room are you in?"

"Not in a room yet. Just in emergency. They should let you in. My mom's here."

"I'll ask when I get there, then. See you in a few minutes."

Micah said goodbye, but Chastity had already disconnected. Micah let out her breath and handed the phone to her mother.

"What's going on?" Marianna asked. "Is everything alright?"

"Well… it will be. I just have to figure out what to do about the police."

Should she trust Bellows or not? She didn't like the way he had looked at her when he found out that she had saved the composite to the EvPro servers. Whether he was the spy or another cop was, she didn't think she should deal with them. Maybe Wes, with his FBI contacts, could point her in the right direction.

She hadn't thought that she would fall back asleep with all of the excitement. She was eager to see Chastity and to find out how she had gotten past security with the USB drive. But as soon as she closed her eyes to rest them, she was gone once more.

52

"Micah? Your friend is here."

Micah opened her eyes and tried to remember where she was and who was there to see her. She looked at Chastity and then looked around for someone else. Marianna had said 'your friend,' and she and Chastity had never been friends.

"Hi," Chastity greeted, looking shy in front of Micah's mother. "You're looking a little worse for wear."

Micah rolled her eyes. She probably did look pretty rough.

"How did you get it out?" she demanded.

Chastity laughed in response. She put her purse on the bed next to Micah. "Go ahead, find it."

Micah picked it up. She would never go through someone else's purse, so she felt a little self-conscious even touching it. She looked at Chastity to make sure that she really wanted Micah to search it, then looked down at it.

It wasn't neat and orderly like Micah's with everything pigeonholed in its appropriate place, but the type of purse where everything was just dumped in the main section. Micah methodically took items out of the purse, examining each. She knew that the USB drive was hidden, somehow, or the guard would have found it. Unless it was still on Chastity's person, hidden in her bra or somewhere else that the guard hadn't patted down carefully enough.

"I'm not seeing it," she said, examining each key and trinket on Chastity's keyring. There were a lot of them, and Micah didn't want to miss it. It would be an easy place to hide a USB drive. But she couldn't find a hidden compartment or removable piece on any of the trinkets. She put the keys down beside her and took out the next item.

Eventually, there wasn't much left but litter and a metal tampon case, with a retro cover and menstrual joke on the front that made Micah roll her eyes in embarrassment. She sifted through the litter, then checked the purse for any hidden compartments. She was beginning to suspect Chastity still had it on her person. In a piece of jewelry, maybe, though Chastity didn't wear much jewelry. Micah had carefully checked every container of lipstick, aspirin, and everything else.

She opened the tampon box, her face heating. She frowned, looking at the contents. She couldn't see the USB drive, but the tampons had been removed from their protective sleeves and lay naked in their applicators. That wasn't sanitary. She raised her eyes and looked at Chastity, who gave her a wide grin. A male guard would not clue in to the fact that they should be in wrappers. He would be too embarrassed and grossed out to examine them any further. Men always acted like tampons were dirty or contaminated, even when they were new and sterile.

Micah took the tampon applicators apart, and found the tiny USB drive jammed inside of one.

Marianna giggled. "What is that? Why is it in your tampon?"

Chastity looked like the cat who had swallowed the canary. She smiled at Micah. "That's how. It didn't show up on the x-ray, because it's in a metal box. And how many men do you know who would touch a tampon?"

They both laughed. Micah held the USB drive in her hand. It was warm and solid. Her evidence was there. No matter what they did with the server. No matter if they burned down the whole EvPro building. She had the evidence.

Raising her eyebrows at Chastity, she slipped the USB drive down the front of her hospital gown and into her bra. Not comfortable, maybe, but out of sight. When Cole and Bellows returned, they would have no idea that she had it.

When Cole got back to Micah's bedside with the Jell-O, Chastity was gone. Micah could tell from Cole's expression and the way he moved that he was on the same page as she was concerning Bellows. He could not be trusted. Maybe he was clean, but maybe he was not, and they couldn't take the risk.

Cole handed Micah her Jell-O with a smile. "Orange."

"Thanks. Orange is the best."

"Well, I should probably be getting on my way," Bellows said casually, looking at the face of his phone. "I'm going to have a lot of paperwork to process tomorrow. Better get a good sleep tonight."

Micah nodded empathetically.

She wished she could trust him. The way that she had felt when they were in the cabin and hiking down the mountain… she had trusted him implicitly. She had known that there was no way he could be a spy. But she just couldn't be sure anymore. He had helped her, but that didn't mean he wasn't working with Kirk Haynes. It just meant that he didn't want her to get killed. Or didn't want to be killed with her. If he couldn't deliver anything to Haynes, then they would dispose of him as well. He knew too much.

Had he always been dirty? Or had they somehow paid him off in the midst of the investigation, directing him to go in a different direction or to give them a heads-up if he got anything that implicated Haynes? Or had they blackmailed him? Threatened his family?

She gazed at him, and he looked back at her with a frank and open expression. If his family was under threat, he was a very good actor. She couldn't see any fear or anger in his eyes. Greed… maybe. Maybe he had become immune to the humanity of what he was doing. He had lost touch with the side of himself that cared what had happened to Trisha and her baby. Or maybe it had never meant anything to him, and he was only in law enforcement for the thrills—those fleeting, adrenaline-powered moments when he really felt alive.

"What is going to happen to Kirk Haynes?" she asked, watching his eyes. "Are you going to be able to arrest him?"

"We'll have to see how the evidence stacks up. Come and see me tomorrow, and I'll take your statement on the kidnapping. Did you actually see his face…?"

Should she admit it? Or would saying that she had seen his face be her death sentence? Micah struggled, unsure what to say to him.

"She might not remember," Cole suggested. "Memories of traumatic events are tricky."

"Yeah." Micah nodded. "I don't remember if I saw his face... or if I was just thinking about him, and thought it was him... it would have been dark. I might not have gotten a very good look."

"Well. Come by anyway and we'll get your written statement. And I'll do my reports, of course. I'll give EvPro a call and make sure that they have the DNA evidence and composite. Even though... it was compromised by your handling of it."

"But when you arrest him, you can still prove he's Sweetie's father." Micah swallowed, unnerved by the fleeting, furtive look that crossed Bellows's face. "Do you know where the baby is? What family she's with?"

Bellows chewed on his lip. "She's safe," he said flatly. "He's not going to find her."

Micah looked at him searchingly. Was he telling the truth, or was that a lie? Would Bellows keep Sweetie safe?

She nodded slowly. He would, she thought, keep Sweetie safe. He would protect an innocent baby. The baby hadn't deliberately gotten into the middle of an investigation. She hadn't poked around like Micah had, carefully gathering together the clues that would compromise Kirk Haynes. She might have provided the evidence that pointed to Haynes's guilt, but it hadn't been intentional.

"See you tomorrow, then."

5 3

Bellows was gone. Micah slurped her Jell-O like a little kid, ridiculously entertained by the wiggly solid that quickly dissolved into a liquid. Even though she knew it was not good for her, she deserved one little treat after the day she'd had.

Cole patted Micah's shoulder. "You and I need to talk."

"I already know."

"I don't think he's safe."

Micah nodded. "I don't either." She shook her head. "I feel terrible, not trusting him. He saved my life out there today."

"And you saved his. You don't owe him anything."

"No… I just wish… We got along together; I wanted him to be a good guy."

Cole nodded his understanding. Marianna looked in the direction of the doors, catching up with them. "What? Deputy Bellows? You think he can't be trusted? But that's ridiculous. He's a cop!"

"Cops can be… corrupted," Cole told her. "Neither of us likes the fact, but we can't ignore it. I don't want Micah to be in any worse danger."

"I don't either," Marianna agreed immediately. "Really, though? He seemed like such a nice man!"

Micah and Cole both nodded, and Marianna sighed.

"He seemed like such a nice man. I really was hoping…"

Micah shook her head. "Even if he wasn't dirty, he is still married."

"That doesn't seem to matter to people these days."

Micah closed her eyes. "Now, I need to sleep."

Micah wasn't sure how long she had slept, but it was mid-morning before she awoke and was ready to do anything. Cole had told her to text him when she needed a ride, and he would drive her over to the sheriff's department. Micah thought she could have driven herself, but her car was at home, so she consented to his picking her up and going with her.

They ran a few errands first, such as stopping at a corner store to buy a pay-as-you-go phone. As soon as she had the new phone, Micah called Wes Watley. She explained the recent developments.

"You could have let me know what was going on before this," Wes pointed out. "I did ask you to let me know if you found anything out about the baby."

"Uh… yeah, I should have given you a couple more updates," Micah admitted.

"You should have called me when you identified the perp."

"I know… but things happened so fast. I called Deputy Bellows, but I couldn't get through to him, and then before I could do anything else, they bricked and jammed my phone, and then… took me and left me in this cabin."

"Go over it one more time for me. Start to finish. What you know and what you only suspect."

Cole and Micah were already at the police station, and they sat in the car while Micah described the evidence, kidnapping, and escape to Wes one more time.

"Are you safe?" Wes asked.

"I'm at the police station."

"The police station where you don't know who is on the side of good and who is not?"

"Well… yes."

"You think that's a good idea?"

"I don't want them to know that I'm suspicious, so I have to behave like I'm not."

"Walking into something like that yourself is not safe and I'm too far away to get to you. I'll make some calls to my contacts, but I don't know how long it will take to get someone to you, or how long it will take to develop enough evidence against Haynes or this cop to make an arrest. Building organized crime cases can take years."

"My dad is with me."

"Your dad."

"He's a retired cop, Wes."

"Oh." There was a new note in Wes's voice. "I don't think you ever told me your father was in law enforcement."

"I might not have."

"And he's okay with you going in there?"

"He'll make sure nothing happens to me. We're just going to go along with Bellows and pretend that we don't suspect anything."

"Okay. Well, keep me updated. I don't want anything to happen to you. Let me know when you're safely out of there. I'll work it from my end."

Micah and Cole walked into the sheriff's office and did their best to pretend not to be suspicions of Bellows. Micah spent a long time writing out her statement, trying to include everything relevant and make sure that her account was perfect.

But she did not include her suspicions of Frank Bellows or the fact that she had seen Haynes's face. It seemed like a good idea to keep those things to herself for the moment.

Bellows grimly informed her that the files at EvPro had been wiped, so there was no way for them to know now whether the initial analysis and Micah's identification of Kirk Haynes were correct. And with the shape that Micah was in, the pain and trauma of the attack, she might have been experiencing some kind of PTSD or dissociative state when she had identified him. As she had always told him, a composite was not enough for an identification. They needed more: a direct DNA match and proper evidence.

Micah didn't look at her father. She didn't look into Bellows's eyes, but down at the table, trying to keep her emotions under control. He would expect her to be devastated. To doubt herself. He didn't know that she still had copies of the information they had tried so hard to delete.

They took a couple of breaks throughout the day. Micah needed coffee and lunch and time to go over her statement and make sure it was all in order.

Bellows got a text on his phone that made him frown, and he excused himself from the room.

Micah expected him to come back pretty quickly, but he did not. Maybe there was another case that something had come up on. She looked at Cole.

"You look pretty tired. About ready to go home?" he suggested.

Micah nodded. "Yeah, pretty soon. I think we've done about all that we can here."

The door opened, and a female cop Micah hadn't met before stood there, looking uncertain.

"Is everything okay?" Cole asked, standing.

She opened her mouth to answer, and then they could hear the yelling. Frank Bellows was living up to his name, shouting angrily and protesting his treatment.

"I'm afraid… there have been some unexpected developments."

"Is that Frank?" Micah asked.

"Well… yes."

"What's going on? What happened?"

The cop's hand was on the doorframe. She looked back over her shoulder anxiously, not sure what to tell them. "Well… there seem to be some FBI agents who… would like to talk to him."

Cole rubbed his upper lip, masking a smile. While the woman's consternation was amusing, Micah felt sorry for her. And for Frank Bellows, even though he had brought it on himself. She felt like a weight had been lifted from her shoulders. She no longer had to worry about what she was going to do or whether she was right or wrong. The FBI would take care of it.

There were voices in the hall, and the female cop moved aside for a man in a suit to enter. He looked at Micah, then looked down at his phone. "Miss Miller?"

"Yes, that's me."

"Are you okay?"

Micah nodded.

The suit shot the woman cop a look that told her to stay out of the way, then stepped into the room and closed the door. "You're not officially part of this investigation, so I was never here. Your friend Deputy Bellows was already under investigation by our team, so when it came to light today that he was trying to get the name of the family that your Baby Sweetgrass Doe is being fostered by, we decided it was time to move in."

There was a lump in Micah's throat at the thought of Bellows giving that information to Kirk Haynes. She swallowed hard and shook her head.

"Thank you. You already knew…?"

"Some of these investigations can take years to develop, ma'am. It's hard to stay back when you know people are being victimized, in order to be able to lay charges against more of the players and to hopefully bring down the whole organization instead of just one or two small fish. But that's part of our job."

"I guess. Yes. Do you know… are you investigating Kirk Haynes and this sex trafficking ring, or just the sheriff's department?"

"Sorry, I can't give you details on that. But you may want to stay away from the EvPro office for a couple of days and keep an eye on the news."

Micah still felt like she needed to sleep for a couple more days, so that wouldn't be a problem. She was relieved that he anticipated things happening that quickly.

"He kidnapped me. He beat me up. I'll testify against him, if that will help."

The FBI agent looked down at the paper in front of her. "Is that your written statement?"

"Yes… but I left some things out. I'll need to spend a few more minutes on it." She reached into her pocket and pulled out a USB drive. Not the original Chastity had smuggled out, but one of a pack of twelve identical copies which she and Cole had scattered across a number of locations, just in case. "And I have this. It includes the DNA evidence that proves he's Sweetie's father and the man who attacked me. And I did a composite sketch of his face before I figured out who he was."

"Sweetie?" the agent repeated.

"The Sweetgrass Hills baby. That's what we've all been calling her."

He smiled and picked up the USB drive from the table. "I imagine Haynes wasn't too happy about you drawing him."

"No. Not very," Micah agreed dryly.

"This will be very helpful, thank you." He slid it into his pocket. "And I'm supposed to tell you hello from 'an old friend.'"

Micah put away her purse and straightened the things on her desk that the cleaners had moved so that everything was square and lined up the way she liked it.

When she opened her email, she noticed a message in the private email that she had set up. She opened the message from a sender she had never heard of before and saw that it was empty except for a video attachment.

Even though she'd kept that address private, shared with only a few close friends or colleagues, she scanned the attachment with her antivirus program before opening it, just in case. When she double-clicked the video, it opened up and filled her screen.

It was a police interview room. Stark and white with a few pieces of furniture and that was it. A blond girl was centered in the frame. Her interviewer was across the wobbly table from her, not in the picture.

The girl was young, probably about eighteen, but she looked unnaturally aged and tired. Her blond hair was dry and matted. There were lines on her face that shouldn't be on any eighteen-year-old's face. She stared off into the distance, not looking at the camera or her interrogator. Her tone was flat and emotionless.

"He liked Trish. He liked 'em young and pregnant—paid good money to be exclusive. But once the baby came… they always disappeared. They told me I had to help him. Do whatever he wanted. And I always did."

"What did he ask you to do?"

"He wanted me to help get rid of the baby. We'd go up in the mountains, and I'd get rid of the baby and he'd get rid of Trish."

"What did he want you to do with the baby? Just leave her up there?"

"No. I was supposed to kill it. Like he did Trish. Hide the body so no one would find it." There was a long pause. The man didn't say anything. The girl scratched at the table, then investigated her fingernails. Her face was blank. She swallowed a couple of times and cleared her throat. "Trish knew what was going to happen. She'd heard about the others. It had happened before."

Another long pause.

"She begged me to protect the baby. She loved it. Said it was the only real family she'd ever had, and she wanted so bad to be its mom forever. But she knew that wasn't going to happen."

"Is that why you abandoned the baby instead of killing her?"

"She really did love that baby. Even before it was born. She was always holding her tummy and talking to it. Like it could hear her, even in there."

More time passed.

"I hid the baby under a bush. I figured, what harm could it do to let it live? It wasn't like the baby could do anything to hurt him. Not like it was old enough to identify him. It was harmless. If somebody stumbled across it, and rescued it, then it was just meant to be. It couldn't hurt Haynes."

Saying the man's name seemed to frighten her into silence again. It was a long time before the girl pushed stray strands of hair back from her face and continued her narrative.

"I scratched my face and got dirt on it. I went back late to where he'd parked the car, way after I was supposed to be there, and I told him I'd gotten lost. I told him no one would ever be able to find it."

"I guess he was surprised when he heard the news."

"I hid out with a friend. I wanted out. I thought there might be something else for me out there… maybe because I helped the baby, God might forgive me for everything I had done and make a way for me to get out. But he didn't."

"How did you get away to hide with your boyfriend?"

"I had privileges. Because I'd been with them for so long, and always did what I was told."

"Until the baby."

"Yeah. Until the baby. I hope wherever Trish is, she knows what I did for her."

It was a moment before her interviewer responded kindly. "I'm sure she does."

Micah left her parents in the living room as she went to the kitchen to check on dinner. She had cooked her own beans for the chili, which never tasted quite the same if she took a shortcut and used canned beans. The flavors of the home-bottled tomato sauce and spices had blended and deepened as it simmered away on the back burner and the hearty, garlicky smell filled the whole house. Marianna said she could smell it all the way outside as soon as they had gotten out of the car.

Micah had split a loaf of hand-shaped bread from the bakery in half and slathered it with butter and garlic and put it in the oven just before Cole and Marianna had arrived. The crusty garlic bread would make a perfect companion to the chili.

Meow chirruped and wound around Micah's legs, eyeing the pot as Micah stirred it, clearly eager for her share.

"It's ready," Micah called. "Why don't you come sit down and we'll eat?"

"It smells so lovely," Marianna gushed as they entered the kitchen. She put a warm hand on Micah's shoulder. "Are you sure you're not doing too much? I don't think you've had long enough to recover."

"Mostly it just cooks itself," Micah said with a shrug. "I just mix together a few ingredients and let it sit on the back of the stove."

They sat down at the table and watched as Micah got out the garlic bread and cut it into large slices, which she put on the table, and then as she spooned a little of the chili into a bowl for the kitten, blowing on it so that it wouldn't be too hot for her.

"You can't give that to the cat," Cole complained. "It doesn't have any meat in it. Won't it upset her stomach?"

"I'm only giving her a little bit. She's used to some beans now and then."

"Cats are carnivores. You can't feed them vegetarian."

"She isn't vegetarian," Micah agreed. "Cats need taurine. And she gets it. She just has a few homemade beans every now and then, and she likes them." Micah put the bowl on the floor, and Meow rushed forward with an eager squeak to gobble them up.

Micah added fresh chopped parsley and cilantro and a squeeze of lime to the chili and stirred it in. She set the pot of chili on a hot pad on the table and sat down with her parents.

"Well, we should toast the resolution of your case," Marianna suggested. "To Micah, carrying on the family tradition of catching criminals!"

Cole raised his glass.

Micah picked up her own glass, fiddling with it. "It wasn't just me. There were a lot of people involved. I couldn't have done it on my own."

"Nobody does it on their own," Cole agreed. "But it was your pictures that put a face on Sweetie's father and your attacker."

"The FDP composites," Micah corrected.

She remembered the LEO from Snohomish who insisted on calling her pictures 'virtual mugshots.'

"The girl who helped save the baby, she said that Sweetie was harmless because she couldn't identify Haynes. But she was wrong. She did identify him."

"The girl was nearly right," Cole said, raising his glass in a toast once more. "She was virtually harmless."

Micah couldn't help feeling anxious as she approached Sara's building. She had done the best she could, but the project had been so different from what she usually did. She was accustomed to working with adult faces, practical models that would be used to identify suspects or victims of violence. People always praised her composites for how lifelike they were, but that was compared to old-style sketches or flat computer composites. She didn't normally do artistic portraits.

Sara or Gregory buzzed her up. As before, it was Gregory who opened the door for her and ushered her in.

"How is she?" Micah asked.

He made a helpless gesture. Not an 'I don't care' shrug, but 'I don't know what to do.'

Micah nodded her understanding and followed Gregory into the living room with the big, empty windows. Sara looked a little better than she had previously. Micah had been worried that she would be much worse, her face skeletal. Time had provided some distance, but she was clearly still grieving. Micah bent down to give her a brief hug.

"How are you, Sara?"

Sara rubbed her forehead, looking tired and pained. "I should be asking you. You're the one who got mugged. I can't believe that happened to you."

"I'm better than I was. The bruises look bad, but they always do when you start to heal."

Sara considered that for a moment, then nodded. "Yes, I guess so."

Micah sat down on the couch next to Sara, putting her art portfolio on the floor and unzipping it. Without any discussion or ceremony, she pulled out the mounted drawing and handed it to Sara.

She waited, watching Sara's face as she took in the picture, waiting for her reaction.

Sara's eyes welled with tears. "Oh, Micah. It's perfect."

Micah studied it with a critical eye. She had done her best to combine Sara's and Gregory's features as they might have appeared on a baby. The pose was the one Marianna had liked, with the baby's fist pressed against his cheek. He was cradled in two pairs of hands, Sara's and Gregory's. It was not a religious picture, but Micah had washed it in light, creating an ethereal effect.

Gregory came over to look at it and touched the edge of the board. "That's amazing," he said. "It's beautiful."

Micah made space for him to sit down, and he cuddled close to his wife, both of them gazing at the picture.

"Our beautiful baby," Sara whispered.

"I hope it helps," Micah told her. "I don't want you to be sad."

"I'm still going to be sad. But this will help. I'm going to put it in our room. Right by the bed." She sniffled. "Oh, he's so sweet."

Micah thought about Sweetie. She was glad that the blond girl in the video had been able to preserve the baby's life. How many other girls and babies had not survived? How many years had Haynes been operating?

Now Sweetie could be adopted by a family that would love her as much as Sara and Gregory loved their baby. A family that would raise her as Micah's parents had raised her after she'd been abandoned. She wasn't sure she'd ever understood the depth of that love before. But she could see it in Sara's eyes.

Trisha had loved Sweetie too. She hadn't begged the older girl to save her own life, but to save her baby.

Even with all Trish had gone through in her young life, her baby was all that had mattered.

It was a new day. Micah was back at EvPro. A few members of the staff had been quietly let go, due, Micah assumed, to their involvement with Haynes. There had been a lot of chatter for the first little while. Micah had avoided even looking at her inbox and, when she had finally felt safe to do so, she had first searched for certain keywords and culled all of the gossipy emails into her trash. Then she had slowly gotten back into the flow of things, checking to see what assignments she had been given and catching up on a few files that had been neglected. Her door was shut, but in a few minutes she would open it and allow herself to be part of the community again.

But first, she had one phone call to make.

She tapped Wes Watley's name on her phone. It rang a few times. He was probably busy and it would go to voicemail. Then there was a click.

"Watley. Oh, hi Micah." He let out a long sigh. "How are you doing? Better?"

"It's going to be a while before I'm completely healed, but at least I look like a normal person now, not all covered with bruises."

"Good. And… emotionally? Are you back at work?"

"Dipping my toes in. So far, so good. I just wanted to thank you… there aren't very many people who could have persuaded the FBI to act when they did. They really think a lot of you."

"It was just luck. They had accumulated a lot of data already, and with what you had on Haynes and that cop, they were ready to close the net. It really wasn't just me."

"But it was partly. And thank you… for the video."

"I didn't send you a video."

Micah smiled. "Okay. You didn't send me a video. I just wanted to let you know how much I appreciated your help."

"Well, I was the one who pointed you at the Baby Sweetgrass case to start with. What kind of jerk would I be to just turn you away when you were in a fix?"

"Speaking of that… who was your client, anyway? Did he get what he wanted?"

"You identified the baby, her mother, father, who was responsible for her abandonment, and a dirty cop. I think I can safely say that he got what he wanted."

Micah waited for a moment to see if he would add any more details, then swiveled her chair to face the door. It was time to get to work.

"If you ever need anything from me, you only need to ask."

There was silence on the other end of the line, and Micah pulled the phone away from her face and looked at it to see if the call had been dropped.

"Wes?"

"I may just take you up on that. We're looking into a possible serial killer here. Weird kind of case. The cause of death is… I don't even know what to say about it. I might have a lead. I'll let you know."

ABOUT HIGH-TECH CRIME SOLVERS

High-Tech Crime Solvers includes:

Virtually Lace by Uvi Poznansky:
Michael Morse, an expert in VR simulation, stumbles on a dead body on the beach. A suspect himself, can Michael stay free for long enough to identify the real culprit?
Virtually Undead by Robert I. Katz:
Neurosurgeon Michael Foreman is drawn into a twisted conspiracy when his best friend is murdered playing a new video game, *Virtually Undead.*
Virtually Harmless by P. D. Workman:
Private consultant Micah Miller's involvement in law enforcement is limited to the composite pictures that she produces with her computer and colored pencils. But everything is turned upside down when she involves herself in the case of an infant found abandoned in the Sweetgrass Hills.
Virtually Dead by Edwin Dasso:
When multiple executives in Vancouver begin disappearing and are then found dead with no signs of trauma, private investigator and former FBI agent Wes Watley is asked by a friend of a friend to investigate.
Virtually Timeless by Casi McLean:
Twins Sydney and Noah Monaco become involved in a conspiracy

involving attempted rape, kidnapping, assault and an ancient artifact that isn't supposed to exist.

Virtually Gone by Jacquie Biggar:

When Detective Matthew Roy and reporter Julie Crenshaw are called on to investigate a string of sexual abuse cases, they don't expect Julie to land in the crosshairs of a serial killer.

Virtually Undetectable by Libby Fischer Hellmann:

Fired Bank Manager Rachel Foreman and her mother, renowned investigator Ellie Foreman, track through the lawless corners of the web to find out who is targeting the female CEO of a Fortune 500 company who is accused of murdering a disgruntled former employee.

Virtually Impossible by Barbara Ebel:

Dr. Hook Hookie extrapolates genetic information that informs patients of their hereditary health risks. But he isn't the only one with a use for the high-tech genetic machinery—a villainess with ill purposes stalks the Medical Center.

In addition, the authors compiled a cookbook with recipes cooked by their characters:

Virtually Yummy: Recipes that Inspire

The recipes in this book come from different sources: some of them are family recipes, some were garnered from our travels around the world, and others—inspired by our research, which enables us to write about the adventures of our characters and their culinary feats. But no matter where these recipes come from, we find them not only delicious but also inspiring. We hope you will too.

Did you enjoy this book? Reviews and recommendations are vital to making a book successful.

Please leave a review at your favorite book store or review site and share it with your friends.

Don't miss the following bonus material:
Sign up for mailing list to get a free ebook
Other books by P.D. Workman
Learn more about the author

Sign up for my mailing list at pdworkman.com and get Gluten-Free Murder for free!

ABOUT THE AUTHOR

Award-winning and USA Today bestselling author P.D. Workman writes riveting mystery/suspense and young adult books dealing with mental illness, addiction, abuse, and other real-life issues. For as long as she can remember, the blank page has held an incredible allure and from a very young age she was trying to write her own books.

Workman wrote her first complete novel at the age of twelve and continued to write as a hobby for many years. She started publishing in 2013. She has won several literary awards from Library Services for Youth in Custody for her young adult fiction. She currently has over 50 published titles and can be found at pdworkman.com.

Born and raised in Alberta, Canada, Workman has been married for over 25 years and has one son.

facebook.com/pdworkmanauthor

twitter.com/pdworkmanauthor

instagram.com/pdworkmanauthor

amazon.com/author/pdworkman

bookbub.com/authors/p-d-workman

goodreads.com/pdworkman

linkedin.com/in/pdworkman

pinterest.com/pdworkmanauthor

youtube.com/pdworkman